AN UNFORGIVABLE
CRIME

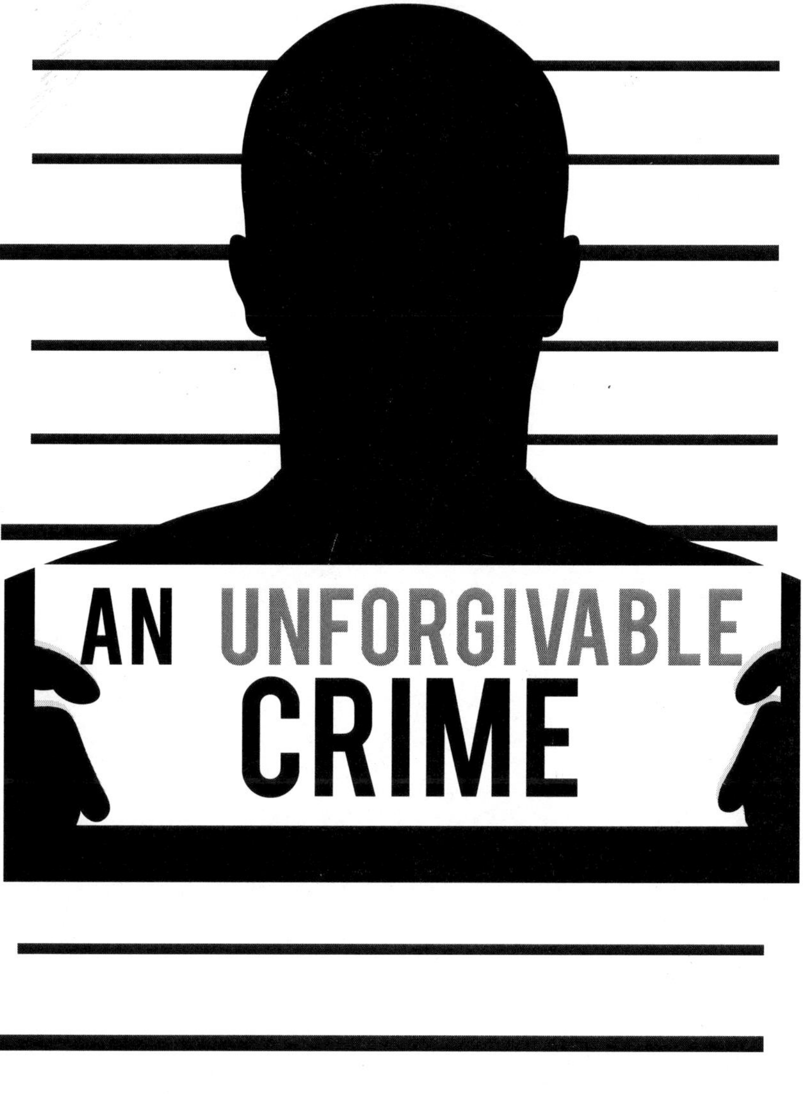

AN UNFORGIVABLE CRIME

JOE PAOLI

TATE PUBLISHING
AND ENTERPRISES, LLC

Published by Tate Publishing & Enterprises, LLC
127 E. Trade Center Terrace | Mustang, Oklahoma 73064 USA
1.888.361.9473 | www.tatepublishing.com

Tate Publishing is committed to excellence in the publishing industry. The company reflects the philosophy established by the founders, based on Psalm 68:11,
"The Lord gave the word and great was the company of those who published it."

Book design copyright © 2012 by Tate Publishing, LLC. All rights reserved.
Cover design by Kenna Davis
Interior design by Stephanie Woloszyn

Published in the United States of America
ISBN: 978-1-62024-064-9
1. Fiction / Christian / General
2. Fiction / General
12.05.22

ACKNOWLEDGMENTS

To my wife, who, for whatever reason,
never ceases to believe in me.

CHAPTER 1

TIM firmly believed that what we can see and touch is not all there is; it's just all our senses allow us to comprehend. The limited data that we are able to perceive only allows us to see what our creator intended us to see. Just about everyone believes in what they can see and touch, but what about everything we don't see and can't touch? Tim knew that there was more going on. He was sure of it.

Tim had trouble understanding how anyone could believe that our knowledge of what's all around us is comprehensive. It was the scientists themselves whom Tim was the most disappointed in. How could these scholars be so simple minded? How could they believe that they could figure out things that were outside of our ability to see and touch or otherwise sense? His conclusion was that any one of these great scientists who chose to believe that the physical was all there is was not the unbiased scientist he or she pretended to be. By no means were they nonreligious. It was Tim's belief that they were actually practicing the religion of materialism. How foolish the knowledge of man was to believe there is no creator behind it all.

Tim was very suspicious about reality, or at least what we call reality. *Are we human beings even living in reality?* he wondered. *Is it possible that we are actually living in a carefully crafted digital simulation?* To his knowledge, everything, at its most basic level, is energy. Even the atom is mostly empty space. The mass of the atom is in the center, the nucleus of the atom, and occupies almost no space compared to the size of the whole. Yet it's this nucleus that determines what that atom is. The electrons complete the cell by providing the opposite charge to stabilize or provide reactivity within the atom, yet the electron truly has virtually no mass. The electrons move so quickly that it only appears that the atom occupies space. Is this not a simulation? Knowing what we know, iron, wood, or any other material is made up mainly of empty space.

The more he learned about what we "understand" about our universe, the more his curiosity grew about what we don't know. For instance, why do the things that are invisible to the human eye look so amazingly complicated yet so strangely similar to the biggest things? In Tim's mind, an atom kind of looked like a solar system. Is that really a coincidence? He also wondered why all life was based on DNA. Does this incredible code that contains unbelievably complex information not testify of a creator?

Through his studies, he had begun to see that everything had unimaginable complexity. Now that it was humanly possible to look deep into the cosmos and really closely at the tiny things through powerful magnification, it was clear to Tim that every-thing was far more complicated than it first appeared to be. What man once called the "simple cell" turned out to be anything but "simple." *How can anyone not be in awe of our creator?* he often asked himself.

Tim's belief that our physical world was only a representation of what is actually there boggled his mind. He had read and heard theories about as many as six additional dimensions in our reality and had even felt like he kind of understood what some of the implications might be of these additional dimensions. With time as our fourth dimension, it would seem that the other dimensions could be almost anything. It also occurred to him that it would be impossible for mankind to even imagine what the other dimen-sions are if we are trapped in our four dimensions, but are we? To Tim, the better question was, Will we always remain as we currently are?

One thing that really perplexed Tim was the idea that our mind is not the brain. The brain is only the tool that our mind uses to control the body. *What does that mean?* he wondered. After much thought about our physical body, the only answer that seemed to make sense to Tim was that our body is only a home for our mind and our soul. Is it only a temporary home, and, if so, what becomes of the mind and soul when the body dies? Why would our minds and souls die if they are nonphysical? Can the nonphysical die a physical death? Tim wondered if it wasn't really the nonphysical mind and soul that were "real." The body and physical things might only be part of the elaborate simulation we are all living in, the simulation that is so finely tuned by our creator that all of these great minds had been fooled into believing that it was all that there is. Could someone earnestly believe that the physical is all there is, or would that person, especially an educated person, be avoiding some greater truth that was far simpler to deny than to accept?

Since the mind and soul reside in the body, is it not possible for other nonphysical beings to reside in a human body? They would have no mass, so room would never be an issue. Just like information, such as gigabytes of information, has no mass and yet still exists. Tim believed that the soul and mind actually existed in some sort of crossover realm—possibly in the additional dimensions we currently have no way of detecting.

Tim believed that he had experienced nonhuman spiritual beings influencing himself, as well as other members of his family. He believed that nonphysical spiritual beings could indwell a person, and he was quite sure he had seen it firsthand. The physical, in Tim's eyes, was only a shell or representation of who a person really was. People are forced to live in the human shell while we are here on earth in this lifetime, but it simply cannot be all there is to reality. Tim was sure that the spiritual world was all around us. There are endless examples and countless stories of its existence. He wondered how any rational person could not believe in its existence.

For most of his life, Tim had known that the spiritual realm was real. He had seen and experienced many things that confirmed his beliefs. At this point in his life, with all he had lived through, the Bible's accounts of the existence of spirits; the creator, God;

a purpose for mankind, and the existence of evil were what he was most sure of. He had looked other places but had come to the conclusion that all other explanations were only attempts to prove the truth wrong. He was convinced that the father of lies was behind all of the misinformation that was accepted as fact by the scientific community and the masses. He knew how it would all end, as he had many times read the final chapter of the Bible. Long ago, he had determined that the truth was simply too difficult for most people to accept. If what the Bible says is true, we would all be held accountable by the creator, the ultimate authority who would one day judge us all against his character.

Tim was sure we were put here on this finely-tuned-for-life planet by God. No chance it just happened on its own. He had never seen anything complex ever "just happen," so he never really struggled with what the Bible had to say about God creating everything. He was thoroughly convinced that every word of the Bible was absolute truth. He had long understood that most people didn't have an issue with the parts of the Bible they didn't understand; it was the parts they did understand that gave them problems. He was not one of the nonbelievers. He believed it all.

Tim's understanding was that our heart, mind, and soul would not die with the body. Why would they? Instead, as the Bible tells us, they would live forever in one of two places. They would live eternally either in heaven or in hell. The good news was that it was our choice where the real "us" would spend eternity. It was very good news for Tim, considering his current predicament.

He had lots of time to think about these things. In only a few days, Tim would be executed. It had been less than two months since his arrest, and his death sentence was already about to be carried out. Everyone else on death row had years to think about their crimes before their execution. Tim's situation was very different, as there was no question of his guilt. There was no need for an appeal of any kind. No one could ever prove him innocent because he wasn't.

CHAPTER 2

TIM, like many of his fellow inmates, had not had an ideal upbringing. His father and mother, though they were never actually married, did have a somewhat exclusive relationship for almost a year before Angela, Tim's mother, had gotten pregnant. About a year after Tim's birth, his father came back but was never really in a traditional loving or even an exclusive relationship with his mother.

Chuck Wiseman, Tim's father, was a heavy drinker and a miserable drunk. As if the drinking wasn't enough, drugs and drug problems were never far from him either. The man was a thief and just about anything else you can imagine a degenerate father to be. Quite possibly, though, his biggest flaw was his addiction to women. He chased them all and cheated on every one of them as much as he could. They didn't even have to be attractive for him to pursue them. As he oftentimes told a young, impressionable Tim, "There is something worth going after in all of them, even the ugly ones. You just have to look hard or drink a lot to find it sometimes."

Chuck treated women like objects. Though he had nothing to offer, his looks and ability to flatter them usually hooked them in spite of his motives. Chuck stood six foot five and maintained an impressive physique through daily weight training. He was very handsome and powerfully built. At one point, Chuck had been a very promising young athlete who had gained the attention of countless college programs. Most people had believed he was a lock for a college scholarship and maybe even good enough to play in the NFL someday. Unfortunately, as he would continue to do the remainder of his life, he got in his own way.

The summer before his senior year, Chuck was caught smoking marijuana with a sixteen-year-old girl. She confessed to their sexual relationship, but he was only seventeen, and it had been

11

consensual, so he only got in trouble for the drugs. Later that same summer, he was arrested for drunk driving. Though he had to spend the night in jail, he learned nothing from it.

When Chuck wasn't getting in trouble for drinking or drugs, he was getting into fights or being asked to leave classes. The vice principal grew sick of seeing his face on practically a daily basis. By the end of his senior football season, no school was willing to take a chance on him, and though he would never admit it, he knew it was his own fault. In spite of his obvious talent, no one wanted a kid who had missed half his games for disciplinary reasons. The drug and alcohol issues, along with the arrests, sealed the deal.

Sadly, Chuck was also extremely intelligent. His intelligence only made it more difficult for those who knew him well to watch him destroy himself and his future. He could have had it all, and he knew it. His regret made him into a bitter young man who was angry at the world. He set the tone for the remainder of his life when he dropped out of high school in the final semester of his senior year.

Chuck's looks and intelligence, along with his completely manufactured charm, was all he needed to reel in the women. The only way he could feel good about himself was to conquer as many women as possible. Nothing else seemed to calm his fire. He'd use his looks to reel them in, and his ability to make them feel attractive and desired to close the deal. In a mind game, he knew he always had an edge. Most girls who operated on the surface and were not wise to his cause were easy targets for him. He prided himself in being able to talk his way into their hearts so he could have his way with them.

Chuck could quickly size up his targets and became so good at it that he wisely passed on the ones who were hopeless. Wasted time on long shots wasn't in his nature. His ability to score with the ladies was truly a gift. Unfortunately, he was even better at making them hate him in the end. Being alone was never his specialty; it only turned up his desire to conquer women.

Chuck didn't really care much for others. He took care of himself and only protected what was his or what he felt was his. When something got in his way, he usually went through it. Guys never stood up to him, and girls usually fell right into his hands. Not only was he physically dominating, he was a master at messing with people's minds as well. He thoroughly enjoyed his superiority over everyone else. Unfortunately, he was measuring his superiority over others in all the wrong things.

CHAPTER 3

CHUCK first met Angela the night after what should have been his high school graduation. He was still undecided on college or work; he wasn't lined out to do either. Since he hadn't graduated, going to college would require some testing and lots of financial help. None of that mattered to Chuck that night, though. He was there to have a good time. Parties were his first love. He loved them almost as much as the girls he went there to meet.

Being the party animal that he was, he knew where all of the cool people were going to be on any given night. Though he never really cared who was cool or not, he understood that the sheep always followed the popular kids. If he wanted to be around all of the insecure young things who were dying to have someone like him take an interest in them, he'd need to be at the cool parties. To him, it was always just another party, though. Whoever the host was, Chuck usually knew them. Regardless of who was throwing the party or where it was at, Chuck always followed the same game plan. He would always get really drunk, he'd get high if the people with money or contacts were there, and he'd always meet and leave with someone of the opposite sex.

Chuck noticed Angela right away that night. He had barely made his way across the living room when he spotted her standing outside by the pool. He made up his mind immediately that she would be his focus for the night. Her beauty jumped out at him. She was truly a knockout, but Chuck always analyzed the entire picture before he jumped into chasing someone. As usual, he started with who they were with. In this case, it was a bunch of losers she was with. Then he looked for body language that might give away how they thought about themselves. He could see it in her face that she didn't even realize that she stood out like a sore thumb in that group. The way she was standing almost deemphasized her curvy physique, as if she were embarrassed of her beautiful adult body. The two girls she was with were overweight and unsure of themselves. They both had bad acne and appeared to be scared to even be there.

Chuck could tell that the guys around her were all checking her out, but she seemed unimpressed by it. She wasn't unaware, though; he could tell that. She just simply wasn't impressed and didn't seem to care that they were attracted to her. It was as if she knew what guys wanted but she didn't need anything from them. Chuck knew that they would all look away if he was out there, talking to her. No one wanted to see him looking at his girl, especially no one in that group of losers.

Chuck quickly decided that he would free her from the fools. From what he saw, she was a beautiful, sexy girl who seemed a bit self-conscious. She didn't like guys checking her out, so he couldn't just compliment her beauty. He could tell that she was self-conscious by the way she was dressed and by her posture. Sure, she knew those guys were looking at her, but why wasn't she flaunting those big breasts? If he were her, they would be sticking out there to tease the guys and piss off all of the girls. It occurred to him that she was likely someone who had been sexually abused. That type always dressed modestly and hated to be stared at. He liked that about her, as he knew exactly how to work the emotionally repressed type. He knew that he had to have her, and he knew that he could get her. He was already working out his strategy, playing it through in his head. She most likely could not be had in a single evening. It would take some time to gain her trust. He'd need it if he was right about her past.

Since it was Jeff's party, Chuck grabbed him by the arm. "Who is that over there by the pool?"

Jeff knew who he was talking about without even looking and without any description, as he had been longingly staring at the beautiful Angela since she had walked through his front door. He knew that she was the only one Chuck could be talking about pointing in that direction, but he was hoping that Chuck was talking about someone other than Angela.

Jeff had been planning to make his move on Angela that night at his party; that night was going to be the night he finally told her what he thought about her. She had been in his mind for months before the party, and, in all honesty, she was the reason for the party. His parents almost never left town, and it was his big chance to get to spend some time with her. He was hoping to impress her with his parents' big, expensive house. He couldn't help but think that he should have already been over there, talking to her. He had just been too much of a chicken. It had taken everything he had just to ask her to come to the party. When he asked her to come, she gave him a big smile while accepting. Now he was beating himself up for not capitalizing on that moment. Why hadn't he told her how he felt then? Now she was in Chuck's crosshairs, and he knew he didn't stand a chance. There was nothing he could do.

Like everyone else, Jeff was deathly afraid of Chuck. He had seen what Chuck could do on the football field, and he had seen him destroy guys in fights off the field. Jeff had even witnessed Chuck beat a guy with a rearview mirror he had ripped off a parked car. Jeff knew that Chuck would get whatever he wanted, whether he helped him or not, and now he was asking about his Angela.

Jeff finally answered with a question. "Which one?"

Chuck gave him a "What the heck are you talking about?" look, and Jeff knew he had to stop hoping and start answering. It had to be Angela he was asking about; who else standing in her group was even kind of attractive?

"Her name is Angela," he finally answered.

In typical Chuck fashion, he didn't ask anything else about her. Hearing her name helped Chuck remember seeing her around school, and he was sure he had had her in a class or two over the years. He began to put the pieces together and remembered that she used to be really skinny and dorky. Now she was a knockout.

Chuck was sure that he had never spoken to her. He would find out all he needed to know about her straight from the source. His policy was to never ask anyone else for advice or permission, as he had found that most people weren't very perceptive anyway. Instead of pumping Jeff for information that would likely be half wrong, he just walked away, straight toward her.

Seeing Chuck honed in on her the way he was, Jeff suddenly felt broken inside. He knew that Chuck would have her. If he were lucky, it would only be a one-time thing and he could still have a chance to get to know her afterward. He felt sorry for Angela. Chuck was never good news for anyone.

What a waste of such a gorgeous creature, he told himself.

Jeff was certain that Chuck would only use her and likely hurt her emotionally and possibly even physically.

As Chuck barreled toward her, Angela spotted him coming her way. It almost seemed as if he was pushing people out of his way. She quickly decided that there was no chance he wasn't coming to talk to her. From the moment she first noticed him heading her way, he was staring right into her eyes. Angela knew who he was and had long since thought that he was the best-looking guy in school. She had been an admirer of his for a couple of years and had even thought about what it would be like to be held by him. He was so powerful, and everyone else seemed so afraid of him. She knew all the bad stuff too, but that didn't really matter to her. She even thought to herself that he could keep her safe.

"I know you from school, right?" He began speaking before he was all the way there, and his stare never broke. Chuck understood that eye contact and focused attention would bring her immediately into his world. The intention was to show her that she had his total attention, as if no one else mattered. It was pretty easy for him to pull off, as no one else did matter to Chuck.

He wanted her to feel as if she was all there was to him. As usual, his plan was working, and it felt to Angela as if they were

17

completely alone, as if no one else was standing there with her or around her. There he was, absolutely locked into her, completely in control. To her, the feeling was exhilarating; she loved the focus and could feel his dominance over her and the party. She felt no competition for his attention. It had been his intention to make it personal between them immediately, and he was very successful.

Why waste time with the rest of her group? he thought.

They were of no consequence to him. They were nothing more than a bunch of losers. It was her he was after. Acknowledging them would only slow him down. If he spoke to any of them or even gave them a look, it would be a total waste of his time. At that point, he couldn't even have told anyone how many people were standing there or if they were guys or girls. It was just him and her. Her experience was as he desired; he was all she knew existed from the second they had made eye contact.

"Yes, and I know who you are, Chuck," she answered.

"It's Angela, right?" he said, ignoring her reference to knowing him, as he knew the reputation he had both as a troublemaker and as a player. As much as it should have mattered, his reputation had rarely hurt his chances in the past. When his reputation mattered to his prey, he knew inside that the person was to virtuous for him anyway. He reasoned that there were just too many fish in the sea to worry about those types of girls. Most girls thought they could change or save someone like him. That usually worked to his advantage.

How arrogant he thought it was for someone to believe they could handle someone like him. How foolish someone would have to be to think that they could improve him; he knew that was up to him to decide. Knowing that people believed they could handle him was just another tool he would use to suck them in. Chuck would show them vulnerability to allow a glimmer of hope that they could change him, but, in the end, he was always in control.

"Yes," she answered, and, unintentionally, she showed him how she felt about him with a shy smile that he knew came from the fact that he had actually known her name.

Chuck saw it and knew immediately that she was his. He never missed a clue, no matter how much he had to drink. Chuck prided himself on knowing when to close the deal, and this was that time.

Before he could make his move, his girlfriend, Stephanie—quite possibly the sexiest girl at the party—pushed her way into their little group and handed him a beer. Stephanie was tall, looked like a model, and was in the most popular crowds at school.

Calmly, Chuck turned to Stephanie. "I need a second to talk with Angela about her brother. We'll be right back."

He took Angela by the hand and walked her across the yard and around the pool. The entire yard was full of people, so they were able to blend into the crowd and escape to the back side of the yard easily.

Angela was both surprised and exhilarated by this move. *Did he just pick me over Stephanie?* she wondered. *Does he plan to hold me tonight? Will I get to kiss him?* The questions began to pop into her head. Suddenly, she started to feel some fear. *How could I ever stop a guy like him? Will I have to try?*

As soon as they were sufficiently hidden behind the crowd in the deepest, darkest part of the backyard, Chuck stopped and took both of Angela's hands in his. He quickly reestablished the eye contact that had initially sucked her in before he began to speak.

"I'm really sorry I lied to Stephanie to get you alone. If you do have a brother, I don't know him. I just needed to be alone with you."

Her expression told him that it was working; he could see it in her face. She needed him to choose her over the beautiful Stephanie; he could see that, so he would give it to her. He also knew that Stephanie would take him back if he left the party. What the heck. He had already slept with her several times anyway.

"I want to take you somewhere we can be alone to talk privately," he said confidently. "I'm not sure why, but I'm willing to walk out on Stephanie to get to know you. You are very attractive, but something more than physical attraction is drawing me to you. If I don't take this chance to figure it out, I'll beat myself up over it later. Can we please go somewhere where we can be alone?"

Angela knew that Chuck was an operator. She also knew that she would likely get hurt by him. She quickly decided that she didn't care about any of that. He was so good looking, so powerful, and it felt like he really wanted her. Something about him made her want to be his, or maybe she was just curious about what he would say or do next. She told herself that she would go with him, but if he hurt her in any way, she would never see him again. She didn't want sex, only to be wanted and protected by him.

She didn't even answer Chuck's question. She just nodded, as she was feeling a rush of fear and excitement all at once. Before she knew what was happening, he was pulling her toward the bushes, away from the house, and into an even darker part of the yard. The bushes turned out to be trees that were covering up a six-foot-tall brick wall.

"No problem," said Chuck, and almost immediately, she could feel his powerful hands around her tiny waist. It felt like he could have thrown her straight over, and she actually felt a jolt of fear before he gently positioned her on the top of the wall. She couldn't help but feel even more attracted to him now that she had felt how powerful he really was.

"Just wait there and I'll go over and bring you down on the other side," he said.

Before she could acknowledge him, he was over it and on the other side. She jumped into his arms and held on a bit longer than she needed to. He loved how she clung to him and knew what she was up to. She found herself holding on to his massive frame and feeling a desire for him that she had never felt for anyone before. Chuck was so powerfully built that she couldn't help but be impressed. Yet he seemed like more of a protector to her than any sort of threat. Was he really this good of an operator, or was some of it real? She had no idea which was true. She was caught up in the moment, and there was nowhere else she would rather be.

He grabbed her hand again but this time pulled her in tight and gently pressed her up against the wall. "You look amazing tonight, and I'm so lucky to be here with you," he said, looking right into her eyes.

She was melting inside. No one had ever made her feel like this. Sure, guys had told her she was pretty, and they were always complimenting her body, but she never believed anyone like she believed Chuck. He really thought she was gorgeous, and he wanted her more than he wanted Stephanie.

Chuck knew how to play this one. He could take his shot now or he could treat her like she was special and set up a more permanent thing with her. Like the rest of them, if he wanted her either way; it would be his choice. He always started with the intention of just trying to hook up with his prey for an evening or at least to forward his cause by setting them up for a second meeting to close the deal. It wasn't any different to this point with Angela. However, he was starting to have some doubts. He really liked how she seemed to believe everything he was saying. It felt like she was counting on him in some way, like she needed him to take care of her. There had been no resistance with her, and he could see the potential to have a hot girlfriend who would allow him to do his own thing as long as he always protected her.

Could she develop into that for me? he wondered.

All of this had happened in only about ten minutes since he had first met her. She had only said a couple of words to him, and he already knew the potential of this relationship. Well, at least he knew the potential in it for him.

Angela hadn't given the situation much thought at all. She was extremely attracted to him both physically and emotionally, but she hadn't really analyzed anything beyond the fact that he wanted her. He had connected with her so quickly that she had just followed.

Even if it is all an act on his part, isn't it worth it to feel this way? she reasoned.

Over the last couple of years, she had felt that guys were attracted to her, but never had she felt this type of desire from someone, especially from someone like him, someone who could have anyone he wanted. At that point, she had decided to follow his lead wherever it took her. Her curiosity, along with the enjoyment of how he was making her feel, was all she needed.

Chuck led her on foot to the house where he and his mother lived. It was a modest place with three small bedrooms and a somewhat undersized living room. They weren't poor, but they didn't have much either. Chuck never knew his father, and his mother was almost never home. She worked a lot and always had some boyfriend who was more important to her than Chuck was. Ever since Chuck could remember, his mother had always chosen men over him. He heard her with them at night, and he hated her for it. His mother seemed needy to him and even somewhat pitiful. He had no respect for her, and she didn't really seem to care how rudely he treated her because of it. Whenever Chuck asked his mother about his father, she had always said, "He was too good for us, so he left." Beyond that, she was completely unwilling to talk about his father. That too was a point of contention for Chuck, and he resented her for it. As desperate as she was for sex, he had decided that she probably didn't even know who his father was.

Chuck kept Angela in the living room, away from his bedroom. "I don't want anything to happen that we'll both regret. I want you too badly to go in there and sit on my bed with you."

He had been with many girls and even some women on that bed. Actually, he had twice been with much older women; both were his mother's friends. His mom was always so busy pleasing whatever guy was in her life that she didn't even realize or care that her high school-aged son was sleeping with her friends.

Chuck gave Angela his absolute attention their entire time together. He asked her all about her family and life. She told him what she wanted to but left out the painful stuff. Most of all, he wanted to manufacture the character he felt she needed to see in him. He knew that he would mess things up, but if he could hook her emotionally, she would stand by him and he wouldn't have to be alone anymore. Although he had a girlfriend in Stephanie, he was still completely alone, and he knew it. He needed someone less plastic than Stephanie to need him. He craved for someone to truly love him, someone who would be there for him no matter what.

Could this be the one? he wondered.

The time flew by, and before they knew it, it was midnight. Angela knew that she needed to be home by 12:30 a.m. or her mother would go off on her when she got in. Her stepfather would likely already be asleep. Actually, this was her second step-father. The first one seemed okay to her, but her mother couldn't manage to hold on to him.

Her real father was driven so far away by her mother's behavior that he broke all ties with them and didn't seem to even want to get to know her. Angela supposed he was so thankful to be free of that nag of a mother of hers that he had left the state or maybe even the country. She wasn't sure which, but she was sure he was gone forever either way.

"I hate to cut the night short, but I really need to get home or I'll break my mother's curfew and have to face the consequences." She hated speaking up and had been seriously considering keeping her mouth shut and breaking curfew.

"No problem. I don't want you getting in trouble. I don't want your mom hating me right from the start." Chuck was being as convincing as he could be, and he could tell that Angela was eating it up.

"Thanks, Chuck." She was impressed that he hadn't even tried to keep her out past her curfew. Maybe he wasn't so bad.

"I'll walk you home." He figured that it couldn't be too far to her house based on the fact that she had told him she walked to school every day.

"That would be great, but it's pretty far to walk. If we leave now, we could probably make it, but I'd bet it's at least twenty to twenty-five minutes to walk there." She hadn't seen a car in front of the house but assumed he had one.

"We better head out then. My car's not running right now, so we've got to walk. Sorry."

She would later find out that his car wasn't the problem at all. He couldn't drive her home because he didn't have a license. He had been pulled over in his mother's car with one of his mother's friends. Both he and the woman were drunk. Chuck had spent the night in jail, and they had confiscated his license for a year. His year without a license would be over in just a few days. The woman got a far worse punishment.

Chuck had made his decision; he would set the hook for a long-term deal. She was the perfect fit for him. She was all kinds of sexy and seemed to have a tremendous need to be loved and protected, and he could tell she would follow his lead going forward. He knew her, but in spite of all of the evidence, she did not know him at all. He was sure she had bought everything. He believed that she thought he was the guy he had projected to be, and, as usual, he was correct.

Chuck walked her home, holding her hand the entire way. He gave her the softest, sweetest kiss she could have ever imagined, and they exchanged a full-body hug. It was done. Their first date was over, and he knew that she would be his. They both knew it.

Angela went straight to bed but got practically no sleep. She was Chuck's if he wanted her. She lay in bed thinking about how great it was going to be to be his girlfriend while Chuck went right back to work. Yes, she would be his, but it wouldn't change who he was.

Chuck headed right back to the party after they parted, found a drunk Stephanie, and took her right back to his place.

Business as usual, he thought as he undressed her.

She was like a beautiful Hollywood actress and just as plastic. Around two in the morning, he found himself staring at the ceiling, thinking of Angela. Stephanie was only a sex toy for him, and he could hardly stand her when she was awake.

Angela was much more desirable to him than Stephanie. Though he had done hardly anything with Angela at that point, he knew that it was only a matter of time until he would violate any innocence she had. If Stephanie found out, he figured she would likely do something really stupid—not because she would be losing him but because she wouldn't understand why someone physically inferior to her had stolen her boyfriend. The more he thought about it, he began to wonder if she would even have an argument. Angela was pretty hot. If she knew how to present herself, people might actually consider her Stephanie's equal or possibly even her superior. That sent him wondering what was under those loose clothes. From what he had seen and felt during their hug, she was pretty amazing. He looked forward to her unveiling.

Based on his evening with Angela, Chuck could tell that she would not be in his business. She had never even asked him about Stephanie. She didn't even seem to care if he planned to stop seeing her. She had tremendous potential.

In two months time, Chuck's and Angela's lives had become intertwined. He had shown her exactly what he wanted to, and she had believed it all. They were officially boyfriend and girlfriend, and they began to spend all of their time together. She practically lived at his house, and Chuck's mom didn't even seem to notice or care. Sexually, they were like a newlywed couple.

Angela became the first and only girl to really captivate Chuck. He could go out on his own and do whatever he wanted, and she would never question him about where he had been or what he had been doing. He drank all the time, did whatever drugs he wanted to do, and stole stuff everywhere he went and even from her and was never questioned about any of it by Angela. She had decided that she wasn't going to be like her mother and drive this man out of her life by complaining and poking at everything he did. During those first two months, he only went out without her a couple of times. Both times he had slept with Stephanie, and he would have liked that deal to continue if it weren't for Stephanie being such a control freak. Once Stephanie was gone from his life, there really was no one else—at least not for a while there wasn't.

CHAPTER 4

ALMOST a year went by with Chuck and Angela living like a married couple. They occasionally went to parties together, but Angela wasn't much for big groups and usually preferred to stay home. When they did go somewhere together, she felt proud to be with him. Even when she noticed him looking at other girls, she knew inside that he would not leave her. She knew he fooled around some but told herself that it was her that he loved. She loved how protective he had become. No one could even look at her without Chuck jumping all over them. She didn't care at all that he didn't like her having her own friends. All she needed was him, and that's all he allowed her to have. That was enough for her.

Angela had a full-time job at a grocery store, and she believed she was making good money. She and Chuck had moved out of Chuck's mom's house and into a low-rent apartment in a sketchy area of town that was near the neighborhood and high school where they had always lived. Angela was paying all of the bills. She felt content and never really worried much about where things were going. Chuck loved the arrangement but wasn't really capable of being content with anything. His compulsive drinking and running around were his way of life. Inside, though, he could not have been more miserable. He was constantly being tormented by his failures and his inability to pull his life together. Being sober had become very painful to Chuck.

Angela's mother was openly disappointed in her decision to not pursue a college education. She could not have hated Chuck more either. She repeatedly told Angela that Chuck was bad news and that he would never change. Prior to their dating, Angela's mother had read about him in the paper. When he was a junior, he had been an all-state football player and had led his team deep into the playoffs. Everything after that read like a train wreck. The article her mother read had been written after Chuck was arrested for being caught on campus with drugs. The article talked about how much he had thrown away, and it had several quotes from his disappointed football coach. To Angela, it seemed like her mother would have hated anyone. She had watched her mother destroy her marriage twice and had never heard her approve of any man. The fact that her mother disapproved of Chuck so strongly actually made her desire for Chuck grow stronger.

Angela agonized over Chuck's situation. His depression over what he had thrown away was destroying him. More than once, he told Angela that he wanted to play football again, though he was sure no one would ever let him play. With no money for college, terrible high school grades, and no test scores or a high school diploma, he had really disqualified and buried himself.

"Why didn't I at least finish that last semester and graduate?" he asked Angela just about every time he drank.

For months, he talked about getting a job, but he kept drinking so much that he never got around to going in for an interview anywhere. Angela was all he had, and she was pulling all the weight. They had been together for almost a year, and he hadn't contributed in any way. All he had ever done for her was beat a couple guys up who had looked her way. For her, his defense of her was a sign of how safe she would always be with him. Of course, she was wrong.

At the height of his depression, he was arrested at Angela's mother's house for almost killing her uncle Larry. Though Angela had never told him about what her uncle Larry had done to her as a child, Chuck always knew someone had. The way Angela spoke about him before Chuck had even met him made him start to theorize. When they finally came face-to-face, the man's arrogance and unacceptable staring at Angela's body confirmed Chuck's suspicions.

Chuck knew people, and he immediately knew that guy was trash. Knowing he was likely the reason Angela was the way she was with intimacy made his blood boil. For more than a year, Chuck had dealt with the damage this creep had done to Angela. Though some of it was pretty subtle, it always came at an inopportune intimate time. Whether it caused her to be protective of what she would allow him to do or, in the worst cases, caused her to make him stop completely, Chuck felt tremendous anger every time it popped up. The anger was never directed at Angela but at her rapist. He knew that man was Uncle Larry.

All of Chuck's anger over Angela's violation was being directed into the man he was face-to-face with. When he first noticed Uncle Larry checking her out, he asked him, "What's your problem, pervert?"

Like Chuck, Uncle Larry was also a heavy drinker. That night was no different. His reply almost cost him his life.

"You got my sloppy seconds, son."

Before he knew what had happened, Chuck had smashed his face in with a full, unopened forty-ounce bottle of beer. The bottle shattered and sliced open his face in several huge gashes. As if that had not been enough, Chuck picked up his limp body and threw him through the sliding glass doors. He then took Angela by the hand and walked right out the front door.

The incident destroyed any chance Chuck had of ever gaining the approval of Angela's mother—not that he cared. He had spent a couple of days in jail when Uncle Larry was released from the hospital and dropped the charges for fear of spending time in prison for what he had done to Angela. Several times between the ages of twelve and fourteen, Uncle Larry had violated Angela sexually. On three separate occasions, Uncle Larry had slept over at their house to sleep off a heavy night of drinking. When he would climb into her bed, he had always threatened to kill her mother if she made any noise. It was like being in hell to Angela, but she was too scared to say anything to her mother or anyone else. Each time she hoped it would never happen again. When her latest stepfather married her mother and moved in with them, Uncle Larry stopped coming over.

Uncle Larry made sure Angela's mom didn't press charges by pleading with her, admitting his crime to her, and paying for all of the damage. Angela successfully begged her mother not to press charges on Chuck for what he had done to her house. She swore to her mother that she would not press charges or even admit to anything Uncle Larry had done to her in exchange for her letting Chuck walk away from this.

In the end, Angela loved Chuck even more for what he had done for her. Thankfully, Chuck hadn't killed her uncle, as he couldn't have walked away from that. Angela finally felt free from what had been done to her, and she loved thinking about Chuck destroying that bum. She now felt as if she owed everything to Chuck for freeing her from the emotional prison her uncle had put her in. She was so deeply in love with Chuck after the incident that he quickly found that he could get away with anything he wanted to do. Chuck had not done what he did to her uncle only for her but for him too. It hurt him to think of anyone touching Angela. She was his.

As time went on, Chuck began to feel majorly depressed over the fact that his life was going nowhere. He began to realize that he could not take control; something inside him began to make him question why he should go on at all. The only thing that made him feel good about himself was conquering women. He knew that he was better than other guys, and it pissed him off that other people were happy.

Are they just too stupid to realize how worthless life is? he wondered.

Even if he had things together, he didn't see the point of life.

With such strong feelings of worthlessness, Chuck became difficult to be around. Angela noticed he didn't seem to desire her the way he once had, and she was pretty sure he was taking care of his needs elsewhere. It became normal for him to stay out all night, and he never told her anything about where he had been or what he had done. She loved him so deeply that she refused to ruin things by nagging him. Though he practically never told her he did, she knew that he loved her. The most difficult thing for her was seeing him so unhappy. She knew he was better than that.

What can I do to help him? she wondered.

Her response to his lack of interest in her was to work out even harder so her body would be more attractive to him. She believed that his lack of attraction to her was her fault. All that mattered to her was him, so she began to wonder if she could bring some hope back into his life.

CHAPTER 5

ANGELA couldn't believe it when he came through her checkout line at the grocery store. He was wearing a coach's shirt, and she recognized him from a TV interview Chuck had been watching the night before. It was really him, Coach Jones. Coach Jones had just taken the reins of the Sam Houston State football program. He had been given the opportunity when the retiring coach, Coach Rollings, recommended him as his replacement. Coach Jones had been a defensive back for Coach Rollings almost twenty years prior. He was never the most talented player but had made up for it with hard work and heady play. In the time between playing for Coach Rollings and now, Coach Jones had been an assistant at UCLA and at Arizona State. He was a promising candidate for getting Sam Houston State's football program back on the map, and it was his big chance at a head coaching job. For Coach Jones, it could be his stepping stone to one of the big programs. At least that was his plan.

Angela could not contain herself when it was his turn to check out. "My boyfriend is the best football player in the state, maybe in the whole country. He's sitting at home instead of going to college because of some really stupid mistakes he made in high school."

"Well, then I better get a look at him," Coach Jones responded in an attempt to be friendly. "Do you guys have any tape on him? Can I talk to his high school coach about him?"

Angela took control from there. She told him yes to both questions and that she would get everything to him. She then visited Chuck's high school coach, Coach Briening, and tried to convince him that Chuck had straightened out. She begged him to talk to Coach Jones on Chuck's behalf. Coach Briening had all the film anyone would need to see on Chuck. Just about every play of every game he played in was a highlight. He agreed to speak with Coach Jones but told Angela that he would have to disclose everything: the arrests, drinking, drugs, stealing, among other things. Angela was quick to point out that he had not been charged with a crime for anything since she had been dating him. She did not mention the arrest and two nights in jail for almost killing her uncle since no charges were ever pressed. It had been almost a year since he had been in any real trouble, she pointed out.

Angela was thrilled at the opportunity for Chuck but didn't say a word to him. She knew he wouldn't want her doing all of that behind his back, but she couldn't help herself. She loved him deeply and only wanted the best for him. She knew he could do it, and she wanted him to succeed. She knew in her heart that playing football and getting his life some direction would cure him. She was sure it would make him happy. Though he had not been running, she knew he lifted weights almost every day. He had told her he was getting much stronger and bigger than he had been in high school, and she could tell.

Coach Jones got the call from Coach Briening, and the two agreed to meet. It didn't take long for Coach Jones to remember who Chuck was. He had seen footage of him before. He was the guy whom everyone had been talking about a couple of years before. Tons of kids had talent and blew it, but not many had Chuck's talent. The guy was an animal. His high school footage had been passed around to all of the major programs and coaches. All of them had interest in the player they saw. By his senior year, no one wanted the trouble he would surely bring. His arrests, suspensions, and the fact that he had dropped out of school had killed any chance he had of playing college football. At least that was what Coach Jones had heard about Chuck.

Coach Briening started explaining the type of athlete Chuck was, but Coach Jones quickly interrupted him.

"I've seen enough to know he can play. I know a smaller school like ours would never even get a shot at a guy like this under normal circumstances. What I want to know is, do you think he has changed? Do you think he can keep himself clean and out of trouble? Would you give him a chance if you were me?"

Coach Briening sat back in his chair to think through his reply before he spoke. Angela had pleaded with him to give Coach Jones a good report on Chuck. She had sworn to him that Chuck had changed, yet when he asked her if he was working, she said, "Not right now." When he asked if he still drank and did drugs, she said, "He drinks some, but I haven't caught him doing drugs in a long time." It just wasn't enough for him to give Coach Jones his word, so he told him, "I'm not sold on him, but I do think he would probably be the best player on your defense right away. He was about two hundred and thirty-five pounds as a junior and about two hundred and fifty as a senior. Now he's about two hundred and seventy pounds, from what Angela told me, he lifts weights almost every day. I hear that he's an animal in the gym now, and that's coming from some of my ex-players who see him at the gym on a regular basis. They say he can bench over four hundred pounds and does his last set of squats with five hundred and eighty-five pounds. I definitely believe he's that strong. I just can't believe he's really any different as a person. He seems to make all of his own decisions and cannot accept or obey authority. Honestly, if I thought he was different, I would tell you, but I don't. I'm really sorry to tell you this."

"No. Thank you for being so honest with me, Coach. I really wanted to hear differently, but I needed to hear the truth. I guess I'll have to think about it and give the kid a call myself to see where I think he is." He truly was sorry to hear Coach Briening say that he wasn't convinced that Chuck had changed.

"That's how I would handle it. Good luck, Coach Jones. We are all pulling for you guys."

Every night for a week, Coach Jones watched the films Coach Briening had given him on Chuck. The footage was keeping him up at night. A player like that could make an immediate impact.

He could make their defense a force right away. The thought of signing Chuck was torturing him.

One day in early June, Chuck got a call from Coach Jones. It had been weeks since Angela had spoken to him at the grocery store. She had left him messages, but he had never called her back. Angela had begun to believe that it just wasn't going to happen for Chuck.

"Hello?"

"Is Chuck Wiseman there?" Coach Jones had never spoken to Chuck, but he was pretty sure it was Chuck's voice when the person had answered.

"You got him." Chuck had absolutely no idea who he was talking to.

"Hello, Chuck. This is Coach Jones from Sam Houston State." After a moment of silence Coach Jones continued. "I met your lovely girlfriend, Angela. She basically told me that I would be making a really big mistake if I didn't try to get you on my football team. She was very persistent."

"I had no idea, sir." He wasn't sure what to say, but the "sir" part was definitely the right way to address the coach.

"Can you come see me in the morning so we can discuss the possibility of you playing football at Sam Houston State?"

Chuck was shocked and excited but didn't show it on the phone. "Sure. What time?" he calmly said.

"Be here at seven a.m.," he said, knowing that that would be a challenge for a heavy drinker. "Meet me at the stadium by Gate A. If you are late, don't bother coming in at all."

Chuck felt like telling him to stuff it, but he wanted this chance so badly that he held his tongue. "I'll be there, Coach."

When Angela got home from work, Chuck had prepared dinner for her. It was so out of character for him to do anything that nice for her, so she was more skeptical than excited.

"Okay. What's going on, Chuck?" she asked.

"I got a call from Coach Jones this afternoon. He invited me to meet with him tomorrow morning to talk about playing football for Sam Houston State. He told me that it's only because of you that I was getting a chance."

She could see that he was actually touched by what she had done by the way he was speaking and by the look on his face. It relieved her that he wasn't angry, as it seemed like everything made him angry lately. She felt so happy for him that she began to tear up a bit. It was the first time in a long while that she felt as if he really was thankful for her. That night they reconnected the way they had when it had all began, and for a while things were great between them.

The evening was truly special; it was the single greatest night in their relationship. Chuck had gone out of his way to prepare a special dinner for her, and they were like first-time lovers the rest of the evening. Angela kept telling herself that it would be this way going forward. Chuck was too smart and too talented to fail now that he was getting a second chance. She was sure their lives would improve.

The next morning, Angela woke up an hour early to make sure Chuck was well fed and prepared to meet Coach Jones. She even drove him to the meeting and waited in her car for him. The meeting actually went pretty well. Chuck acted as if he was trying to pick up on some hot chick so he wouldn't lose his focus and tell the high-and-mighty coach where to go. He had convinced himself that he could fool the guy just like he had so many girls. He knew that he could play football at that level, and if he put any effort into it at all, school would be easy. Still, under all of his feelings of superiority, he knew that he would blow it. He could feel that pressure building inside of him already. They would expect him to change, but could he?

Coach Jones started in on some ground rules and terms for the agreement they were about to make. "I am putting my name on the line in giving you this chance, Chuck. I need you to guarantee that I won't be sorry for taking this chance. Will you sign an agreement for me? It will boil down to one thing: if you mess up even once, you are gone. No second chances. Can you do that?"

"Sure," Chuck answered. He was doing his best to act like the good kid everyone always wanted him to be. Inside, though, his stomach was churning. The thought of one mistake costing him this second chance was intimidating to him.

"Additionally, I'll need you to take the ACT so we can get you admitted. Your high school grade point average is too low to get you admitted even if you had graduated. You'll also need to take the GED test to give you a high school diploma equivalency. Will you take the tests?"

"No problem. I'm pretty good at tests."

Chuck was an avid reader. He loved math and liked to read about science and technology in magazines. School was never difficult to him, but showing up to class had been. Chuck had no fears about his ability to pass the tests; it was everything else that would be difficult for him, and he knew it.

As promised, Chuck signed the agreement and took the tests. He got a 31 on the ACT, with near-perfect scores in both math and science. The GED was a breeze. No problem there. Angela bought him test prep books for both the GED and the ACT. After a quick studying of each, he was more prepared than most high school students were after four years of studying. The entire coaching staff was amazed at his scores, but Chuck wasn't.

Due to Angela's hard work, Chuck was getting another opportunity. His God-given gifts, athletic ability, and high IQ afforded him that second chance. His books, tuition, and all fees were covered by the athletic department, and he had Angela for the rest of his needs. His talent was never in question; it was everything else that was in question. With Angela's help, Chuck had been convinced that he could pull it together and take advantage of the opportunity. Angela really believed in him, and based on his size, ability, and the tapes of him destroying quarterbacks as an all-state defensive end, this new head coach was willing to take a chance on him in spite of his poor grades and multiple brushes with the law.

Things finally seemed to be coming together for the couple. The few weeks between Chuck signing the agreement with Coach Jones and the start of practice were the best times Chuck and Angela ever had together. They were all over each other. She could not get enough of him, and he was a new man now that she had gotten his life back for him. It didn't even seem to Angela that he was drinking anymore, though he was. He was only having a beer or two instead of getting stinking drunk every night. Chuck stayed home every night and worked hard to pass the tests and get his body into outstanding shape. Angela felt like he was becoming the man she knew he could be.

Unfortunately, things would soon change. Chuck was starting to feel the stableness of his situation, and it made him uncomfortable. How could he let her be the one calling the shots? It didn't feel right, and he just wasn't capable of giving up control. It needed to end.

CHAPTER 6

T didn't take long for Chuck to begin to erode the high path he was on. As usual, the football part was easy for him. He quickly rose to first string. At six feet five inches and two hundred and seventy pounds of solid muscle, the only thing freshman about him was his academic standing. Chuck's style of play was nasty—almost dirty. He didn't just tackle guys; he tried to end them. He actually wanted to hurt people when he hit them. He used all of his anger on anyone who got in his way, and he was known for holding guys down, late hits, and for taking cheap shots whenever he could. His teammates began to turn against him, but he just kept on laying them out. It had always been his way. He wanted them to know what he could do to them. He didn't want anyone to think they were even close to as tough as he was. Keeping them intimidated made him feel unstoppable. He was only nice to the women he was trying to seduce. Guys only got in his way, and he had never met one he couldn't run over or outsmart.

In typical Chuck fashion, he began to focus his attention on the ladies. Now that he was someone again, he felt like conquering the women who would surely be impressed by who he was. It didn't take long for him to find a target. Her name was Jennifer Tines, and she was, in Chuck's view, the best-looking cheerleader on the cheerleading squad. She was tall, curvy, and blonde, and to Chuck, she looked just like a Barbie doll. Her body was solid from top to bottom, and Chuck really wanted to examine her to see if she was made out of plastic like her Barbie doll twin.

Jennifer had a boyfriend. His name was Derrick Smith, and he was one of the linebackers on the football team. Jennifer and Derrick met religiously every day after practice to hug and kiss on each other. Chuck liked what he saw and began to follow Derrick out of the locker room every day to watch his prey tease him. He knew that she noticed him staring at her day after day, and he felt like she was encouraging him by making eye contact and smiling back at him.

Jennifer was in a sorority, which was a world Chuck knew little about. He knew the Greek type, though, and he knew that he would never be one of them. As a member of a sorority, she likely came from money. These types always seemed to stay in their too-good-for-anyone-not-in-a-sorority-or-fraternity mind-set.

How can I get closer to her? he wondered.

He decided that he would just continue to stare at her every time their paths crossed until an opportunity arose for him to make a move.

After a couple of weeks of staring at one another, the cheerleaders moved their practice into the gym. That was very good news for Chuck, as the football team spent their last ninety minutes of practice in the weight room. The weight room was on the north end of the gym while the locker room was on the south side of the gym. The players were forced to walk across the gym to get to their lockers after their workouts. On the first occasion, as soon as he noticed that the cheerleaders were in the gym, he stopped about halfway across the gym to see if he could find her in the group. It didn't take him long, as she was right up front. As the cheerleading team captain, she was always in the front.

Jennifer had been waiting for that moment. It could not have gone better for her. She had hoped that he would look for her, but she was ecstatic that he had actually stopped to look for her. Her confirmation came when he gave her a big smile as soon as their eyes met. Not only was he well built, but he was very handsome—movie-star handsome—in her eyes. She couldn't help but think of him as a perfect physical specimen, and she had heard what an animal he was on the field and in the weight room. His fearsome play was all her boyfriend could talk about. She didn't know why, but his very presence made her tingle inside and act giddy outwardly. It was so obvious that her best friend on the team, Brandi, noticed it and confronted her after practice.

40

"What's going on here, Jennifer?"

Jennifer knew she could not hide it from Brandi, as no one knew her better than Brandi did. She couldn't help but feel bad about it, though. Derrick was such a good guy, and she knew he really cared for her. She knew that Brandi knew it too.

"I can't help myself. This guy is so—I don't know—forbidden, I guess. I can tell he's bad news, but I only want a fling with him. I can't stop thinking about him and what it would be like for him to take me with all of that power." She knew it sounded bad and figured Brandi would try to straighten her out.

"You are acting like a spoiled little rich girl who has to have everything she wants. I hope you realize that you are risking the loss of a great thing with Derrick. He is a great guy with a great future, and he worships you. You know this would kill him."

Brandi was not like the others. Sure, she was beautiful, but she was much more focused on doing something with her life than the others. Cheerleading was a passion for her, but she was not a cheerleader first in life. Although many of the girls were good students, Brandi was the best. She was committed to following her dreams. The wisdom she possessed made her incapable of acting as if things like what Jennifer was about to do didn't matter. Honestly, it was this quality that drew Jennifer to her. Jennifer's family had a great deal of money. She was used to getting whatever she wanted. Her beauty was both an asset and a curse in that she was not always mature enough to keep her looks from getting her unneeded attention. Jennifer projected a strong personality with tons of self-confidence, but inside, she was unsure of herself and desired admiration from others for her looks and for her family's money. Brandi understood all of this about her, and Jennifer knew she did.

"I know, Brandi, but I just can't control myself. I have to have this guy."

Brandi was disappointed in her and told her so. Jennifer was set on getting what she wanted and wasn't going to listen to any reasoning on this subject. She had made up her mind. She was going to have this guy, even if it destroyed Derrick. She needed Chuck.

Chuck looked forward to seeing her every day, especially when he was leaving the weight room in his little muscle shirts and tiny little shorts. Jennifer was always in there practicing and waiting for her chance to see him. Chuck would pump up his body as much as he could before making the walk. He had even noticed her talking to the other girls and giggling when he went by. He started to wonder if he could have them all, but, at that point, she was the only one he needed. He knew someone like her would not stand for any competition from inferior females. He could blow it before he got his shot if she even noticed him looking at any of the other girls, and there was no chance he was blowing it.

One day after practice, he found a folded piece of paper in his gym bag. He always left his bag near the backdoor of the gym. Everyone knew it was his bag, and he knew no one would ever dare mess with it. The note was actually a printed advertisement for a car wash fund-raiser the sorority was putting on the following Saturday. In big red letters, Jennifer had written, "Come see me at 3:00 p.m. J." She had signed it, "J," but he knew it was her.

This is a done deal, he told himself.

He could hardly wait to touch that body and kiss those lips. It crossed his mind that he might even get to kick Derrick's ass.

Will that get me thrown off the team? he wondered. *I'll have to play it a bit smarter than I've played things in the past. Too bad, because I can't stand the cheerleader type of player that Derrick is. Why is this guy always so upbeat?*

Chuck could hardly stand that the other players followed Derrick the way they did. To him, Derrick was an average player with a put-on over-the-top, upbeat attitude.

When Saturday rolled around, Chuck borrowed Angela's car and headed to the car wash. He had his license back but had to share a car with Angela. It was all her money, and the car was in her name, but he never thought of it that way, and neither did Angela. He had dropped Angela off at work at 2:00 p.m., and she was not getting off until 10:00 p.m. Chuck knew that she wasn't stupid. Actually, he was pretty impressed with how sharp she was. He knew she loved him no matter what, though. He didn't even consider that he could ever lose her. Even if she got hurt, he could always tell her he screwed up and that she was the only one for him. How could she find out, though? She never asked him about anything, and, if she did, he knew that he wouldn't have to answer. She would drop it and move on. That was why he loved her so much.

With Angela dropped off, it didn't take long for Chuck's thoughts and fantasies to turn to Jennifer.

Will I get to have her today while the others are out there, washing cars? he wondered. *Man, that would be sexy.*

Whatever happened, he would be ready for it. If she gave him the go-ahead, he would do it to her right there in the parking lot. He really didn't care. It would never be any reservation that he would have that would postpone the encounter. The only thing that would be unacceptable to him would be for things not to move a step closer to intercourse. That had to happen, and he would not stop until it had.

When he pulled up to the sorority house parking lot, he saw a bunch of sexy girls in their bathing suits. He almost forgot that it was Jennifer he was there for until he saw her. She looked like a Playboy centerfold to him. Her bikini was tiny, but her body wasn't. The strings could barely hold those little pads of material that were barely covering those tiny amounts of skin that they were designed to cover. Her stomach was thin and flat and showed some incredible definition. She definitely had all of the right curves.

Jennifer had been thinking about him while she waited for him to arrive. As soon as he drove in, she quickly spotted him.

It is really going to happen, she started to tell herself. *Can I really handle this?*

Her bet was that he was in awe of her physique. All guys were. She worked on it harder than anyone and knew that she had been truly blessed with what she had to work with.

Chuck noticed immediately that she was far too confident in herself for him to actually date. He hated people who were difficult to manipulate, and girls with confidence had long been his enemy. Of course, that wouldn't stop him from sleeping with her. Maybe her confidence was just the manufactured façade she projected for people to believe what she was trying to sell about herself. He saw a strong, sexy, confident centerfold, but something told him that she was just a spoiled little brat who would crumble if things got tough.

"Hey, Chuck," she hollered as she gestured for him to pull up into a parking spot away from the others.

While he was still parking, she jumped in the car with him. She appeared to be oiled up, and it crossed his mind that something might just pop right out of that little top of hers. He hoped the oil wouldn't get all over the passenger seat, as Angela would be sitting there later.

Jennifer was the most amazing creature that he had ever seen. Her eyes seemed almost too good to be true.

Is it even possible to have eyes that green? he asked himself.

Unlike most of those over-groomed girls he had been close to in the past, it almost looked as if she had no makeup on. Her face was just naturally the right color in the right places. Her hair was beyond blonde, and he began to wonder if it was her real color until he noticed that her eyebrows were the same golden color. As he quickly scanned her practically naked body, he decided that she had been blessed with the looks of an angel. Every part of her body was perfect, as if it had been designed as the ideal. Every part of her appeared to be perfectly tanned as well. He couldn't help but wonder how much time she must put in to keep her complexion just right. He was sure that it wasn't nearly as much time as she must have put in to get her every muscle toned up the way she had. He knew most of what he saw was just God given, but he could tell that she had worked tirelessly to make it better than anyone else's body. He figured her for a perfectionist.

How shallow she must be, he decided.

"What do you think?" she asked him.

"I think you are amazing."

He loved what he saw, but he already hated who she was. Angela looked almost that good but was a hundred times better than that idiot. He hated that he loved Angela so much. It made him have to deal with feelings he thought he would never have to deal with.

Why am I feeling this way?

He decided that he needed to get past any such feelings, and Jennifer's hot body was helping him do just that. If he didn't manage the feelings he was having for her, she would eventually begin to control him. He told himself that he didn't need Angela or anyone else, but down deep he knew that that was a lie.

"What about Derrick? I see you two hugging and kissing all over each other out in the open all the time."

He was really curious to hear what she would have to say. He knew she was ready to cheat on him, but he had no clue what her long-term expectations were. He was hoping she had none but was wondering if she was just trying to use him to make Derrick jealous or something. If she was, he could help her with that. Beating the crap out of Derrick would just be a bonus. He just didn't want it to get him thrown off the team.

"Derrick is sweet, but we're not married. He's not even around this weekend. Don't you live with someone anyway?"

She had seen Angela pick him up a couple of times. She had even felt some jealousy watching him climb into that car with her. When she asked around, she had learned that he had a live-in girlfriend. Angela never dressed in anything revealing from what she had seen, but from what she had noticed, Angela was a very worthy opponent. Jennifer didn't expect any less of someone who could get Chuck to live with her.

What would it be like to live with Chuck? she wondered.

Knowing that he was in a committed relationship made him even more attractive to Jennifer. She knew Derrick was a good guy, and she also knew that Chuck wasn't. He was nasty and rough, and that was what she liked about him.

"Yes, I do live with my girlfriend."

He didn't like admitting that, but he knew it meant that he could have Jennifer without affecting Angela. Certainly, the risk would be minimized if Jennifer wasn't going to expect him to be around for her. Angela never bothered him about where he was or who he was with, so a convenient, sex-only relationship would be low risk for him. If Jennifer knew about Angela and wouldn't be a risk to confront her, it would be an easy score for him. It sounded like she wanted a purely sexual relationship with him, but in his past experience, girls tended to become pretty clingy once he had slept with them. Why would she be any different? He knew that it was very unlikely that she had ever been with anyone who could please her the way he knew he was about to please her.

"Well, maybe I'm not so terrible then. What are you doing tonight?"

Jennifer almost looked vulnerable, but Chuck knew it was likely just the technique she used to get what she wanted. She was a natural at that. He felt sorry for her father, but not for Derrick. He assumed that she had them both wrapped around her finger.

Good thing that can't happen with me, he thought.

"I have no plans, and I'd like nothing more than to spend some time with you tonight."

He was working her too. He had already done an assessment and felt confident that he knew how to handle her. He was doing his best to cultivate her interests, and he knew she was not in need of someone who would get close and personal with her. What she needed was a forbidden affair, his specialty. All he wanted was sex, and from what he could see, it would be amazing. He knew it was his looks and reputation she was after, and he wished it could be that way with every girl he wanted to sleep with. His bet was that she liked the idea of being manhandled and that she would get off on being a little afraid of him. He would show her the best time of her life with the intent of getting her talking to those other hot cheerleaders about how great he was. She was likely the key to the vault, as he was aware that all of the others admired her popularity and beauty. If he could get her talking about him to her friends, he could most certainly get some of the other cheerleaders into the sack. That's what he was really after. He wanted them all if he could have them.

"I'm free after eleven p.m.," he said, remembering he had to pick up Angela at 10:00 p.m.

He had a thought that Angela might not like him taking off right after they got home alone together, but he dismissed the thought quickly, knowing she wouldn't resist. She wouldn't even question him. That was why he loved her.

"Okay. I'll see you after eleven p.m. then. We are having a party, so the place will be a madhouse. Maybe I can wear something more comfortable when we're alone tonight."

What a tease, he thought. *She's wearing a micro bikini right now.*

He knew she was trying to suggest that they would get naked, but he hated stupid games. He only played along with morons like her because they were the easiest prey. Heck, they wanted to be prey. In his mind, they were begging for it. She would get just what she deserved.

"I'll hunt for you whenever I get there." He knew that it was already a done deal. Showing up early or even on time was not necessary. She would wait for him, but her ego wouldn't allow her to get over it if he didn't show up. He could be late, but a no show would end it for him.

She leaned over to kiss him, and he felt her hand on his stomach. He knew that she could feel his abs, and it made him feel in control. Her tongue was deep in his mouth, and her oversized breasts were all over his chest. It was exciting for the both of them. Almost as quickly as she had jumped in the car, she was out again. Her smell was still in the car, and he couldn't stop staring at her butt as she walked away. He could tell that she knew he was watching and that she liked that he was watching. She was so confident in her appearance that she didn't even have to turn to look back to know that he was looking. He left without ever getting the car washed.

As soon as she was gone, he rolled down the windows to get her oily scent out of the car. As he pulled out of the parking lot, he began going through the scenario in his head. It seemed perfect. She knew he lived with someone but didn't really care. She was just having fun, and so would he. He really didn't like her much, so he didn't even care if she liked it, though he did want the word to get around to the cheerleaders and to the hot sorority chicks that he was an amazing lover. He knew he was very good at his craft based on the reactions and emotions he had always brought out of his lovers. He had a lot of practice and even some very experienced coaching from the older women he had been with.

It was a long wait until Angela would get off work. He had lots of time to kill, so he headed to the gym to pump iron while he thought about his evening. As usual, he tore down his body like no one else in the gym. He spent more than three hours in the gym, not talking or wasting time but getting after it. No one could keep up with him in the gym, and he loved the feeling he got from being there and knowing he was better than anyone else in there.

Chuck picked up Angela from work at 10:00 p.m., as planned. She was tired and wanted to unwind and get to bed. Since he was feeling a little guilty about what he was planning to do, he made love to her, told her he loved her, and took a shower. He was also feeling guilty that he had just made love to her while thinking about Jennifer. Thankfully, he had not mentioned Jennifer's name on mistake. He had been thinking about being with Jennifer for so long that he began to wonder if the real thing would even compare to his expectations.

Angela was already falling asleep when he got out of the shower, so he simply kissed her good night and headed out.

How perfect she is for me, he told himself.

Although he loved Angela, he had no respect for her. He knew she was perfect for him, and he knew she was intelligent, but the fact that she allowed him to sleep around made him feel like she was weak. It wasn't that Jennifer would be that much better in the sack than Angela. Angela was fantastic in bed. Chuck just wanted to sleep with everyone he was attracted to for his own pleasure. They would all be different, and he desired that. It was never for them, it was all for him. Although he needed other women, Angela was the only he could ever imagine staying with. She was really smart but refused to believe it. She was extremely good looking but never used it or acted like she knew it. He fiercely protected her as his property, but he could not stay home at night for her. Since he had no fear of ever losing her, he saw no reason not to satisfy all of his needs whenever and wherever he pleased.

Chuck was at the party just after 11:00 p.m. He didn't recognize hardly anyone but was amazed at how many good-looking girls were there. As usual, he was the biggest guy in the place. There were a couple of pretty tall guys, but they were just tall, rich geeks or soft doughboys. He felt as if he could have the run of the place if he wanted to. Chuck knew that he could pick up any girl he wanted—not just because he was big and good looking, but because of all that along with his ability to charm them.

Since Chuck and Angela had moved in together, he had not been out much. He didn't really have friends to hang out with, and he was getting all the action he could handle from Angela, who seemed to desire him constantly. He couldn't understand why she wanted him so often. All he could figure was that she knew that he needed lots of sex and she was throwing herself at him to keep him from going anywhere else for sex. His failures had put him in a place in which he had begun to need her, and he really didn't like it. Though he had missed the thrill of the new catch, he had not needed anyone for quite some time. Now that he was becoming something again, his ego needed women to want him. His pride and his sex drive for unfamiliar women seemed to be connected. He could hardly wait to start sleeping with all of the sexy girls who would surely start coming his way since everyone would know who he was again.

After walking the yard and part of the first floor of the sorority house, he noticed three of the cheerleaders standing together. They were all looking his way, so he walked right over to them. He had never been the shy type.

One of them—he didn't even know these fools' names—said, "Are you looking for Jennifer?"

She was really sexy, so he gave her his best smile and sexy look before he answered. "I sure am."

"She told us to tell you to go upstairs and knock on the door at the very end of the hallway. It's her room." Though she delivered the message Jennifer had given her, Brandi's face was full of disapproval. She actually looked angry to Chuck.

What a slut Jennifer is, he thought. *She told her friends to send a guy up to her room for sex, some guy she had never even been on a date with. She is definitely my kind of girl. What is it with this cheerleader, though? Why does she seem to be so pissed off?*

The other two were smiling seductively at him, but the one that seemed in charge, though she delivered the message, seemed kind of aggravated with him or Jennifer; he could not decide which.

"Thanks. What are your names?" He couldn't walk away from the opportunity to meet some of his future conquests.

"I'm Brandi, and this is Jada and Kristi."

Brandi looked Indian or something to him. She had a beautiful face and a great body. Her complexion was very dark, as were her eyes.

Jada and Kristi are both average looking for cheerleaders, Chuck thought. *Cute and perky, but nothing special.*

All of them were idiots to him.

"Nice to meet you guys. I've got to ask, is Jennifer a little controlling?"

"You have no idea. That's one reason she's the captain. She is used to getting whatever she wants," answered Brandi. "She is amazing, and we would all like to look like her. Actually, if you think about it, I'm kind of like her negative."

Chuck was very attracted to Brandi. She seemed to be very bright. He took it back; maybe the others were idiots, but Brandi was almost certainly not. He liked girls like her but didn't have much luck with them. If they weren't emotionally shallow, insecure, drunk, or didn't have some other handicap, he usually didn't have the patience to pursue them. Why bother? He couldn't be stuck with someone who controlled him, and Brandi was certainly that type. Even though she was being funny now, she still looked pretty angry about something.

"Thanks for the direction. I hope we can get to know each other better, Brandi." He ignored the other two, and they both looked bothered by it from what he saw out of the corner of his eye.

"Maybe, but I'm not sure I can follow the Jennifer show."

Brandi knew far less about Chuck than Jennifer and the other girls did. She was not a big gossiper. She had no clue that Chuck had a live-in girlfriend or she would have told him no way to the possibility of them ever getting to know each other. For all she knew, he was just another guy who was attracted to the beautiful Jennifer, and she couldn't blame him for that, though she wondered how it was possible for him to not know about Derrick. He must, and that made him a major jerk in her eyes.

That face; her wit; her tight but conservative clothing; and those perky, full breasts—she was quite a package. He thought about changing his plans and telling her that he wouldn't go up there, but it just didn't compute. As attracted as he was to her, Brandi was more of a girlfriend type. He already had one of those, one who let him do whatever he wanted. Angela was smart too, but she was loyal and loved him no matter what. Brandi could almost certainly never be that way. He could tell that she had too much self-confidence for that. If he had to guess, Brandi was going to do something with her life. That type was never a good fit for him. They would nag him to death about his drinking and lack of direction. He decided to keep his mouth closed, as it would be nuts to not go up there and take Jennifer right now. Jennifer was a knockout and a sure thing. Guys would kill for her. So he told Brandi that he was hoping to see her around, and he headed for the sure thing.

On his way through the living room and up the stairs, people just got out of his way. He never had to say excuse me like most people did. He just walked and they moved. At one point he turned back to see if the cheerleaders were still watching him, though it was only Brandi he wanted to see looking. He was happy to see all three of them looking his way. Brandi looked somewhat disappointed, though. He wondered if she was disappointed in him, or perhaps she was disappointed in Jennifer. Was he blowing a shot with her?

Maybe, but I'm following the odds, he told himself.

At the top of the stairs, he noticed a familiar face coming the other way. It was one of the other football players, but Chuck could not come up with his name.

"What's up, dude?" the guy said while he was taking a break from his girl's face.

"Hey," Chuck said.

It crossed his mind that that guy might tell Derrick if he saw Chuck going into Jennifer's room, but he decided that it was her problem, not his. Derrick was no threat to him. He just kept walking. He was on a mission.

When he finally got to the door at the end of the hall, he stopped and popped a couple of mints into his mouth before he knocked on the door.

"Who is it?" she asked through the door.

"It's Chuck," he quickly responded.

The door cracked open. He pushed it open just enough to get in and quickly turned around to lock it as he felt her naked body immediately on his backside. The room was dark, but his eyes quickly adjusted. He decided to be really rough with her, not to hurt her, but to fulfill the fantasy he was sure she was having about him. He threw her down on the bed and took her with enormous passion. He was sure she was experiencing something she had never experienced before by the amount of noise she was making. She almost sounded like he was hurting her, but she wasn't trying to stop him. Still, he had never heard anyone scream and cry the way she was. He was thankful that the party was so loud.

Throughout their experience together, she kept telling him she had never felt anything like what he was doing to her. He had lots of practice and had been taught things from older women that most guys his age had no clue about. Sure, she was a slut and didn't deserve so much of his effort to please her in the way that he was, but he knew he was setting the expectations for her entire sorority and the cheerleading squad that night. The concern for her pleasure was not for her; it was for him. Surely she was shallow enough to brag about what he was doing to her. He was banking on it.

I'd better give her something to rave about, he told himself.

When he was through with her, he relaxed and lay down beside her. She lay beside him, shaking and trembling but didn't say a thing. Though she clung to him tightly, he managed to doze off. When he woke up, it was 3:00 a.m. Since she hadn't said a word since they had quit, he assumed she would let him leave without a bunch of useless talking. He was ready to go, so he started to stand up to leave. When she noticed he was trying to leave, she jumped to her knees on the bed and grabbed him around the waist. He told her he had to go home to his girlfriend, and she was immediately reduced to tears.

Inside, he was thinking that she was crazy, but he knew that there was a good chance for more sex, so he jumped on it and took her again. When he was through, she was a teary mess, but she begged him to promise that they would see each other again. He promised, and she let go with no further restraint. He had officially lost what little respect he had for her. It was she who acted like it was no big deal that he had a girlfriend and she had Derrick. Maybe she wasn't so confident. She gave him her phone number and a long hug, and he left.

Only a few people were still hanging around in the sorority house. He recognized none of them.

When he got home, Angela was out cold and snoring, none the wiser. It was always easy with her.

For the next two weeks, Chuck met Jennifer often. Sometimes they would meet in the middle of the night. The place was always different, but there was always lots of aggressive sex. Chuck loved the sex but was getting worried that Jennifer was starting to get too attached. Could this spill over into his life with Angela? He would not allow it, he decided. She was still seeing Derrick and even told him that she loved Derrick.

Will that keep her in check? he wondered.

During the affair, Derrick knew something was wrong. Jennifer had suddenly become very emotional. She never acted like she had much in the way of feelings in the past. Now she was crying and telling him she loved him all the time. Finally, one night, she broke down and told him about Chuck. She just couldn't live with herself any longer. She knew what she was doing was wrong, but she found herself becoming addicted to Chuck's animal aggression. Though Chuck didn't care about her in the least, she loved how badly he wanted her. After every encounter, she would cry herself to sleep. When she had unloaded everything on Brandi, Brandi urged her to stop and to tell Derrick.

Derrick was furious when she told him about Chuck. He loved her so intensely that he made sure she understood that he still loved her. He didn't know if he could get past this or not, but he knew he loved her with everything he had. The feelings of pain, betrayal, and his love for Jennifer were completely consuming him. He was shaking and even began to cry. Jennifer held him and told him how sorry she was. She told him that she wanted to quit with Chuck but that he had some sort of power over her. The filthiness of it cut Derrick so deeply that he began to shake even worse than Jennifer was. The two huddled together as if they had already decided to work it out together.

Derrick knew Chuck was a scumbag. No one on the team liked him. No one had befriended him. Unfortunately, no one challenged him either. Chuck was different. He was better than the rest of them. He was the type of talent and had the type of body to play professional football. Everyone knew he didn't belong at their little school. Derrick was tough but knew that Chuck would kill him in a fight. He actually wondered if Chuck literally would kill him in a fight. The guy seemed pretty angry all the time, and his ability to hit people with it was becoming legendary.

"Do you really love me, Jennifer?" Derrick asked.

"Yes, I know I do now. I am so sorry. I only want you. Please don't leave me. I will die without you."

"Then you have to tell him that you two are through. If you really want me, you will never let him touch you again."

She knew he was right, but she too was a little scared of Chuck. He was an animal with her. It was amazing every time, but she always left feeling so terrible, like she was just a sex object and nothing more to him. It was Chuck who showed her how much she loved Derrick. Derrick wasn't like Chuck in any way. He was honest, hardworking, had lots of direction, and got good grades, and she knew that he really loved her. Chuck was the opposite and made her feel so dirty. She knew he was going home to Angela after they were together, and she had heard that he had slept with one of her sorority sisters. She was broken inside and was in awe that Derrick was willing to forgive her. She knew that things would never be the same, but she loved him for having such a forgiving heart. She had to do it; she had to tell Chuck it was over.

At 2:00 a.m. that night, Jennifer got a call from Chuck. He wanted her to meet him at the gym. Somehow Chuck had gotten a key to the gym and could sneak in there anytime he wanted to. She knew she had to do this in person, so she agreed to meet him to get it over with as quickly as possible.

This was going to be the scariest thing that she had ever had to do, but she was convinced that she had to do it. She wasn't even sure if Derrick would be able to get over what she had done to him, but he was telling her there was a chance he could put it behind them if she quit Chuck. For all of her flirting around, she had never actually slept around on him until Chuck came around. This truly had been a first, and it was definitely going to be the last. She had learned her lesson and was sure she would never make such a stupid mistake again.

When she arrived at the gym, she noticed that the door had been left open a bit. She slipped in and made sure it was closed behind her. She heard some grunting and started to wonder if he was working out. As she entered the weight room, she saw him in there with one of her friends. It was one of the younger cheerleaders. They were going at it, and when Jennifer got a good look at what was going on and who it was, she immediately felt sick to her stomach. He had invited her to get her to walk in on this.

She turned to leave but suddenly realized that she could use this to make the break from him. It would be easier this way, and Derrick would not be put in harm's way.

"What are you doing?" she screamed. He turned to look at her, and she yelled, "You are a disgusting pig!"

He immediately left her friend to chase her. He was chasing her completely naked but still managed to catch her before she opened the door to leave. He grabbed her arm and looked her in the eyes.

"I was trying to get her here tonight, not you. I thought I was talking to her. You know I have a girlfriend. Why would this matter?"

"It just does. Good-bye." She shook free and left. As soon as she was out, she stopped on the other side of the door and collapsed in a heap. As she lay there crying, she couldn't believe what she heard Chuck saying to Kim, her sorority sister and cheerleading teammate. He was telling her that he had just broken up with her. Then they started back at it.

How could I have slept with this guy, and why does this hurt so badly? She had to stop herself from throwing up, and the tears started back up.

Chuck didn't give up easily. He had been hoping to get Jennifer to jump in with him and Kim but was pretty sure it wouldn't work. He had to give it a shot. He visited Jennifer the next day before practice. While he was in her room, Derrick called. Chuck went running out of her room as soon as he knew who it was. He was at Derrick's apartment in a matter of minutes and proceeded to beat him and his roommate up so badly that they might have been killed had Jennifer not followed him and threatened to call the police. The relationship between Chuck and Jennifer was officially over, and the rumors began to spread all over campus.

Chuck was back. He was sleeping with everyone in sight and beating up any guy who got in the way. In Chuck's mind, things were great. Too bad he didn't actually feel great. For some reason, even though he was getting everything he thought he wanted, he was miserable inside. He had all the pleasure he could have ever wanted, yet he was not able to feel any peace. Without Angela to come home to, he would have had no comfort. She always accepted him and provided for him. She was proud of his success in football, and she was happy that he was back in school. She didn't care if he ever made any money; she just wanted to see him get what he wanted. She knew he had started sleeping around again, but she knew he loved her and would always come home to her.

CHAPTER 7

WHILE Chuck was achieving so much with the ladies off the field, on the field things were going even better. The first couple of games were showcases of Chuck's talents. He sacked the quarterback five times in those two games. Nothing came to his side without him stuffing it, and he actually knocked a guy out in one of the games. They had to take the guy off on a stretcher, and he ended up in the hospital. On the downside, Chuck also got three offsides penalties and two unnecessary roughness penalties in those two games. Unfortunately for Chuck's future, he had already begun to alienate himself from his team and from the coach who had stepped up to the plate for him.

It wasn't his play or the penalties that started what became the end of Chuck's football career; it was his off-field problems and lack of respect for his teammates and coaches. It wouldn't have hurt him to go to a class now and then either.

When the head defensive coach confronted him about the penalties, Chuck became enraged and told the coach, "That's how I play football." The two got heated, and it ended when Chuck grabbed the coach by the throat and pinned him to the lockers. The result was a two-game suspension and a requirement to submit to a weekly drug test.

The failed drug test was the final straw. He tested positive for both marijuana and steroids. He even failed the retest. The positive steroids result bought him a one-year suspension. Coach Jones told him to turn in his stuff and promised Chuck that he would never play football again for Sam Houston State. He also pointed out to him that what he had done was exactly the kind of stuff he had agreed not to do in the agreement he had signed.

On Chuck's way out, Coach Jones asked him earnestly why he didn't want a better life. Chuck didn't answer. He rudely walked away, knowing that the coach had a question he couldn't answer.

Why didn't he want a better life? He was smart enough to realize what he was throwing away. His anger and lusts had taken his future from him again. He knew deep inside that it would never be any different for him. There was something inside telling him that that was his lot in life. Unfortunately, he chose to believe it.

His coaches had all felt that Chuck had NFL written all over him. Any one of them would have loved to have had his gifts. Chuck knew it was true; he could have done great things with his talents. The failure was too great for him to bear. He completely stopped going to class even though he was paid through the end of the first semester. Almost immediately, he became an alcoholic. He began taking whatever drugs he could get his hands on as well.

Soon he had turned on everyone who loved him, especially Angela. He treated her like trash from then on. She should have seen it coming, but she had her own issues and loved the man more than anything else in the world. He began pushing her around, he cheated on her (even with her friends and people she worked with), he stole her money, he came home drunk at all hours, and he did not permit her to question him about anything. For the first time in their relationship, she began to fear him.

All the cheerleaders were now wise to him, and everyone in Jennifer's sorority house hated him, especially the ones he had slept with. In his last efforts to hook up with one of the cheer-leaders, he appealed to Brandi to meet and talk with him. He told her that he was dying inside and that he really needed to talk to someone. She reluctantly agreed to meet with him, but her intent was not to comfort him but to tell him to grow up and to start becoming a man. Brandi had been dealing with a broken Jennifer since the day everything had blown up between her and Chuck. She was so angry with Chuck over what he had done to her friend and to Derrick that she felt like she needed to set him straight. Her big mistake was agreeing to meet him at his apartment.

She had agreed to meet at his apartment because she didn't want anyone to see them together. It was her intent to get ugly with him, and she didn't want an audience for that. As usual, he had been underestimated. He was waiting for her in a tank top with the intent of getting her into the sack. He knew that it would be difficult, but he told himself she wouldn't be coming to his place if she didn't want to have sex with him. She would have wanted to meet in a public place if she wasn't planning on having sex; he was sure of it. Sure, she had probably told herself that she didn't want him, but she must want him deep inside or she wouldn't come to his apartment like that.

Chuck was pumping up his arms when he heard the knock on his door. Angela had left for work an hour earlier, so he had all day if he needed it. When he opened the door, he tried his best to look dejected and defeated. He noticed right away that Brandi was angry.

"Thanks for coming, Brandi," he said softly.

Just seeing him pretending to be hurt cranked up her anger even more. "I'm not here to have sex with you, Chuck, so you can knock off the act."

Her mistake was not walking away. Instead, she came in and let him shut the door behind her.

Chuck had always been impressed with her intelligence. He knew when a jig was up, so he confessed. "Brandi, I've wanted you since the first time we spoke. No one will ever know this happened. Aren't you curious what it would be like with me?" *She has to be*, he told himself.

"You are a pig! Are you even human? You act like an animal in heat. I came here to tell you what I thought of you and to urge you to get some real help. You have an obvious drinking problem, you're a sex addict, and you don't care about anyone but yourself."

Though she would later realize that she should have had better sense than to speak to him like that, she didn't. It happened so quickly that she woke up in the hospital without even seeing it coming or feeling a thing. He had slapped her across the face so hard that she was unconscious before she even hit the floor.

She woke up in the hospital, and she didn't even remember what had happened. It wasn't until she saw her face in a mirror that she remembered what had happened to her. The swelling was pretty bad, but considering who had hit her, she knew she had gotten off easy. The policeman who had shown her her reflection in the mirror was pressing her pretty hard to tell him who had done this to her. She wisely chose not to tell on Chuck but did ask how she had gotten to the hospital. She was told that someone had called from her cell phone, reporting that she was unconscious and needed medical attention. The police sent a car to the location and found her lying on a bench. It was a man's voice on the recording they played her, but Chuck had done an outstanding job disguising his voice. Even though she knew it was him, she knew that no one else would ever know. She prayed she was done with that guy.

Why had I been so stupid to think that I could tell this guy to get his act together? Thank God he didn't kill me, she told herself.

Chuck was a mess inside, now more than ever. He could feel it all slipping away. He thought he didn't need anyone to comfort him but could not stop going back to Angela every night. It didn't matter where he was or who he was with; he needed her there for him even though he would not even admit it to himself. He knew she loved him, and he loved her, though he didn't treat her like it. Angela was his only constant. She knew he was sleeping around on her, but he always came home, and she loved him.

Angela came up with the only plan she thought would turn him around. She stopped taking the pill. She told herself that everything would change if he knew he was going to be a father. He would stop running around and slow down on the drinking. She thought he would stop yelling at her and sleeping around on her if he knew she was going to be the mother of his child. She even thought that he might try to find a steady job if they were going to be parents. Maybe she could finally get him to marry her.

The plan didn't take long to execute. One morning after Chuck had been out all night, Angela dropped the bomb on him that she was pregnant. Though part of him felt happy at the idea of having a child with her, he knew that whatever was inside of him would not allow him to be a father to anyone. He knew the kid would be damned with him as a father, so he ran out, telling Angela that he couldn't do it.

CHAPTER 8

TIM was pretty young when Chuck first entered his life; actually, he was only a few months old. Though Chuck had abandoned Angela when he found out she was pregnant, she thought nothing of taking him back when he staggered back into her life a year later. Chuck had tried to live without her, but he had failed at that too. It had gotten so bad for him that he had actually thought about taking his own life several times. These suicidal thoughts made him even more miserable inside. To survive, he had attached himself to an older woman who had pretty much controlled him by providing for all his needs. He hated her so much that he had actually considered killing her at one point. Thankfully for her, he changed his mind and decided to go back to his Angela.

So what if we have a kid together? he decided. *She will be a good mother and I can still live my own life.*

She had always made him feel better and would take care of him no matter what. He needed to be loved again, and he knew she was the only one who really could love him.

It had been almost a year since he had left, but, as Chuck had expected she would, Angela took him back and treated him as if he had never left. He had shown up at her door just before dark one night. She jumped at him and wrapped her arms around him almost as quickly as the door had opened. She told him that she was happy to see him and that she wanted him to stay with her and Tim. Then she made love to him with Tim's crib in the next room. Chuck didn't even ask to see his son Tim. He felt like he had already failed this kid.

Chuck was overwhelmed by Angela's love and forgiveness for him. Though he had expected it, it was still difficult for him to accept. Unfortunately, his gratitude only lasted a few days before he started back at his old habits.

Angela had gone through pregnancy alone, and she was forced to rely on her angry mother for help watching Tim while she was at work. Her mother never failed to remind her how she had been a fool to let Chuck screw up her life. She had always felt like asking her mother about the three guys she had married. Were they all losers too? She knew the answer to that one; it was her mother who was the real loser. Her mother had driven them all off with her constant picking and complaining. Angela could not afford to upset her mother since Tim had been born, as she really needed the help. Instead, she kept her mouth shut and took her punishment daily.

Angela's mother was getting enough alimony to live on and lived in a paid-off house that she had gotten from her first marriage. At forty-three, she was a stay-at-home grandmother. Since her mother never actually came over to her place to pick up or drop off Tim, she figured she could pull it off for a while before she would have to let her know that Chuck had returned. Angela knew Chuck wouldn't be able to watch a baby. She knew he would be out until all hours of the night, but she also knew she still loved him and that Tim was his too.

It didn't take Angela long to figure out that Chuck was actually much worse than when he had left. At this point, Chuck had no hope. He hadn't returned to her because he had changed in any way or to repair things. He hadn't decided to become a model father and provider. He didn't even pretend to be that guy. Angela didn't require that he change either. In all honesty, he was there for himself. He could sleep with her, steal from her, and run around on her and she would take care of him and love him. Angela still loved him deeply and wanted to believe he could change. She swore to herself that she would never complain like her mother always did if he didn't, though. Of course, that was all Chuck needed to operate.

Unfortunately, it only took about a month for Angela's mother to figure out what was going on. Chuck had given Angela a black eye for trying to stop him from having his way with her in front of baby Tim. As Angela would soon find out, that was only a foreshadowing of things to come. Though Angela tried to hide the black eye with sunglasses, her mother saw it right away and knew instantly that Chuck had returned. Her mother knew Angela would never see another man for fear that her darling Chuck would return and catch her with someone else. There was no question that the black eye was Chuck's handiwork, and her mother would not stand for it.

Angela knew what was coming, and she was right; her mother went on and on about how terrible Chuck was. It was over, and Angela knew it. Her mother would not watch Tim if Chuck was going to be in their lives.

What will we do? she wondered.

Chuck knew he had to do something if he wanted to stay. He either had to take care of Tim or he had to find some other way to get Tim watched during the day. His mother immediately came to mind. She was working nights and would probably be happy to watch Tim during the day. She had told Chuck a couple of months ago that she was working from 5:00 p.m. until 1:00 a.m. five days a week. In his mind, she would be available by 8:00 a.m. when Angela went to work. Angela had become the day manager at the grocery store, and she had the freedom to come in a bit late and could leave a bit early. He might not have to take on any responsibility if he could get his mother to watch Tim for them. Though his mother had always chased after men, during the day perhaps she was available and willing. He wasn't really sure, as she had never been willing to put him in front of all of those men in the past. If she accepted, it would leave her with no free time on her work days.

Chuck's mom, Kathy, seemed to be their only hope, so they gathered up Tim and headed to Grandma's place for an introduction. Angela had gotten to know Chuck's mom during their time living with her but wasn't sure how willing she would be to watch

Tim or even how reliable she would be. It did seem to be the only solution since they had almost no money. The discussion on the way over seemed very adult to Angela.

Chuck seems to really care about this. Is he starting to change? she wondered.

Kathy was thrilled to meet baby Tim. She had no idea that she was a grandmother. When she saw baby Tim, her heart melted and she could not hold in the tears. It had been less than two years since Chuck and Angela had moved out, but she had not been a part of their lives since they had left.

Kathy was honored that they would ask her to watch Tim. She had always felt as if Chuck thought she was a joke, and she knew he had never respected her. As a matter of fact, she had not even heard from Chuck in almost a year before he had called a couple of months back to see how she was doing. During the call, she had tried to ask about Angela, but Chuck changed the subject. She had the feeling that Chuck and Angela had split, but Chuck wasn't willing to even discuss it. Seeing them together really made her happy. She knew that Angela really loved her son, even with all his faults.

For the next six years, Kathy watched Tim all day while Angela worked to provide for her family. She admired Angela for her strength and began to despise her son for how he was treating his family. She knew he was unfaithful, and she knew he was both physically and verbally abusive. Little Tim was such a smart little guy that she wondered how much he understood about his parents' relationship. She wondered how much he had seen.

Kathy had changed herself since Tim had come into her life and was in a loving relationship with a good man named John Taylor. She was acting the way she had always wished she had acted when Chuck was a baby. Tim got her full attention, and she knew she would have never met John if it had not been for the stability Tim had brought into her life. John treated her well, and she no longer was drinking and jumping from man to man.

Kathy was amazed how special Tim was. He seemed completely unselfish and, in some ways, not childlike at all. His almost adult sense of humor and ability to notice the suffering of others was unusual for a child his age. He had brought a settling calm into her life. Everything just seemed right when he was with her. She wondered if it was him who was making her able to become worthwhile and lovable to a good man like John.

John too felt that Tim was unusual. He didn't know why, but from the first time he saw him, he had taken an immediate liking to him. It was Tim's interaction with Kathy that had sparked his interest in her. He wasn't like other kids his age. John noticed that right from the beginning.

Tim and Kathy were sitting on a park bench, talking back and forth like a couple of adults, when John first spotted them. He was walking by, minding his own business, when he noticed five-year-old Tim chatting it up with a woman he assumed was his mother. They seemed to be communicating like two close friends. John couldn't help but stare at them as he walked by the park bench the two were sitting on.

Almost as soon as he had taken his focus off the two sitting side by side, he heard the little boy say, "That seems like a nice man."

"Why do you say that, Tim?" the woman John assumed was his mother responded.

It was Tim's reply that got him.

"He's listening to us and wants to know our story," Tim answered.

John couldn't help but stop in his tracks. He turned and apologized for listening in on their conversation. Inside, he was amazed at the little boy. It felt as if this little person knew his heart—as if he could sense a good man from an average guy.

"May I sit down?" His curiosity had the best of him.

"Yes," answered Tim. "I want you to meet my grandma, Kathy."

Is this kid always trying to introduce his grandmother to men? John wondered.

Something told him the kid knew what he was doing. It felt like the kid knew him from just being in his presence. It wasn't at all strange, though—just amazing.

Tim had been right. John was a great guy. He quickly fell in love with Kathy and really enjoyed being around Tim too. Within a year's time, John popped the question. With Tim entering kindergarten, Kathy felt as if the time was right. She accepted John's proposal and offered her house to Chuck and Angela if they would only pick up the payments. It was a deal, and the family suddenly had a house to call home. Since Chuck had no credit, the house was put solely in Angela's name, like everything else.

Before Tim turned seven, John's company required him to move. It would be well over a thousand miles away. As painful as it would be for both of them to be away from Tim, they had to make the move. Tim had experienced a loving relationship with his grandparents. Now that was going away. In true Tim form, he told his grandparents he was happy for them and really glad they would always be together. They knew it was hard for him to see them go, but Tim was too strong and mature at the age of seven to make them feel bad about doing something he knew they had no choice but to do.

CHAPTER 9

DURING Tim's early years, he saw his mother thrown around and treated like trash. Dad wasn't the type to just beat on Mom, but if she pushed or resisted him at all, he'd knock her down just to show her who was in control. Tim hated how his mother was treated, but he felt as if it was out of his control. He wanted to help her, but he saw that she too was partially to blame. Both of them were out of control in his young mind, but he loved them in spite of their behavior. He also knew they loved each other. They only treated each other that way due to the pain they had inside.

Tim saw his dad with other women—lots of them. On more than one occasion, Chuck actually brought women home and did his dirty business in the living room or on Tim's bed with Angela in the next room, crying. During one of those home visits, Chuck had forced Tim to do things to a woman who was passed out on his bed. Tim was only ten years old at the time of the encounter, and the whole experience was traumatic for him. Though he did what he was told to do out of fear of his father, it wasn't really him. To Tim, it didn't even feel real.

Tim understood something was going on inside of his father—something evil. He could see his father's heart and knew he was a man being tortured. His father got no rest, and he didn't even seem to be able to relax until he had done harm to someone who cared about him. By the time Tim was ten years old, he was as mature as most young adults. It might have been due to the amount of trauma in his life, or perhaps it was something else— something innate.

More than once, Tim had confronted his father by staring into his eyes and telling him he knew how much he loved him and Mom. Chuck would become uncomfortable but always shook his head in agreement before starting to well up. Being the macho man he was, Chuck couldn't stay and face Tim's psychological forcing of the truth on him. In most cases, he would simply run away. Sometimes he would be gone for several days.

Tim loved his father very much, but Chuck wasn't capable of facing it. Chuck was so proud of young Tim and, deep inside, didn't feel as if he deserved such a good kid. It made Chuck so uncomfortable that he either ran or pushed back by being downright mean to Tim and Angela. Through it all, Tim could always see the truth and knew his Dad loved him and his mother.

The womanizing and drinking were damaging, but it was the mind games that his father always played that really messed up Tim and Angela's minds. Dad liked to get Tim and Angela feeling like things were their fault. He would tell Angela he had to do something with someone else because she wasn't very good at it or that she had disappointed him in some way. He would tell Tim that his mother wasn't pleasing him and that was why he had to have all of those other women. Chuck often told Tim that he needed to learn how please a woman so he wouldn't disappoint them and force them to run out to find someone like him to take care of their needs. Everything was related to his pleasures, but he projected everything onto others. Tim could tell that his father lacked the character to do what was right, but he couldn't fully understand it.

Tim hated it when his father told his mother that she was getting fat or not doing enough to stay in shape. He saw how hard his mother worked to keep herself in shape for him. He couldn't believe his father was actually displeased with anything his mother did, especially in this area. From what he could see, his mother was really pretty. He had even had his friends tell him that their dads said she was pretty. It wasn't her looks that made Dad the way he was. Tim was sure of that.

When Tim was twelve years old, he came home from school earlier than normal one day to find his father with one of his conquests. He opened the door to find a naked woman on the living room couch with his father in the kitchen retrieving another beer.

Tim recognized the woman, as she was the mother of one of his friends. Mom had become good friends with this woman, and Tim knew the lady was married.

Seeing his friend's mother naked on the couch caused Tim to explode with anger. He yelled out at the top of his lungs, "Quit screwing your family away!" He slammed the door and started running. Though no one chased him, he ran all the way to his mother's grocery store.

Angela had worked at the same grocery store for about fourteen years. She was pretty much in charge at that point and could come and go as she pleased. When Tim came running in and told her she needed to go home right away because Dad really needed her, she didn't hesitate to leave for home immediately. Tim, knowing exactly what she would walk in on, turned and ran out of the store as soon as he could tell she would follow. In Tim's mind, she needed to stop Dad. It was her duty as his wife, not his. As she jumped in her car, she could see Tim running across the field that would allow him the shortest route home.

Angela easily beat Tim home and hurriedly stormed in on round two. It was about an hour before she normally got home, and when she saw what was going on, she was sure that Chuck thought he had more time. He must not have remembered that Tim didn't have football practice that day. It was difficult to see him with Sandy, but, as usual, she didn't challenge him or go after him. Instead, she turned and left. Both Chuck and Sandy had looked her right in the eye. There was no chance they had not seen her.

Sandy fell apart after seeing Angela. She felt shame and disappointment rush through her body. Even after Tim had walked in on them, she had allowed him to have her again. He had been so powerful and good looking; she had allowed him to seduce her.

"What the hell is wrong with you?" she screamed at Chuck.

Inside, it was herself that she was really mad at. She knew about him. She had seen him drunk before. For months he had been coming by, trying to get her to have sex with him while her hardworking husband was at work. She had begun to fantasize about him, and he had assured her it would only be physical. She had talked herself into letting it happen, but now she knew it was a terrible mistake.

As she pulled away from Chuck, questions began to run through her mind. *Is my marriage over? What have I done to myself and my family? Why was I so stupid?* There was no way it was worth it, and now she was feeling repulsed by the pig of a man that Chuck was.

Chuck, sensing that she had turned on him the way all women eventually did, grabbed her, turned her around, and took her again one more time. That time it was against her will. In all honesty, it felt better to him than the other two times. He loved dominating women like that. Sandy was screaming and fighting so hard that she passed out. Chuck finished up and threw her out in the yard, completely naked. He was really drunk and had taken some of those pills that seemed to give him even greater strength.

Chuck knew he had gone too far that time. He jumped into Angela's car with Angela watching from the side of the house and drove away.

Angela slowly walked over to Sandy's lifeless body. From what she could see, Sandy wasn't badly hurt. Not knowing how to handle someone who might be suffering from some sort of head injury, Angela turned and ran inside to get a blanket to cover her up with rather than try to get her into the house in her current condition. Almost as soon as the blanket touched Sandy's naked back, she snapped out of it and began crying profusely. Angela almost felt sorry for her but, knowing what Sandy had just done with Chuck, quickly decided against comforting her.

The two staggered inside while holding on to one another for balance. Once inside, Angela sat Sandy on the couch and told her to take her time getting herself together and to let herself out. Then she ran from it by leaving. She watched from well down the street until she saw Sandy leave before she returned. Tim didn't return for quite some time.

That night Chuck drank like never before. He got in a really bad fight that normally he would have dominated. That time, however, because of his drunken condition, he got beat up pretty badly. Dragging himself to his feet, he crawled back into Angela's car. He decided to go home, where he knew Angela would take care of him, but he was in no condition to drive. Unfortunately, that didn't stop him from trying.

Chuck never even noticed the stop sign. The car he collided with had stopped at the four-way stop before proceeding into the intersection to turn left in front of Chuck. He caught them head-on and was dead instantly.

The woman and her daughter both died as well, but their deaths were not instant. The mother was still alive when the police got there. She could hardly speak but managed to push out, "My daughter stopped breathing. Please help her." By the time the ambulance arrived, both had breathed their last.

It was over. Chuck was gone. Angela and Tim were alone— devastated and alone. Tim was both angry and sad about his father's death. Angela was mess. More than anything, she was haunted by feelings that it was partially her fault for not being able to completely satisfy him. He was always telling her that his misery was her fault. Since he was gone, she felt more than ever that he was right.

Tim had many times felt that he had been face-to-face with evil when his father had gotten intoxicated and transformed into the beast. Because it was his father, in some strange way, he still admired him. He knew his father had been a tremendous athlete, and he fully understood his father was smarter than anyone else he knew. He couldn't help wanting to be like his dad, at least in some ways. Thankfully, Tim was too smart to think that what his father had done to his mother and to all of those other women was acceptable in any way. He felt as if his father was fighting something inside. He had begun to believe that it wasn't entirely his father's fault, though he knew that his dad had no one else to blame but himself. Tim knew something had control of his father. Why else would he act like that?

Tim also knew deep down in his heart that his father deeply loved his mother. He had seen the way his father had protected her. If someone ever hurt her feelings, Dad was all over it. His father had even gotten arrested one time for badly beating a guy who had called his mother stupid at the grocery store. No one else could treat Mom like crap; that was his dad's job.

Tim had also seen the regret in his father's eyes in the mornings after he had slept off the alcohol. He had seen his dad's pain when he had to drive some floozy out of the house. Tim had seen his father's attempts to be a better man. Something was terribly wrong in his father, and Tim knew it. Still, it was his father, and Tim had no choice but to love him.

Angela felt completely empty after Chuck passed away. She had always loved him, even though he constantly broke her heart. The pain he had put her through was unbearable at times, but she lived with it all to keep him in her life. After his death, she cried herself to sleep for months. She had always believed she deserved everything he had done to her.

Tim never understood why his mother felt like she deserved to be treated the way his father treated her. She must have because she never complained about it or tried to end it. Tim knew how she felt, as he always seemed to know how others were feeling. He didn't need her to tell him about it. At times he found himself feeling that she was as worthless as his father had treated her, but something inside him told him he was wrong. He inherently knew it wasn't who she really was; it was who she believed she was. Why did she believe that? Was it all because of how his father had treated her, or was she dealing with something else also—something evil?

In Tim's mind, both his mother and father were influenced by something external. They both struggled with something, and that something won in his dad and was winning in his mother. How could he stop it?

CHAPTER 10

THE night of the collision, Angela was called to the scene of the accident, as the car was registered in her name. Chuck had no ID on him. When she arrived, Angela felt as if she was stuck in a dream. Chuck had wrecked their only car, so it took her some time to get there, as she had to wait on a friend to pick her up.

She was asked to identify the person who had been driving her car. Though he was almost unrecognizable, Angela had no trouble identifying him. Inside, she was feeling a strange nothingness, as if it weren't real. Outwardly, her complexion had gone white and her face completely stoic.

After ten minutes of processing what was happening, Angela noticed a man who was being counseled by some police and medics. The guy was a pretty normal-looking guy, though he did appear to be pretty well-off. She heard someone call him Mr. Brooks and was told that he was the husband of the woman and the father of the daughter whom Chuck had just killed.

She was really starting to feel guilty, so much so that she could not even speak to him when they came face-to-face. He seemed strangely calm to her, though he was clearly shaken. Roger looked deeply hurt to her, but he didn't appear to have any anger toward her. Chuck had just destroyed his life, yet he seemed to only feel pain.

It really threw her off when he asked her, "Are you going to be okay?"

He seemed worried about her condition. It made her uncomfortable. She could tell right away there was something really different about that guy. He had some sort of peace she couldn't understand.

Before Roger Brooks left with the police officers, he gave Angela his card and told her that the accident wasn't her fault and that it wouldn't help anyone for her to feel any responsibility in what had happened. He told her that if she loved her husband as much as he loved his wife and daughter, she was in for some difficult times. He encouraged her to go to her church, friends, and family for support. She wasn't able to respond but felt like telling him she was completely alone. She had none of those things in her life.

From his business card, she found out that he was an engineer. She wasn't entirely sure what they did though. That guy had put her at ease in the midst of the most difficult situation she could ever imagine.

What is it about him that makes him this way? she wondered.

In about two weeks' time, Angela got a call from Roger. It had been difficult for her to even get out of bed in the mornings, and she and Tim had hardly spoken since Chuck died. She was going through the deepest, darkest time of her life. The hardest part for her was her feelings that Chuck's death could have been prevented had she been a better person. If she could have only kept him satisfied, maybe he would still be alive.

Roger's voice was soothing over the phone. He seemed even more caring on the phone than he had been that night. Roger told her he just wanted to check up on her to see if she was doing okay with everything. Throughout the call, he kept telling her that he and his younger daughter, Jessica, did not blame her. He explained that he and Jessica had stayed home the night of the accident and that he had left her with family before rushing to the scene of the accident when he had gotten the call. Now he and Jessica were going through a painful grieving process together.

Roger earnestly asked Angela about her family and learned about Tim. Then he shared with her that he was a Christian. It intimidated Angela a little, as she feared being judged. Every Christian Angela had ever met had looked down on her, and she knew it. Sure, they would try to get her to come to church where they could act interested in her and Tim, but, at least in her eyes, it was only so they could feel like they were doing something good. Several times churches had tried to "reach out to them" by giving them things like Christmas gifts and money. It was always an insult to her. Sure, they took the gifts and money, but that was all that came from it. Angela knew that no one really wanted to be around scum like her. They wanted to do a good deed, feel like they were helping the less fortunate, and then get out before they got some of it on them.

When the call ended, Angela was surprised to learn that they had spoken for almost thirty minutes. It had felt like ten or fifteen minutes to her. She couldn't help but feel better after they hung up. Roger had calmed her and repeatedly told her that she had done no wrong and had no blame in anything that had happened. He had been so convincing that she almost believed him.

Although he was a Christian, Roger seemed different than the other Christians she had met. He was obviously destroyed by the death of his wife and daughter, but he seemed forgiving of Chuck and earnest in his concern for Angela and Tim. Why wasn't he angry at the sinners for spilling their mess over into his life? She couldn't help but feel that the death of Roger's wife and daughter was partially her fault since she could not please Chuck in a way that would have kept him home that night. These types of thoughts dominated her thinking. Constant damnation was the norm for Angela, especially now that Chuck was gone. Why couldn't she be good enough for Chuck? Why did he need all those other girls? She knew it was her fault. She felt so lucky to have had Chuck for so long. Her delusion was reality to her, though any rational outsider would have told her she was crazy to think that Chuck had been a good man.

Angela had also learned that Roger had not been left completely alone by the accident. He still had a thirteen-year-old daughter, Jessica. Based on her short meeting with Roger and their telephone conversation, Angela felt like Jessica was really lucky to have a dad like him. In the few minutes she had been with Roger, he had made her feel accepted. In thirty minutes on the phone, he had succeeded at making her feel like he cared about her and Tim. Roger seemed to know that she felt guilty about the accident, and she could tell that it really bothered him. He had taken the pressure off her that night by telling her that he was so sorry for her loss. During their phone conversation, he had asked her if she and Tim were okay and if there was anything he and Jessica could do for them. No one had ever treated her that way. Why would he care? What were his motives? She couldn't understand why he was the way he was. His behavior seemed somewhat against nature to her.

Chuck had made her feel special in the beginning, but he didn't always treat her that way. Actually, he almost never had treated her that way. She told herself that he only treated her that way because she had disappointed him so often. Roger seemed to be the opposite of Chuck. Was he for real, or did he want something from her? He seemed like such a genuine, caring man, but was she missing something? Roger's wife must have been a really great woman based on all of the great things he told Angela about her. It sounded to Angela that Roger's wife had been a far better wife than she had been for Chuck, even though she was never actually his wife.

CHAPTER 11

ALMOST two years after the accident, Roger called Angela out of the blue. He told her that he had been thinking about her, and he wasn't lying. Roger had been feeling a sense of responsibility for her that just wouldn't go away. The more time that went by, the more he felt a responsibility to check on her. He wasn't sure why, but his internal turmoil seemed to be getting worse and worse with time. When he finally picked up the phone to call Angela, he knew he was doing the right thing. Hearing her voice was oddly settling for him. Though he wasn't sure why, he felt a sense of calm when he was speaking with her.

Angela was surprised by the call but was very happy to hear from Roger. She too had been thinking of him. His kindness and concern had left an impression on her. Over the last few months, she had begun to think about him and his daughter. She wondered if their lives were as empty as hers and if they were still as broken as she was over their loss. When she first realized who she was speaking with, she felt very excited inside. As she remembered, his voice was calm and soothing. When he asked if they could meet, she felt like a school girl again. She had been almost hiding from life since Chuck died. She had decided to totally avoid men because they would only hurt her. They always had. Even as a kid, she had been hurt by men.

Her answer was quick and lacked any attempt to hide her excitement. "Yes, I would love to meet with you." Inside, though, almost the second she had blurted out her answer, she began to panic a bit. *What if he is just being nice and doesn't really want to meet with me?* she worried. Her haunting condemnation went on. *Why would he want to see a piece of trash like me? I don't deserve someone as good as this guy is.* She quickly decided he wouldn't like her once he got to know her.

Angela felt like a failure in so many ways. She just couldn't get it through her head that Roger could actually want to meet with her. Why would he care how she was doing? She finally decided he was just meeting with her for himself, to close the loop on his dead wife and daughter, and that would be okay with her. Maybe she needed more closure as well.

They set up a time, and in what Angela would learn was Roger's typical way, he showed up ten minutes early to pick her up. When she saw his shiny new car pull up, she hoped he wouldn't be upset that she wasn't ready to go yet. She ran to the door to let him in but didn't even have the towel out of her hair yet. When he saw her, he was blown away. He honestly didn't remember her being such a beautiful woman. With her long brown hair, dark eyes, and slender figure, he was smitten. He immediately felt guilty inside, as he had never intended for this to be a romantic meeting.

Why am I feeling such an attraction? he wondered. *Is it only her beauty?* He knew his intention had been pure in contacting her, but seeing her then all he could think about was how attractive she was.

Though he had been thinking about her often, it had never been in any sort of romantic way. He only wanted to make sure Angela had moved forward with her life and that she and Tim were recovering emotionally. Now he was severely distracted by her beauty.

Did I make a mistake setting up a personal meeting like this? he wondered. *Did I notice how beautiful she was when we first met but not allow myself to remember it? How could I not remember her looking this way?*

It was baffling to him, and it caused him to go to the Lord in prayer for strength. Like Angela, he too had completely turned off his interests in the opposite sex since the accident. For the first time in almost two years, Roger was suddenly incapable of not being attracted to a woman.

Angela told him that she was really sorry she wasn't ready yet and explained that she had dropped off Tim at a friend's place, which had put her a little behind schedule. Roger could not have cared less about the time. He told her there was no hurry and took a seat in the living room. As he sat, he began to pray that he would honor Angela with respect and not violate her with his eyes and his mind. She was attractive, so he would have to be on special alert all night. Roger treated everyone as he wanted to be treated, and he respected all women as if they were his mother. At least that was his goal. That night would be a challenge though. He was already sure of that. He had just seen more than he had intended, and the image of her body and beautiful smile was tempting him to want to stare when she came back in the room. He decided that no matter how good she looked, he would look only into her eyes.

Roger's attraction to her was so strong that he actually felt a desire to protect her. Almost the second he made eye contact with her as she opened that door, he wanted to hold her and shield her from the world. It was such a powerful impulse that he almost forgot the circumstances. He almost forgot what she had gone through and about his own loss. The strangest part about his attraction for her was the fact that he felt it was right, that he owed it to her to take care of her, that they were somehow bound for one another. Having such a revelation at first sight made Roger question himself and his motives. He knew he needed to control what he had decided must only be lust for Angela.

Roger knew that Chuck had been a heavy drinker from his phone conversation with Angela. He had no idea how bad their relationship had been, though, as Angela didn't complain in any way about it. Roger was curious based on his exposure to families affected by alcoholics. He didn't want to pry for more information, but he knew alcoholism would likely have left some scars on the loved ones of the alcoholic. Though he was no expert at diagnosing anyone's emotional state, he knew Angela was struggling with guilt and the feelings of failure. He could hear it in her answers and even in her voice. He felt concerned for her.

Roger had been suffering the death of his wife and child for almost two years, and he just wanted to follow his heart, which was telling him to meet with Angela. Something was telling him that they were the only two who could understand the other's pain. He knew she had to be hurting too. Inside, though, he knew he felt more than just concern for Angela. From the time he had met her, he felt a connection. He had not noticed then how attractive she was, but he had felt something for her. It was something that now, two years later, had to be looked into. As he sat on her couch, waiting, he began to realize that he had been attracted all along—not physically, as her looks truly were a surprise, but on an emotional or spiritual level.

Roger felt loved by God and found it easy to love others. He truly treasured the people in his life. For that reason, he was surrounded by loving friends and family. He had suppressed some of his feelings from those close to him but had healed much more thoroughly than Angela had due to his supporting cast and his relationship with God. Roger had put most of the pieces of his life back together, but he had this burning in his heart for Angela. He knew down deep that Angela and Tim were dealing with darkness and hopelessness, and something was telling him that he and the Lord would be their relief.

Their first evening together was almost magical. Roger was a perfect gentleman, and Angela could tell that she was his only priority. He impressed Angela by never looking around the room. Instead, she had his full attention. Even when beautiful women walked by, he never diverted his attention from her. It felt as if no one else was in the room, even in a crowded restaurant.

They connected immediately in a profoundly deep way. Roger felt like she was something out of a dream, while Angela couldn't believe how he was treating her. She had never been around someone who was as into her as Roger definitely was who didn't stare at her body. He only looked into her eyes, and he seemed to be hanging on her every word. He was really listening, and he got her talking about things she had never talked to anyone about. It was amazing.

The physical attraction to one another was immediate for Roger and grew exponentially for Angela as the evening went on. Roger wasn't exceptionally good looking, but, maybe for first time in her life, Angela was looking at the inside. What she was seeing was drawing her in. What she was feeling was all new to her. He made her feel special and worth his time. The fact that he almost never said anything about himself other than how much he had been blessed with family and friends was definitely a first for Angela. Chuck always talked about himself and how unfair everything had always been. She sensed none of that in Roger.

Roger spoke in glowing terms about his family, his church, and even his job. His openness was like nothing Angela had ever experienced. What she didn't like about him was the way she felt about herself when she was in his presence. She felt inferior to him in almost every way. He seemed to be such a good man with lots of love in his life and a great career while she felt like she had not achieved anything with her life and knew that no one but Tim and Chuck's mom loved her. As she had felt earlier that evening, she knew he wouldn't like her once he got to know her. It was only a matter of time until he figured out that she was not worth his time.

Roger, on the other hand, was feeling quite the opposite. He thought she was amazing. She seemed so caring and devoted to Tim that he couldn't help but admire her for it. Her looks were somewhat intimidating to him though. This type of girl never paid someone like him much attention. She was out of his league, and he knew it.

From the first date on, Angela took to Roger. He was everything that Chuck hadn't been for her. He had no motives and seemed to be a rock with work and with his daughter. He was a good-looking guy, though nowhere near as good looking as Chuck had been.

Maybe that's a good thing, she thought.

What really jumped out at her was his concern for her and Tim. At first it set off some alarms with her. She was so used to being manipulated by Chuck that she had great difficulty accepting anyone's concern for her and Tim. She wanted to trust him but found herself holding back.

The feelings of unworthiness were sometimes too overwhelming for Angela to bear. It was such a burden for her that she felt uneasy most of the time. When Roger came over to her place, she couldn't get her thoughts off how she wasn't good enough for him. The feelings weren't as strong at his place, so she preferred to go there. His place was much nicer, had lots of room, and harbored no memories.

Angela really liked how Roger understood how important Tim was in her life. He seemed to treat everyone as if they mattered, and it was no different with Tim. Tim was very intelligent, and Angela knew he would size up Roger quickly. The beauty of Roger was that he too was intelligent and he wasn't trying to pretend to be someone he wasn't. Tim would know if Roger tried to fool him. Thankfully, Roger was who he was, no strings attached. Actually, Angela knew that Tim would know if Roger was a fake quicker than she ever could. The fact that Tim seemed okay with Roger validated Angela's feelings for him.

Since Chuck passed away, Angela had not even considered moving on. Now all she could do is thank God for this guy.

She felt joy that she couldn't ever remember having in her life. This guy connected with her like Chuck had emotionally, but he was everything Chuck never was. Unfortunately, she had always believed she didn't deserve someone like Roger. Chuck had always treated her the way she felt she deserved to be treated. Roger was treating her like she was of tremendous value, as if he was the one who was lucky to be with her. It was always about her with Roger, and she was certain that she didn't deserve it.

There was one thing about him that really bothered her. For some reason, he would hardly touch her. He had given her a hug every time he had seen her since the first date, but he would keep it very nonsexual by keeping his distance and not allowing their bodies to touch. Even when she had attempted to press her breasts up against him, he had succeeded in pulling away. Roger wouldn't kiss her with his tongue or touch her body at all. No matter how hard she tried to get him to look at her finely sculpted body, she had never even caught him checking her out. Most men couldn't help but stare at her body.

She had done her best to be available and inviting to him, but he didn't seem to want her in that way. Several times, when they were not going to go out into public, she had purposely worn revealing clothing. He didn't treat her any differently, and she was hurt by it but never said anything to him.

What is wrong? she wondered. *Why isn't he attracted to me physically? He treats me so well, but he doesn't desire me.*

Angela wanted to please him sexually because she knew how important that was to men. His lack of interest in her was beginning to make her feel unattractive. Roger telling her that she was pretty was just not enough; she needed to share herself with him. That was the only way she knew how to really show a man how she felt about him.

Angela had struggled with her body most of her adult life. Ever since she hit puberty, she had blossomed in such a way that men were always looking at her. It made her so uncomfortable that she often wore no makeup and never dressed in a way that might turn a man on. Now, when she wanted Roger to notice her body and all of the hard work she had done to get it and keep it that way, he was treating her like his sister or something. She had even tried to give him a massage one night, but he told her that he didn't think they should.

Roger assumed that she understood why, but it never crossed his mind that it was hurting her. Had he known, he would have done his best to explain himself to her. He was falling for her big time, but he would not destroy the purity of their young relationship. Sex and all the other intimate things she wanted to do with him were meant only for married couples. He wanted to tell her that, but he knew it wouldn't make much sense to her, so he foolishly avoided it. Now it was causing her pain.

CHAPTER 12

TIM was fourteen now. For the last couple of years, he had been the man of the house, and he really wasn't crazy about his mother hanging out with any man. He was having some trouble understanding why his mother would want to spend any time with Roger. After all, Dad had destroyed this guy's life. Roger did seem nice enough though. He really didn't seem like he wanted to take advantage of Mom. Mom actually seemed happy for the first time in a long time. Still, he couldn't help but think what his father would have done to the guy for even talking to Mom. Roger was maybe six feet tall and, to Tim, didn't seem very athletic. He was sure that Dad would give this joker a beating for even looking at her.

What Tim did like was Roger's daughter, Jessica. Though she was a year older than he was—well, actually only about seven months—he couldn't help but find her attractive. Tim had seen her around school and knew she was a sophomore, but he didn't know her name until Roger brought her over to meet him and his mother. Tim had already singled her out as one of the best-looking girls in the school prior to their meeting.

Jessica was blonde and beautiful in Tim's eyes. He noticed that she always seemed to be surrounded by friends and that she and her friends always seemed to be having a good time. Although he was a freshman, he had inherited his dad's physique and was already well over six feet tall. He was one of the best players on the football team and was great at every other sport he played. He wondered if Jessica had ever noticed him. Since her father had brought her over to meet him and his Mom, Tim couldn't help but stare at her every day at lunch. Most of the time she smiled back at him, and she had even waved to him a few times. Whenever their paths crossed in the halls at school, she always acknowledged him. Tim had figured out how to make the crossing in the halls happen as much as possible. He began to crave seeing her.

Before long, Tim couldn't get Jessica out of his mind. She became all he thought about day and night. As much as he wanted to talk to her, an internal battle he was fighting held him back. He could vividly remember his dad's advice about women and the stuff he had seen his father doing with women. Thankfully, he also remembered the torture he saw his mother go through. He knew that almost everything his father had done with women was wrong, but he feared it was in some way a part of him. Something seemed to be coercing him to take Jessica for himself, to treat her like the great conquest that she was.

Why is this even crossing my mind? he wondered. *Is this coming from the memories of my father, or is it part of me?*

Though he had never had intercourse, he had fooled around with a couple of girls. On those occasions he had felt the potential of losing control. It scared him.

Tim wanted this girl so badly that it frightened him. He didn't want to just touch her; he wanted her to be his. In a short period of time, he began to realize that he didn't just want to have sex with her; he wanted her to be completely his. Her beautiful face and body might have attracted him to her, but he wanted to get to know her, not just her body. It seemed crazy to him, but he felt like she was the girl for him—not *a* girl for him; *the* girl for him. Just thinking about it made him feel like a joke. He knew he was far too young to be thinking about anyone in that way.

Is this something common that other kids my age feel? he wondered.

Tim knew very little about her, but from what he had seen of her personality, he felt like she was a good person. He wondered if he could respect her the way he was thinking she deserved to be respected. He was truly torn and began to really struggle with the two sides living inside of him. Did he have the strength to control his beastly desire to have sex with her, or would he be unable to control himself? As much as he wanted to know the answer to that question, his fear of failing Jessica was paralyzing.

Is it really in my hands or will I be tugged one way or another by my father's sins? he thought. *Will I become my father? Will I be a drunk, and will I treat women the way he did?*

So far he had completely avoided alcohol, and he had never treated a girl badly. Still, Tim feared the worst.

If it were up to him, he decided, he would not be like his father. He would be in total control if it were at all possible. Tim knew there were forces at work, and he decided he had to be in control of them or they would destroy him.

How can I do that? he wondered.

He had seen his father's demons completely consume him. His father was either helpless against them or he just didn't care to fight back. Tim knew everyone was responsible for their own actions. He would do whatever it took to be in charge of his actions. He knew instinctively that drinking alcohol or taking drugs simply could not be a part of his life if he were to stand any chance of defeating the dark side. The way he felt about drinking and drugs helped him stay away, and he promised himself that he would never get started. He swore them off for life.

Where can I find answers? he asked himself.

Roger was the only guy he could think of.

He's a Christian and probably knows a lot about the Bible, he surmised.

Although Tim had never read anything in the Bible, he had heard that the Bible talked about the devil, demons, and right and wrong. Roger would most definitely know something about those subjects. As smart as his father had been, he had never talked about any of those things with Tim. When Tim had asked about God, his father had exploded in anger and told him not to believe any stories about God.

"You don't want to know a God who would allow people to suffer the way that they do," was his standard answer.

CHAPTER 13

ROGER had just pulled into his driveway when he noticed Tim sitting over by the entryway. Instead of pulling into the garage, he parked and rolled down the window to acknowledge Tim sitting there. Tim immediately felt like he had made the right decision. He knew Roger was the right guy to ask about this stuff.

If there is a good side, this guy will know all about it.

Tim knew he could trust his instincts about people. It was something that came naturally to him, and his instincts had never failed him. He had often wondered if it was some sort of gift.

As Roger walked up the walkway, Tim suddenly felt relief that this guy had come into he and his mother's lives. He was definitely not the enemy, even if it felt wrong to have someone other than his father hug his mother. Roger seemed very bright and obviously had it together. Everyone seemed to respect Roger, and Tim could see why.

"Hey, Tim. What brings you by?" Roger asked as he walked up the walkway.

He seems very happy to see me, Tim thought. It was a strange feeling for Tim. *Why would this guy give a crap about me?*

Still, Tim knew he really was happy to see him. It made him feel certain that Roger would give him the truth or tell him he didn't know if he didn't.

"I was hoping we could talk about something."

Tim wondered if Roger might think he was there to warn him about his mother or maybe even to ask him to stay away from his mother. It also occurred to him that Roger might think he was there waiting on his beautiful daughter. Though he was hoping to see her, it was not why he was there.

"Sure. Did you ring the doorbell? Jessica should be home by now."

"No. I was waiting for you, and I didn't want to bother her." At least he had established that he wasn't there for Jessica.

"No problem. I'm really glad to see you. Can I get you a Coke or something?" Roger was unlocking the door.

"A Coke would be great, Mr. Brooks."

He almost never had Coke at home, as his mother felt it was a waste of money. They usually drank water or tea.

Tim followed Roger into the kitchen. As they passed the stairs, Tim caught a glimpse of Jessica's figure out of the corner of his eye. She was gliding down the stairs as they went by. She had constantly been on his mind since that first time Roger had brought her over to his place. Just being in her presence made him feel a little self-conscious, and he wondered if he had any effect at all on her. There were lots of pretty girls all over campus, but she was the only one he thought about. It was as if no other girls existed to him anymore. He wondered if his father had ever felt that way about anyone. Maybe he was different than his dad.

"Hi, Dad," Jessica said so sweetly that Tim fell even deeper in love with her than he had been ten seconds earlier.

She was dressed in her school clothes, but, to Tim, it was like she was in a fine evening dress. She had such a classy look that he couldn't help but feel like she was different. He fought himself to not wonder what she looked like in a bathing suit or even in the raw. For some reason, thinking of her body that way seemed wrong to him. She definitely had a great body, but her face was even more amazing to him. It was something inside her that he felt he was really attracted to though. The outside was just a bonus.

Could I love her any more? Tim wondered.

If what he was feeling was really just lust, why did he want to treat her so well? Why did he feel unworthy? How could he be in love with someone he really didn't know, especially at fourteen years old? Was any fourteen-year-old capable of true love? It sure felt like love to him. If it wasn't love, he was pretty sure that real love would kill him.

"Hello, sweetheart," Roger replied.

"Hi, Tim. How are you?"

He loved the way her mouth moved when she spoke. She was looking right into his eyes. He suddenly became aware of every flaw he had.

Did she notice that big zit on my nose? he wondered.

Tim wanted to remember every moment that he was in her presence, as he knew it would soon be over and he would have to work from memory again. He was taking it all in. Every movement, every sound, her heavenly smell—it was all being committed to memory. He wished he could record it somehow so he could play it all back a hundred or more times.

"I'm okay," he managed to get out. *Man, my father would have been so smooth right there*, he thought.

"What's up? Are we doing something with the Wisemans tonight?" Jessica asked her father.

Tim was grateful that his mother had her last name changed to Wiseman years ago even though she and his father were never actually married. It had made things a lot easier on everyone that way.

"No. Tim just came over to have a word with me."

"Well, I'm going back up to my room then. Good to see you, Tim."

Hearing her say his name was truly amazing to him. It sounded different off those lips. In just a few minutes, he had heard her say it twice.

Jessica turned and ran up the stairs. She too was very self-conscious when Tim was around, though she didn't let on to it. She ran into her room to check her appearance in the mirror. She felt something for Tim that she didn't understand, and she didn't know how to deal with it. As she looked at herself in the mirror, she told herself to grow up. If he liked her, she didn't want it to be only because of her looks anyway. Still, though, he had to like her. The way he had been staring at her at school assured her that he did.

What will I do if he doesn't like me? she wondered.

"I'll come up to talk with you when Tim and I are done," Roger hollered up the stairs.

Tim wanted to say something else to let her know he was hers, but he didn't have the courage. He didn't want to tip his hand in front of her father either, so he just stood there and let it go for now.

Roger and Tim sat down at the kitchen table. Tim had heard no sound when the hundred-pound girl had run up the stairs. He was impressed at how well the house must have been built. At his place you had to deal with rowdy neighbors, and everything squeaked when anyone walked across the floor.

Roger started the conversation. "So what's on your mind, Tim?"

"I was hoping you could help me out with some answers and maybe some direction," Tim replied.

"I'd be happy to try." By that time, Roger was really curious what it was Tim was there to talk about.

"Well, you and my mom have been getting pretty close. I know you are aware that my dad was about as far away as he could be from being anything like you."

Tim wasn't trying to insult Roger. Actually, it was anything but insulting. He just wanted to make sure Roger knew where he was coming from. He wanted to establish that things had not been ideal for his mother. He wanted to make sure Roger was aware that his mother had been abused both physically and emotionally for more than twelve years.

"I've been gathering that from your mother. Honestly, from what I've heard, I'm very concerned."

He knew more about Chuck from what he was told by the police about him than he did from talking with Angela. Angela seemed unwilling to discuss her feelings, especially her feelings about Chuck and his passing. It was her yearning for meaning and for his approval that interested him the most. He could feel a need in her. From their first date, Roger felt like Angela wanted to pay him back for what Chuck had done. He wanted her to understand that none of it was her fault but, so far, hadn't gotten far in convincing her. Roger knew she was carrying a lot of unwarranted blame, and he wanted nothing more than to help her get over it. He wanted her to be able to move on and forgive herself.

"Concerned about what?" Tim wanted to make sure this guy wasn't dating his mom because he felt sorry for her. That wasn't his impression of Roger, but he still felt compelled to ask. He needed that validation to move on.

"About what you two have been through and what you might still be dealing with."

Roger did care for them, and he wanted them to know it. He was not trying to use their past against them or orchestrate anything to benefit himself. He could tell that Tim was very perceptive and was only asking what he'd been concerned with because he wanted to know that he could trust him.

"Like what? What do you know about our past? What do you know about my mom and dad's relationship?" Tim was really more curious to see how much this guy had figured out on his own. He knew that he was aware of his father being an alcoholic but figured that he didn't know how his father had beat on her and cheated on her all the time.

"I'm sorry, Tim, but I just don't feel comfortable talking about your mother without her here. I will say that I fear she has been led to believe that she is not the beautiful, intelligent woman that I have come to realize that she is. There are likely deep scars there. I see her as a glorious creation of God. She has an inner beauty that far exceeds her external beauty, but she feels unworthy of a good life. She has been lied to, and she's been buying into it for years. I care deeply for her, and I hate this pain she carries around with her. Although we have only been seeing each other for a few months, I can honestly say that I love her." That last part made him feel some emotion that he was unable to hide.

Tim noticed it. "I believe you. Don't ask me why, because I have no clue why I know these things." It made him feel really good for his mother to hear Roger say that he loved her. He wondered if Roger had told his mother yet about his feelings. Then he changed the subject. "You seem to know a lot about God."

"Why do you say that?" Roger was glad that the conversation was starting to go this direction. He was hoping to find a way to talk to Tim about what he believed in. He had wanted to ask Tim if he knew anything about Jesus or if he had ever read any of the Bible.

"You are always saying stuff about him, and I know you took my mom to your church, where they talk about Jesus and God and all of that stuff all the time."

Angela had gone to church with Roger the previous Sunday but had not even woken Tim up before they left. It was almost as if she was embarrassed to let him know she was going. Tim had been really disappointed. He was curious about God and the Bible. He also knew Jessica went to church every week, and he knew most of her friends were kids from her church. Just being around her would have been enough for him. Of course, he had not mentioned his interest in Jessica to his mother and certainly not to Roger.

"Yes, God is very important to me. I know that Jesus loves me, and his love makes me who I am and comes through in everything I do." Roger had spent some time around young people and understood how tricky it is to talk about Jesus with people who have no background in the concept of sin and our need of a savior. Roger was painfully aware of this, and he knew he had to establish that the Bible was true in every way or Tim would back away as quickly as he had headed into this conversation.

"Do you think God made my dad crash into your family that night?" Tim was really curious about this. He had heard that nothing happens that God is not aware of, and he wondered if God allowed this to happen or if he wasn't involved at all.

"That's a really good question, Tim. It's not that easy to answer. Honestly, I don't know. It hadn't crossed my mind until just a few weeks ago. My wife was an amazing woman. She and I made a perfect couple, and our daughter, Maria, was made in her image." A tear was coming to his eye, and he began to get a bit choked up. "They are in a better place right now. Knowing that makes it much easier to bear. I can't think of a reason why God would take them from Jessica and me, but knowing that they are with Jesus in heaven, it's hard for me to feel sorry for them. It's those of us who are left here on this fallen, sinful earth who struggle. You see, we are created for something better than our life here on this cursed earth. The Bible tells us that God has a purpose for mankind while we are here and that we will live with him in a perfect new world for eternity if we accept Jesus as our Lord and Savior.

"As for your father, I don't know enough about him to say what I think God's plan was in all of this. If he was not saved, he will be doomed to hell in which he will be tormented for all eternity. It's probably not what you want to hear, Tim, but I don't want to lie to you. The truth is the truth. Whether you believe it or not, God's Word is the truth. That's why it's so important for each of us to search for the answers for ourselves. We are all going to be held accountable to God, and where we spend eternity, heaven or hell, all rides on our decision and acceptance of the free gift of salvation in Jesus. How good or bad we are while we are here has no bearing on where we spend eternity. Our salvation is based solely on our acceptance and belief that Jesus died on the cross for our sins. As Jesus tells us in Scripture, 'Jesus saith unto him, "I am the way, the truth, and the life: no man cometh unto the Father, but by me.¹"'

"When it comes to you and your mother, I will say that I am very thankful to have the two of you in my and Jessica's life. I thank God for you and your mother and hope to help you both realize that God loves you too. He created mankind and tells us that he had a hand in every one of us. He tells us in the Bible that he does not wish that any of us perish but that we all accept his Son, Jesus, and get to spend eternity with him in heaven."

Seeing the pain in his face and the honesty of what he was saying, Tim felt a rush of emotion overtake him. He almost started to cry, as he knew Roger was right about his father. How could he be anywhere else than hell? He didn't really grasp all of the other stuff, but he did want to understand. For now, though, he wanted to see if Roger knew anything about the evil side, so he pressed on.

"Do you believe in the devil, demons, and evil spirits?"

"Yes, I certainly do. I believe in their existence as much as I believe in the existence of God. God's Word, the Bible, is full of stories and information about them." Roger was always amazed at how many people didn't believe in spirits, the devil, or even hell. A person could not take the Bible literally without believing in these things.

"I've heard that about the Bible, and I know that evil spirits are real." Tim was excited to hear that Mr. Brooks was a believer in spirits and evil forces. He felt confident to discuss what he felt had been happening to him and his family.

Roger was taken a bit by surprise. "How do you know they are real?" He had sensed that something terrible had happened in their lives, but it sounded to him that it might have been much more blatant than he had originally thought.

"I know they exist because I've lived with someone who had demons, evil spirits, or whatever they are." Tim's look turned from interest to anger.

Roger could tell that this was just the tip of the iceberg. Tim was deeply affected by what he had seen and lived through. The change in Tim's demeanor was pretty unsettling. He was becoming stern and angry looking. It actually made Roger feel uncomfortable.

Roger suddenly felt anxiety building inside of him. He wanted to make sure they were talking about who he assumed they were talking about. "Are you talking about your dad?"

"Yes, but not only him. I believe he had one, or something. I think my mother might have something influencing her, and I'm really scared that I might get one if I don't already have something."

The anger on his face had turned to despair. He appeared to be somewhat defeated by the thought that he too might have a demon or evil spirit. Roger could certainly understand why he'd feel that way and began to pray inside that Tim and Angela were not being tormented in that way.

"Do you want to go see my pastor about it?" Roger worried that he might be in over his head.

He would stand by Angela and Tim no matter how bad things got, but he knew how serious a situation they could be in, and he wanted to make sure he did everything he could to make sure they got all of the help they needed. He had no actual experience with this sort of thing, though he had heard and read about possession. Roger knew these things needed to be taken seriously. The advisory was very clever, and it was very unsettling to think that he could come face-to-face with something that he was ill prepared for. If something demonic was in their lives, Roger knew that the Lord could drive it out. He just wasn't sure he was the guy to tackle it straight on.

Roger's life had not been much of a struggle. Sure, he had worked hard to get his education and had dealt with all of the usual stresses and obstacles people deal with. However, his family was pretty sound, with no major distractions. Both he and his wife had come from Christian families. Roger had known some people who had been through some serious stuff, but he had never dealt with anything like what he might be getting into.

"No way," Tim quickly answered. "I'm talking to you about it. Can't you help me?" He was clearly uncomfortable with the thought of taking this beyond Roger for help or otherwise.

"Sure. I just wanted to offer. My pastor has lots of experience with this type of thing. He's got a big heart for God, and I trust him. Let's hold off for now though. I don't want you doing anything that makes you uncomfortable, Tim. Let's work on it ourselves for a while."

He hoped Tim wouldn't back down since he had admitted that he needed help. He really was scared for all of them. His praying continued.

"Thanks, Mr. Brooks. I was thinking that it would be really uncomfortable for my mom at your church if I went in there talking about this kind of stuff. What if she starts taking me to that church with you and Jessica? I don't want them to think we are crazy."

Tim was very curious about Roger's church. It seemed like Roger knew what he believed in. He seemed to know the answers to the biggest questions about life. If those were the kinds of things they taught people at their church, he wanted to go check it out. Tim was also hoping to get to go to church, or anywhere else, with Jessica.

"Okay. Let's take another approach. How about you and I start to read the Bible together? You see, the Bible is God's Word. He actually talks to us through it. The Bible is a living document, and he will begin to talk to you through it."

"Really? I've never heard that." Tim was surprised. That was great news.

"Yes, if you earnestly seek him, he will reveal himself to you. Reading his Word is the best way to find him."

Roger was feeling good about where it was going. He understood that people cannot be convinced that the God of the Bible is who he claims to be without God convicting them himself. The Bible is clear that man's understanding is like foolishness to him. No reasoning of man can ever definitively prove or define God. Yet God has revealed himself to man in the Bible. If Tim would look for God in the Bible, he would find him there.

"I don't have a Bible. My dad told my mom that he would burn it if she ever tried to bring one in our house. He used to tell us it was written by clever men trying to come up with something they could convince everyone else to believe in so they could control them. He said it was full of rules to control people. He told us that if there really was a God, he didn't care about us. It made him really angry when anyone said anything about God or church. He told us that only simpleminded idiots believed in God and that everything in the Bible had been proven wrong anyway. Maybe people believed in it once, but no educated person does now."

"Well, I've got several Bibles and am very happy to give you one. I'm so excited that we are going to read this together. I don't think it will take you long to figure out how wrong your dad was. Sadly, everything your dad told you is exactly what the devil wants us to think. All the devil has to do is convince you that God's Word is not true. He doesn't have to get you to worship him, though he would surely love that. All he has to get you to do is ignore God's Word until you die. Ignoring it does not absolve anyone from judgment. We will all be held accountable before God for what we did with the free gift of salvation he sent us in Jesus. Nothing is more important than our response to Jesus."

Roger excused himself but quickly came back with what looked like a brand-new Bible and two notepads. "Here you go, Tim. Let's start right at the beginning so we can establish who God is and why we are here. After that we'll move to the New Testament to see how he tells our generation to live and where we can find true fulfillment. The notebook is for your notes and questions." Before handing the notebook to Tim, Roger wrote "Tim" on the cover of both notebooks.

"Great. The beginning sounds like a good place to start." Tim was excited about reading the Bible. Part of it might have been due to the fact that his father had forbidden him from even talking about it, but it was mostly exciting to him because of the answers he was hoping it could give him. Now that his dad wasn't around anymore, he could look back and recognize that his dad hadn't been right about much. Actually, it seemed now that he had been wrong about just about everything.

"Tell me, Tim, it seems like you are unusually mature for a fourteen-year-old. Why do you think that is?" Roger had a good idea why but wanted to see what Tim thought.

"I had to be. I loved my dad, even though he was terrible to my mother. For years I didn't really know how wrong it was for him to push Mom around and sleep with other women. The older I got, the more I noticed that my friend's families weren't at all like ours was. No one else had a dad who had girlfriends, drank, and did drugs right in front of his family, and none of their fathers came home to smack their wife around or to have sex with someone in front of her. That was how my dad was. Mom just kept taking it. She would even tell me that it was all her fault. She never stopped telling Dad how much she loved him. I know Dad loved us both, but he didn't know how to deal with his demons." Tim seemed coldly detached from his feelings while he spoke. He seemed angry yet calm and accepting about what he was saying.

Roger felt sick to his stomach. He knew that Chuck was a bad guy, but what he had just heard was far more than he had bargained for. He was aching inside for both Tim and Angela. He just wanted to tell them that it would be all right. Could Angela ever get over being treated that way? How could Tim tell him all of that so soon? He really was an exceptional young man.

"You are an amazing young man, Tim. To go through what you have been through and be able to see out from all of it is truly amazing for someone of any age. To understand that your father loved you guys even though he did unspeakable harm to you both is very perceptive. It was his fault, but you are also right in believing that he had surrendered to something evil. Men are capable of unimaginable evil, but they must first turn from God. To get to where your father was, one must be given over to it by God. God does not have any part in evil, but he does give us free will. If we follow our own way and neglect to honor his wisdom, we will be deceived by the enemy. I am so sorry for what you two have been through."

Roger was doing his best to not get emotional. He decided it was best to not overreact, though he wasn't sure what reaction would be an overreaction to hearing that Chuck had slept with other women in front of Tim and Angela. Tim was right; Roger was in total agreement that Chuck had been influenced by something evil.

The praise felt really good to Tim. He was not used to hearing praise from a father figure. His father never praised him and had told him more than once, "You need to look out for yourself. Everyone else is only looking out for themselves. Me telling you that you are good all of the time won't make you tough enough to survive in this world." If he ever cried, his dad just called him a baby and made fun of him. What Roger was saying made a lot of sense to him. If everything God says is true, just about everything his father had said was false. His father had clearly pushed God out of his life. Had God given up on his father? He knew he would have if he had been God.

"Thanks, Mr. Brooks. I'm glad you are here for my mom. She really needs someone who will actually look out for her best interests."

Tim was so thankful that he wanted Roger to know how great it was that he was there for his mother. He knew that his mother needed what Roger was giving her, and the changes in her were easy to see. She was smiling all of the time and seemed excessively happy. He had never seen her this way before, and he loved it. More than anything, he didn't want it to end for her.

Roger felt as if God had brought Tim and Angela to him. What Tim was saying made him realize just how important it was that he honors God's will by loving them as God does. He already had deep feelings for Angela, and he just wanted to find a way to take away all of the pain he was sure she was carrying. He knew the type of emotional torture she had been through would not be easy to subdue. It occurred to him that it could take years for Angela to truly feel loved. Could he even handle the challenge? At that point, he was positive he could. Either way, he was completely committed to do whatever it took to make her feel loved. She was not only beautiful; she was one of the most giving people he had ever met. She was always putting him first, and he wanted to do the same for her. He was praying inside that God would give him the strength to be the man he needed to be for her. For now, he would begin to work with Tim. Reading the Bible and meeting regularly to talk about it was surely the best thing they could do.

"Let's meet back here every other day to talk about a chapter of the Bible. When do you get home from practice, Tim?" It would be difficult with Jessica and his other commitments, but it would have to take priority if it was going to work.

"I'm usually done by five thirty p.m. I head home to eat right afterward."

"Okay. I'll talk to your mom about this. If you want to eat with Jessica and me a couple times each week, that would be nice. I know your mom usually gets home around five thirty also. Perhaps the four of us can eat before you and I meet. Can you please mention it to her when you get home?"

"Yes, sir, I will. Thanks." Dinner with Jessica was all he could think about. He would read the entire Bible every night if it meant he would get to eat dinner with her.

"Do you need a ride home?"

"No, sir. I'll walk. Can you do me a favor and not mention the questions about possession, demons, and the devil to Jessica or my mom?"

"I won't. That's between you and me. Please, just call me Mr. Brooks. *Sir* makes me a little uncomfortable." There was no chance he would betray Tim's trust.

"Thank you, Mr. Brooks."

Tim knew he could trust Mr. Brooks to not tell anyone. It was really only Jessica he was afraid of freaking out with the demon stuff. He really didn't care that much about what his mom might think, though he knew that that needed to change. It was part of the legacy his father had left him, but he knew it was not an acceptable excuse for not caring what she thought.

As he got up to leave, his thoughts went immediately to that gorgeous creature living upstairs. When he passed the stairs, he hollered, "Good-bye, Jessica." Her response came quickly, as if she was waiting on him.

All she had said was, "Good-bye, Tim," but that was more than enough for him.

As his fingers hit the doorknob, he noticed her bouncing down the stairs behind him. He stopped and turned as she ran right up to him.

"I'll see you tomorrow at school, Tim," she managed to get out through her amazing smile.

He wanted to hug her so badly that he almost reached out for her before he came to his senses. "Yep. I'll see you there for sure." He couldn't believe what a moron he was around her.

"Okay. It's a date then." She grinned back at him. Then she leaned in and gave him a hug.

Tim was beside himself. He couldn't believe he was hugging her. He could feel his heart beating as he breathed in her heavenly smell. As he pulled her in, her tiny frame came in contact with the right side of his body. It was more than he could handle, so he quickly released her. Their eyes met, and both of them felt awkward.

"Good-bye, Jessica," Tim managed. Then he turned and left.

On the way home, he was as excited as he had ever been in his life. His concerns over whether or not she liked him were suddenly gone. He was only a freshman and understood that girls usually liked older boys. Before the hug, he had been concerned that she would not be interested in him. Now he felt like there was more than a chance.

It kept running though his head that he might not be able to treat her the way he knew she deserved to be treated. Where were these doubts coming from? Whatever it took, he committed to himself to become someone worthy of her love.

When he finally got his thoughts off Jessica, he began to think about his time with Roger and their commitment to read the Bible. He hoped that the Bible and Mr. Brooks had some answers. Tim hoped they could help him become what he needed to be for Jessica.

CHAPTER 14

JESSICA turned around to find her father standing there watching her awkward good-bye to Tim. He had a notebook in his hand that had "Tim" written on the cover.

"What's that?" she asked.

"Tim and I are going to start reading through the Bible together." As excited as he was that he and Tim were going to read the Bible together, he was now consumed with what he had just seen between Jessica and Tim.

"Great! I've been thinking a lot about him since we started spending time with them. I was thinking that they probably know nothing about God or the Bible. Am I right?" She was hoping to avoid any conversation about the hug she had just given Tim.

"That's right. They have actually avoided it. Both of them seem to have quite a lot of interest right now, Tim in particular. He seems like a really smart kid."

"That's what everybody says about him, Dad. I've also heard that he's the best football player in his grade. I hear the varsity coach is very excited about getting him next year. Everyone says he's the nicest guy and that he's always helping people with school work and even on the football field."

"Wow. You seem to know a lot about the guy."

It actually worried him quite a bit. He knew some of what Tim had been exposed to. Additionally, Tim was already taller than him. In a year or two, Tim would be able to physically dominate him.

What if he acts out any of his father's sins against my daughter? He quickly stopped himself. *I can't do this to Tim. I've got to give him the benefit of the doubt while remaining aware of what's going on.*

Still, how could he not have concerns since he knew about his daughter's obvious interest in Tim? He had never seen her this way. He had never heard her say anything about an attraction to any boy. He had always known that day would come, and he knew he wouldn't be ready for it.

Jessica blushed and smiled a bit. "I don't know that much about him, Dad. Knock it off."

She really liked him. He was on her mind constantly, and she was always looking for him at school. She had never noticed him until she and her father had visited Tim and his mom at their house a few weeks back. Once they had met, she started asking around about him. Her interests were so obvious that her friends were already teasing her about him.

Jessica had been a perfect daughter and had never had a boyfriend. She had been through lots of heartache over the loss of her mother and sister, and her interest in boys was really nonexistent. Now her mind was being dominated with thoughts of Tim. He was sweet and good looking, but there was much more she liked about him that she just didn't understand but couldn't deny. It felt like she belonged with him. No one had anything bad to say about him. He was smart, a great athlete, and seemed to be going somewhere with his life. Mostly, though, she could tell that he was interested in her. Though she occasionally had her doubts, she was pretty sure he was feeling something like she was feeling.

"I would ask you to join us for the Bible study, but I think he and I need to do this alone."

"I understand, Dad. You will do great!" She knew she didn't belong in their group.

Roger couldn't get over how similar Jessica's personality was to her mother's. Although Maria looked more like her mother, Jessica got all of her mother's personality while Maria had his. Jessica's blonde hair and slender figure made her look like his side of the family, but the way she cared about others was straight from her mother. Roger had learned to care for others through his deceased wife, Caroline. Caroline had always been the one bringing things to him to ask if it was okay if they did this or that for so-and-so. It was she who had opened his eyes to the pain in other's lives. Sure, he understood that everyone went through pain. What he didn't get before she came into his life was that it was his responsibility to take care of the less fortunate. She showed him that he could change someone's life with a kind word, act, or even by simply listening to them. Looking at Jessica, Roger didn't see the physical differences between she and her mother anymore; he only saw her pure heart. She was a really good person, just like her mother.

CHAPTER 15

TIM could hardly wait to start reading what God had written. He wasted no time telling his mother about the deal to read through the Bible he had just made with Mr. Brooks. As soon as it sank in, Angela felt a sudden fear rush over her.

What would Chuck do if he knew this was happening?

It quickly faded as she realized that he was gone. The time that had passed since Chuck's death hadn't been enough to wipe away all of her fears. She still found herself measuring every situation and decision against what Chuck would think.

As soon as Tim got to his room, he started reading. He read the first chapter, and then the second, and the third; he couldn't stop. He had read much longer than he had planned, and before he knew it, he had read all fifty chapters of Genesis.

He found it totally contradictory to what they had been teaching him in school. Ever since he could remember, he had been told we came from apes. Everyone had always talked about how things were millions of years old. That's not what God says. God says that he created it all. He says that everything was created in six days, including all of the animals. How could anything have evolved if God created everything the way the Bible says he did? It just didn't make sense to him. How could people believe in a God who got it all wrong?

If he didn't get it wrong, what in the world is going on? he wondered. *Roger must believe this stuff or he wouldn't have asked me to read it, right?*

Tim decided that he couldn't wait two days to talk about what he had read. He decided that he would go after practice the next day to see if Roger would have time for him.

Though he had read much of the Bible in bed, he had not been able to relax or feel even a little tired. As he lay awake, he tossed and turned but got no rest. Why were they teaching lies?

One side certainly is. Two things can't be true if they are contradictory. He knew that much for sure. If the Bible was God's Word, how could he be wrong?

Tim knew that he was outmatched with all of it. He knew very little about science and history. He knew even less about the Bible. He did find it interesting, though, that the devil was right there at the beginning of what the Bible called "the curse" and at the start of man's sinful nature. It was Satan himself who had told the first lie. It was he who put doubt about the truth of God's Word into Eve's mind. It was because of Satan that man sinned. Sure, man was guilty of not obeying God's Word, but Satan sure had a lot to do with it.

The flood seemed very drastic to him. Why wipe everything out? It sounded like God had made a mistake. Was that possible?

He noticed two places where giants were mentioned.

Was that for real?

Then there was all of this "God's chosen people" stuff. Why had he chosen a group of people? It seemed strange to him. He seemed to give them all sorts of favor, but why? The story of Joseph and how God used him to preserve his people fascinated Tim.

He finally got up out of bed to write some of these questions and others down so he wouldn't forget them. He had forgotten about the notebook Roger had given him but remembered as he started to write stuff on a loose piece of paper.

The notebook is way better, he thought. *Now I will have it all in one place.*

Roger really knew what he was doing. If there were answers to those questions, he needed to hear them, and Roger was definitely the right guy to answer them.

CHAPTER 16

WHEN Tim's alarm went off, it felt to him as if he had only gotten a few minutes of sleep. He didn't really care, though. He was full of excitement over what he had read in the Bible, and he could hardly wait to start getting some answers. Deep inside, he had always known that there was a God. From what he had read, God created everything. Tim was sure of it. If God had created us, he had to have created us for a reason. The Bible had even said that God created man "in his own image."

What does that mean? he wondered.

School seemed to drag on, but football practice flew by. It was just after 5:30 p.m. when Tim hopped on his bike on a fact-finding mission. He hoped Mr. Brooks would be home and have time for him. If he had Mr. Brooks pegged right, he would be more than willing to talk about the Bible that day or any day.

When he got to the Brooks' house, he didn't see the car in the driveway, but since Mr. Brooks would likely park in the garage, he went right to the front door and knocked. Jessica answered. He hadn't even thought about the possibility that she might be home alone. She opened the door with a big smile on her face, as she had seen him through the window before she opened the door. As happy as he was to see her, he suddenly felt awkward and ill prepared.

"Hi, Jessica. Is your dad home?"

"Not yet, but he should be here any minute. I didn't expect to see you again until tomorrow. By the way, I saw you at school today, but you seemed really distracted and I don't think you noticed me."

She was pretty sure he hadn't noticed her, but it still bothered her that he had not acknowledged her. She was sure he had been looking for her at lunch and between classes most days. When they had crossed paths earlier that day, though, he had not even made eye contact with her. She had been telling herself all day that he just hadn't noticed her.

"No, I didn't see you. I would have said hi or something if I had seen you."

He feared that he might have hurt her feelings. He could tell by the expression on her face that she was disappointed. It was the last thing he wanted to do. Since he had met her, he had done everything in his power to make sure their paths crossed as much as possible. Now she thought he had purposely snubbed her.

"I didn't think you saw me. I tried to get your attention, but you were really focused on something else." She could tell by the way he answered that he really hadn't noticed her. She felt better already. "Why don't you come in and wait for my dad?" She was smiling again.

Wow. What a smile she has, Tim thought. "I'll wait, but can we wait out here on the porch? I don't want your dad to get the wrong idea." He didn't want to offend her, but he didn't want her dad to think anything was going on either. He really wanted her to wait with him, so he added, "Do you mind coming out here with me to wait?"

"Not at all," she replied.

It felt really good to her that he wanted her to wait with him. Though they had hardly spoken, she felt safe with him. She felt like he was someone she could trust. His staring at her had never made her feel uncomfortable. He looked at her longingly, like he wanted to be around her all the time. It made her feel desired and special. His stares never felt dirty or lustful to her. She had the strangest feelings inside for him—feelings she had never felt before.

"I read Genesis last night." He wanted to see her reaction, so he made the statement and shut up to see what she would say. He wondered if she believed it was all true, like he was sure her father did.

"That's great!" She was so excited and didn't hide it.

It was easy for Tim to see her approval in her smile and reaction. She knew he wasn't a Christian, but for them to ever have a future together, she knew he would have to become a believer. She had long known that the man she would one day marry would be a Christian.

That will be a long time from now, she thought, *but it is important to me that he becomes eligible.*

Inside, she knew it was more important that he find the truth and that he chose to make Jesus the Lord of his life, but her immediate thoughts were about their future together. She wanted him to be saved for more than her selfish reasons, but at that moment, the thought of him someday marrying her was dominating her thoughts.

"I read the whole thing last night, and my notebook is full of questions for your dad."

The sheer joy written all over her face was enough to let him know that she was supportive of him reading the Bible. It felt good to see her so excited. He loved her smile, her eyes—all of it.

"Wow. You read all of Genesis in one night? My dad is definitely the right guy to answer your questions. He reads the Bible every day, and he's taught several Bible studies. He's also a really smart guy."

She loved her dad more than anything. He was so good to her and everyone else he came across. She often felt that he was someone who truly wanted to be like Christ in character.

Tim must really be searching for the truth, she thought. *He read the whole first book of the Bible in one night.*

She felt guilty for not going after it the way he was. She had been in Sunday school and Wednesday night church groups all of her life. She had read bits and pieces of the Bible her whole life, but she had never been focused enough to just read straight through the Bible. Her father had read Genesis with her when she was younger, but she had not read it on her own since. He talked a lot about what things meant, and she had just enjoyed his company rather than taking advantage of the chance she was being given to ask questions.

Tim must be really motivated, she thought.

She admired that about him already. Her father was a hard worker who never took shortcuts. She really admired that quality about him, and it appeared to her that Tim too might have that quality.

"I couldn't help it. It was just so cool to be reading something God wrote. It raised so many questions in my mind. Do you believe it's really God's Word and therefore all true?"

He had to press her to confirm his assumption. He hoped she believed it. He hated knowing that it would affect the way he felt about it if she didn't believe it, but he knew it would. It would affect him, but he would still press through to make up his own mind either way.

"Yes, I believe every word. I only wish I knew it the way my father does."

It was overwhelming to her to think that she could have an impact on this guy's decision to believe and ultimately on his salvation. The responsibility she had always been told about, that others will push you to see what you really believe, was now right in front of her. This guy's salvation could be in her hands, and she didn't feel adequate. She didn't feel properly prepared, and it made her feel some disappointment in herself. She knew she could answer the basics, but why hadn't she searched harder for the difficult answers? Why had she so easily believed? She knew nonbelievers who were honestly seeking would want to know why she believed, but she just hadn't taken that responsibility seriously enough. She knew that now, and she began to pray inside for the strength and wisdom to show Tim she was certain about God's Word. It occurred to her that her father had done what God commanded in bringing up his children in the fear and admiration of the Lord. She concluded that she believed because of him, because of his example, well, also because of her mother's example.

"I'm really happy to hear that. I hope to get some answers from your dad. I've got a list of questions for him. I can tell he believes what the Bible has to say, and I'm looking forward to learning from him."

He could sense that she was a bit nervous that he might ask her something she didn't know, so he backed off and decided to save the questions for her father.

"I'm so glad you two are doing this. My dad is really pumped. He told me that he is so happy to have someone who really wants answers to study with. He can hardly wait to meet with you again."

She had not seen her father this excited about anything in a long while. Her dad had told her how excited he was when Angela had gone to church with them, but he admitted that she was not really seeking and didn't seem to have much curiosity about God. His feeling was that she had only gone to church for him. He already knew that it was her tendency to try to please others and she was only trying to do things he wanted. Angela wasn't really opening up with him, and he felt that there was still quite a bit to sort through before she would be truly ready to move on from her past. With Tim, though, her dad had said that it was different. He told her that Tim was hungry for answers. He went on and on about how great it was to see someone who just wanted to find out the truth.

Just then, Mr. Brooks pulled into the driveway. He was happy to see the two of them standing out front. All day he had been hoping that Tim would not be able to wait to talk about the Bible after starting to read it. As he drove in, he noticed how happy they both seemed. He rolled down the window and told them that he was going to park in the garage and would meet them inside.

As they turned to walk into the house, Tim's eyes strayed down at Jessica's behind. It was perfect in every way, but he found himself feeling uncomfortable looking at her that way. He was beginning to notice something strange about himself when he was around her. For whatever reason, he could not allow himself to violate her with his eyes or thoughts. At first he had, but as he spent more time thinking about her, he began to feel more like her protector than anything else. He began to wonder what he would do if someone else tried to take her out or, God forbid, hurt her in any way.

Roger was just opening the door from the garage when Jessica said, "Hi, Dad. Your study buddy is here." She walked right up to him and gave him a hug.

Tim wished he could change places with Roger for the hug. He'd had one of those and knew that there was nothing better.

"Thanks for taking care of him until I got here, honey. Tim, what brings you back so quickly? I hope this is a result of you reading the Bible." Roger was already painfully aware of Jessica's attraction to Tim. He was pretty sure Tim was attracted to her too, though he had nothing more than common sense to go on.

"Yes, sir. I read all of Genesis last night and couldn't sleep at all. I've written down a bunch of questions for you in the notebook you gave me." He could tell that Roger was excited about the chance to answer his questions, and he could hardly wait for answers.

"What about your mom? Does she know where you are? Should we invite her over? We could all have dinner before you and I get started."

He wanted to make sure Angela didn't get offended that he was taking Tim away from her like that. From what he had seen, Tim kind of did what he wanted to. Roger felt like it was important to bring them together with him and Jessica as soon as possible so they could all get better acquainted. Tim didn't have a cell phone, but his mother did.

"She has no idea where I am, but she won't be worried. If you want to invite her over, that's fine with me. I'm not sure if I can keep from asking questions while we eat, though." He didn't want to come off like he didn't care about what his mother thought, because he did.

"I'll give her a quick call. Perhaps we can talk for an hour or so before we eat and for a while again after we eat." He wanted to be available for Tim, and he knew that it would likely take a couple of hours to cover what he imagined Tim would crave to have answered, but he also knew it was important to involve Angela.

"That would work great! We can eat around seven then."

He was happy with the proposed solution. As badly as he needed to get his questions answered, food was always a major priority for him.

Roger made the call to Angela, who happily agreed to be over by 7:00 p.m. He then gave Jessica instructions to call in an order for pizza at 6:30 p.m. for a 7:00 p.m. delivery. Roger also gave her cash to pay the delivery person for the pizza and tip.

Jessica was happy that they were having company for dinner, especially Tim. She took the cash and promised to order and to answer the door and pay for the pizza when it arrived. She then turned and ran up the stairs to change out of her school clothes. Tim watched longingly.

"Tim, I've got to run up to my room to change and to get my Bible and other material for our Bible study. I'll be right back."

Roger turned for the stairs and headed out of the room while Tim took a seat at the table and began to dig in his backpack for the Bible and notepad Roger had given him.

It was almost 6:00 p.m. when Roger reappeared. He had his Bible, the notebook with "Tim" written on it, and a bunch of other papers and a couple of books.

"Okay. Let's get started," said Roger as he sat down with Tim at the table.

For the next hour, Tim asked the questions he had written down in his notebook. Roger was well equipped with answers. He did his best to work from the beginning forward. He explained that every word of the Bible was true, that God created everything, including the heavens and earth, in only six literal days and that we have a good feel for how old the earth is based on the life spans of the people in the Bible. For instance, Adam lived a hundred and thirty years before he had Seth, and then Adam lived eight hundred more years. He lived a total of nine hundred and thirty years and had sons and daughters, which was where all the other people came from. God tells us that he only created Adam and that Eve was taken from Adam's body to create a helpmate. Roger explained that that is God's purpose for marriage, that a man leaves his father and mother to become one flesh with his wife. The Bible provides a time line from each ancestor to the next, from Adam all the way to recorded time in which outside resources could be used to put actual dates to things. As a matter of fact, the Bible has the genealogy from Adam all the way to Jesus. The text shows that Adam died only 126 years before Noah was born. Noah's father was alive for fifty-six years before Adam's death. They might have known each other firsthand.

According to the timelines in the Bible, the flood occurred 1,656 years after creation. Roger pointed out that around the world, enormous layers of sedimentary rock (rock that is formed in water) have been found. This, along with many other observable phenomena, proves that at one time, the earth was covered in water. Signs of massive runoff, such as the Grand Canyon, show that it happened quickly. There are many facts that point to rapid, catastrophic conditions that killed without warning. This also points to a worldwide catastrophic flood as described in the Bible. Some examples include large groups of animals killed simultaneously, fossilized creatures found eating each other, and marine mammals, including whales, found in huge deposits of dead algae. Roger told Tim that anyone who is earnestly interested in finding the truth can look into the evidence and decide for themselves. Just because something is accepted by academia doesn't necessarily mean that it's true.

Scientists claim that coal formed many millions of years ago, while human objects, such as handmade metal objects and pottery, have been found inside coal beds. This proves that humans existed before the formation of coal. Additionally, oil is frequently found at extremely high pressures. It is not possible for the rock to have contained that pressure for millions of years; therefore, the oil was formed recently under great pressure. The size of the deposits indicates that they must have been produced in a recent catastrophe like Noah's flood.

Roger was reading most of his information from several printed articles and papers from Dr. Hovind, Ken Ham, and Dr. Chuck Missler. He pointed out to Tim that, at this point in history, information is more easily accessible than at any other time in history, yet many people continue to reject the truth. Unfortunately, this is reflected in all aspects of life. He told Tim that it's usually not an intellectual discussion that leads people to God. It's always a matter of faith, and they must be called by God to even seek him. The Bible teaches that we are all born knowing that there is a God, but, like children trying to avoid obeying their parents, people grow up and try to deny God and his character.

Science proves that humans can only produce humans, dogs only produce dogs, and trees only produce trees. There are no missing links. Genesis tells us over and over that God created everything in its kind, and this is still what we see today. Though man has now successfully blurred these lines by creating hybrid animals and perhaps even hybrid animal-humans, these things are not natural. Evolution from species to species has never been observed. Man tinkering with genes to produce hybrids actually proves intelligence is required to create hybrids, not randomness and lots of time. That is if *create* is even a proper word for mixing two or more previously existing creations of God.

Roger told Tim that at the time of the flood, it is very likely that there were more than one billion people on the face of the earth. He also pointed out that dinosaurs were created along with all of the other animals and that they were created of their own kind. The Bible tells us that everything he created ate fruit and vegetation at least until after the fall and very likely all the way to the flood. After the flood, God told Noah that he and his family could eat meat when they came out of the ark.

Roger showed Tim in the book of Job, where the Bible gives details of two dinosaurs: behemoth and leviathan. Behemoth is described as having a tail like a cedar while leviathan is described as a fire-breathing dragon. Then he pointed out all the cultures that had dragon stories in their history, especially in the Orient. One unique characteristic of reptiles is that they continue to grow throughout their lives. Before the flood, it is possible that they lived much longer lives under different conditions than our current conditions. The long lives of people are well documented in the Bible, so it makes good sense that the animals also lived much longer lives before things changed radically with the flood.

They dove into details about the early earth. Roger showed Tim where in the Bible God told us it had never rained on the earth before the flood. It took Noah more than a hundred years to build the ark, and he, no doubt, was teased and harassed to no end while building the ark. Noah and his family were the only people God saved through the flood. They were chosen because God said, "Noah was a just man [and] perfect in his generations, [and] Noah walked with God" (Genesis 6:9, KJV). The "just man" part had to do with following God's commandments, but the "perfect in his generations" part might have meant something more than simply pure in the sense of his motives and actions or even that he was seeking or walking with God. He explained that many scholars believe that perfect in his generations had to do with his actual human DNA. There are signs in the text that humans were having a DNA pollution issue due to fallen angels conceiving children with human women. Roger gave Tim two pieces of text that led people to believe this. First:

And it came to pass, when men began to multiply on the face of the earth, and daughters were born unto them, that the sons of God saw the daughters of men that they [were] fair; and they took them wives of all which they chose. There were giants in the earth in those days; and also after that, when the sons of God came in unto the daughters of men, and they bare [children] to them, the same [became] mighty men which [were] of old, men of renown.

Genesis 6:1, 2, 4 (KJV)

Secondly: "And the angels which kept not their first estate, but left their own habitation, he hath reserved in everlasting chains under darkness unto the judgment of the great day" (Jude 1:6, KJV). What the text suggested was that angels, heavenly beings, had come down to earth and had offspring with human women. These children were part fallen spiritual beings, angels, and part human. The ramifications are staggering, as the stories of gods and half gods are found everywhere throughout most secular history. Even the stories of aliens visiting Earth are likely tied to these fallen angels. God makes it clear that he created everything and that there is only one God. He created everything else that claims to be god.

Tim had asked about giants. They were mentioned in the verse Roger had just read to him, Genesis 6:4. Roger told him that the giants are mentioned several other times. They continue to appear and are always in opposition to God's plan. They are always threatening to his people, and God is always delivering his people from them or using his people to defeat them. He told him about David and Goliath and explained about David's faith, that he was a man after God's own heart and yet was still a sinner guilty of adultery and murder but forgiven by God after he suffered great loss as a consequence. The giants were real, and they were most likely supernatural.

Roger explained that with the ark, God delivered mankind like he will deliver believers in the end-times. He promised to spend a lot more time on the subject and told him that the Old Testament was full of events that foreshadow what God's plan for us is.

"It all boils down to Jesus," he told him, and he promised to spend a lot more time on the subject in the future.

They were interrupted when the doorbell rang. It was Angela. She was actually on time and had even beaten the pizza delivery guy to the house.

Tim was so amazed that he told Roger, "Boy she is really into you to be here on time. She can't even make it to work on time."

Roger was happy to see Angela. She had been the only thing on his mind for several weeks. He loved being around her, not just because she was so beautiful, but also because she seemed to want to see him as much as he wanted to see her. She was dressed in some sort of running outfit, and he could tell she was a serious runner just by the way the outfit was stretched by her powerful thighs while highlighting how in shape the rest of her body was. As usual, it would be a struggle not to stare at her body. The outfit was tight in all of the right places, and he knew immediately that her wearing it to dinner meant she had plans to work out after they ate.

Perhaps I should start working out, he thought.

While Tim and Roger tore into the pizza, Jessica and Angela got drinks for everyone. The conversation during the meal was mostly playful and fun. None of the heavy stuff Tim and Roger had been talking about came up, but Roger noticed Tim sitting back quietly a couple of times. He was pretty sure Tim was thinking about what they had been talking about.

After the meal, Tim helped clean up the table and told his mom that he'd ride his bike home by 10:00 p.m. at the latest. She hugged him and Roger and asked Jessica if she would like to go on a walk with her before she left.

Jessica jumped at the opportunity. "Yes, I would love to. Do you run also?" She was hoping to start doing some sort of exercise, but none of her friends worked out and she was not into any sports. She was just too petite for sports, and her dad wasn't crazy about any of them either.

"Yes, I run almost every day. If you want to run some, we can do that too. We can actually do both or either tonight. It's your call."

Angela had only eaten two pieces of pizza and had noticed that Jessica only had one. Roger had several pieces while Tim ate an entire pizza by himself. Eating light wasn't always easy for Angela, but Chuck had trained her well with his condescending comments and threats about going after better-looking women. She had learned to control herself and actually craved the working out.

"I'll do my best to keep up with you. I'd hate to slow you down." She was actually feeling really excited to have someone asking her to work out. Maybe she could learn to love it like Angela seemed to.

"I planned to ask you to walk. I wasn't counting on running, so you won't slow me down. We'll move at your pace."

Angela had never had anyone to work out with. The possibility of finding a workout partner in Jessica was appealing to her. Early on, she had never wanted to spend time with anyone but Chuck. Every time she had tried to get close to anyone, they would start in on her about Chuck and how she shouldn't put up with him. She would always back away to avoid that.

Tim sat there thinking about how running could make Jessica even more perfect. *Stop it*, he told himself. *She is Mr. Brooks's daughter, and he's my Bible study teacher and could end up with my mom.* He knew he needed to stop thinking about her like that, but it wasn't easy.

As the ladies set out for their workout, Tim and Roger sat down at the dining room table and jumped right back into their study and discussion. Tim was curious about the devil, and he had several questions written down in his notebook on the subject. One of the questions was why God would create the devil.

If he knew the beginning from the end, why would he create the devil? Why would he allow evil to enter the world?

Roger explained that God created the devil so that he could find true love with people. He explained that God is love and that he created people for relationships. Since God made us, he knows we cannot love without free will. God chose to give us free will and knew it would have to be our choice to love him. Without the devil and sin, we would have no reason to not choose him. He explained that as a man, you don't want your wife to love you because of what you have or how you look. You want her to have true love for you, which has to be based on her absolute free will to choose you or not choose you. If there was no devil, we would have no alternative to God. He explained that everything about God is the opposite of the devil.

Roger went on to explain that the devil was the father of lies. He showed him how the devil worked in the beginning by creating doubt about God's Word. They talked about how this strategy has never changed and how the devil is still trying to create doubt about God's Word. The attack on Genesis and when and where we came from has been effective—so effective that much of the church has accepted man's evolutionary time line that is in complete opposition to God's time line, known as the truth. This acceptance has started the erosion of the church, as Genesis is the foundation of everything else in the Bible. He explained how the devil is far craftier than people think and that the devil didn't have to convince us to love or choose him to win. All he has to do is get us to reject God and we will go to hell, just like he will.

When Tim asked why the devil continues if he will not win in the end, Roger explained that the devil knows God's Word far better than we do. He told him that the devil knows what God's Word says but that the devil, being a liar himself, is not able to believe God. He might actually believe that he can become like God, like the Bible tells us he proclaimed to God before he was cast down to the earth with one-third of the angels that chose to follow him. The Bible teaches that the devil was so filled with envy when the creator created mankind in his own image that he rebelled and became the sworn enemy of God. The angels who fell with him are believed to be demons here on earth. They are spiritual beings that tempt, condemn, and even possess people who give them the right to enter them. Roger told Tim that some believe that the demons are actually the disembodied spirits of the offspring from the union of fallen angels and human women. They agreed to make that a subject of focus of their studies, as Tim was convinced he and his mother had been dealing with something demonic. Tim firmly believed that his father had a serious problem that was likely rooted in some sort of evil spirituality.

As they reluctantly moved on to another subject, Tim told Roger that he was confused by the long life spans of the people in the early parts of the Bible. Roger told him that no one knows for sure what the earth was like before the flood. Only God knows, as he was there. For the rest of us, we have to examine the text of the Bible for answers. He shared with Tim that there was not much said in the Bible about the pre-flood world, as the flood took place in only the sixth chapter of the first book in the Bible. However, he encouraged Tim by saying that there had been quite a bit of work done to better understand the pre-flood earth. Roger told him that there are some clues in the Bible, and one of them has to do with the description of the early earth in the first chapter of the Bible. In the second day of creation, God tells us:

> And God said, let there be a firmament in the midst of the waters, and let it divide the waters from the waters. And God made the firmament, and divided the waters which [were] under the firmament from the waters which [were] above the firmament: and it was so.
>
> Genesis 1:7-8 (KJV)

If the earth was made with a protective canopy of water around it, it would protect the earth from harmful rays from the sun, much like a greenhouse does. The atmosphere might have been different, allowing pterodactyls to fly and providing for much higher levels of oxygen. Studies have been done that have proven that a high level of oxygen improves recovery time in people while allowing for heightened growth rates in vegetation. Based on the life spans given in the Bible, Noah and his sons were the last ones to live long lives. Over the next few generations after the flood, life spans came down to a hundred years fairly quickly.

The Bible tells us that the flood was such a catastrophic worldwide event that everything that walked the earth or flew above the earth and was not in the ark died. Then he read Tim two passages:

In the six hundredth year of Noah's life, in the second month, the seventeenth day of the month, the same day were all the fountains of the great deep broken up, and the windows of heaven were opened. And the rain was upon the earth forty days and forty nights.

Genesis 7:11-12 (KJV)

And all flesh died that moved upon the earth, both of fowl, and of cattle, and of beast, and of every creeping thing that creepeth upon the earth, and every man: All in whose nostrils [was] the breath of life, of all that [was] in the dry [land], died. And every living substance was destroyed which was upon the face of the ground, both man, and cattle, and the creeping things, and the fowl of the heaven; and they were destroyed from the earth: and Noah only remained [alive], and they that [were] with him in the ark.

Genesis 7:21-23 (KJV)

The events were so radical that it is believed that everything was different after the flood. The ice age was likely a result to the loss of the greenhouse effect, the protective layer of water that might have made up part of our atmosphere before the flood. The equator quickly became much warmer, while the top and bottom of the earth began to freeze. The changes might have taken years to reach equilibrium.

Roger pointed out that most modern-day scientists are totally blind to any possibility that things on the earth were radically different in the past. For this reason they make the false assumption that it is possible to tell things about the past based on current conditions and our limited understanding. God reminds us several times about the foolishness of man's understanding. Roger showed Tim several examples, including:

Professing themselves to be wise, they became fools.

Romans 1:22 (KJV)

For it is written, I will destroy the wisdom of the wise, and will bring to nothing the understanding of the prudent.

1 Corinthians 1:19 (KJV)

But the natural man receiveth not the things of the Spirit of God: for they are foolishness unto him: neither can he know [them], because they are spiritually discerned.

1 Corinthians 2:14 (KJV)

Roger pulled out a book written by Ken Ham and others called *The New Answers: Book One.* He told Tim that the book would go well with their studies about Genesis and the literal truth of every word in the Bible.

Tim took the book and started to flip through it when the two heard some commotion at the door. It was Jessica and Angela returning from their exercise. Jessica opened the door and walked right through the kitchen to get a bottle of water out of the refrigerator. Her face was red, and she was perspiring profusely.

"That lady is a machine," she told them. "She's not even breathing hard or sweating."

"That's why I never run with her," Tim responded. "I'd better get going, Mr. Brooks. Thanks so much for doing this with me. Can we do it again tomorrow?"

Angela walked in and accepted a bottle of water from the exhausted Jessica. She looked the same as she did when they left well over an hour earlier. Roger was impressed. He knew he couldn't run around the block without passing out.

"Thanks, Jessica. You did really well tonight."

"As difficult as it was, I'm really glad we did it. I want to keep running with you. Maybe next time I can walk a little less and run a little more." She loved feeling like she was working hard and knew that it would help her get in shape and feel better. Angela's fitness level impressed Jessica greatly. Angela hadn't even breathed hard at any point that night.

"We can do this every night if you guys are up for it." Roger's response was hopeful, and he knew that it sounded that way. He really wanted to spend as much time as possible with both Angela and Tim. It was his chance to invite them deeper into his and Jessica's life. He knew that every night would cause him to change some of his commitments, but he knew that was where he needed to be.

"Count me in," said Tim.

"Me too," added Angela. "I'll bring something to cook tomorrow night, though."

"Great. It's a date then," Roger responded. He felt satisfied and couldn't help but hug Angela good-bye.

Tim wanted to hug Jessica with every part of his being but knew it wasn't possible at that point. He didn't realize that Roger had seen him and Jessica hug the day before, and he felt it would freak out everyone if he even looked at her too long. He took some more mental photos of her and grabbed his backpack on his way out.

"See you guys tomorrow night. I'll be looking for you at school tomorrow, Jessica. I'm really sorry about missing you today."

"You'd better not walk right by me anymore. We are almost family now."

She was definitely flirting, and her father new it. Tim was pretty sure she was as well, and he loved it.

CHAPTER 17

FOR the next few weeks, the four met for dinner, studying for the guys, and running for the girls. They met almost every night and spent even more time together on the weekends. Jessica and Angela made dinner, and the guys cleaned it all up.

Tim almost always arrived early to spend time with Jessica out on the porch, talking. He loved how caring she was. She always talked about how things made her dad happy or about something one of her friends was going through. She never talked about herself or how good she was at school or anything else. She was funny and smart, and her looks were amazing and seemed to improve daily. Tim was so smitten that he was almost in a trance whenever she spoke. Most times he just listened and watched as she spoke to him.

Jessica was equally infatuated with Tim. She loved how dedicated he was to his Bible study with her father. Dad had told her that he was an amazing student who was pushing him to become a better disciple of God's Word just to keep up. Jessica admired that Tim wanted to be like her father. She knew her father was continually trying to be more Christlike, and Tim was following him there now. Though the physical part wasn't important to Jessica—at least that's what she kept telling herself—she could not stop looking at him when he was around. She never looked around or even noticed anything else going on when he was with her. They just locked in on one another, and everything else melted away. Everything felt perfect when Tim was around. She loved how he never bragged about how good he was. Everyone at school talked about him, but he never seemed to want to use it with her. He seemed to want to be there for her and never seemed to be trying to impress her. She loved that about him.

Tim pushed Roger hard for information, and he began to understand what it meant to be a Christian. The fact that sin had entered the world through one man made sense to him. Man, through his own choices, had rebelled against God and created a chasm between himself and God. The fact that Jesus had come to earth; lived a perfect, sinless life; and then sacrificed it for man wasn't completely clear to him, but he knew it was true. Roger had told him that Jesus gave up his heavenly body and became a man to save us. For all eternity, Jesus would be both man and God, and Scripture tells us we will have resurrected bodies like his. Tim had read enough to know it was all true.

Still, there were things like the talking snake thing that he just couldn't understand. Roger had told him that there are things in the Bible that we will not understand until Jesus returns. Whether some animals were able to speak before the fall of man, or whether this was the only occurrence as the Scripture tells us that Satan himself entered the serpent, we are simply not told.

Their Bible study had been going on about a month when Tim told Jessica that he was going to ask her father to help him accept Christ into his life. He asked her if she could be there with them when they prayed. She was so touched by the fact that he wanted her there for such an important moment in his life that she couldn't help but lunge at him for their second embrace.

"I would love to be there for that, Tim." Her voice was being muffled by the beginning of her joyous cry.

The hug alone made him feel like melting, but hearing her cry made it impossible for him not to cry. He wanted to kiss her so badly that he struggled to control himself. As she pulled away, he felt like her face looked like an angel's face. He had just felt her heart up against his. It was the first time they had touched since their one brief awkward hug—the one he thought about constantly. When her arms had gone around his neck, he was pretty sure he felt his heart leap inside his chest. She felt so tiny and vulnerable in his arms that he felt like he could easily break her. That thought made him feel the responsibility to respect her as the precious creation of God that she was. There was no way he would ever hurt her, he decided.

"Thank you, Jessica. There is no one I want to be there more than you."

She couldn't believe she had actually attacked him with her hug like that. She was glad she had, though. He was solid, and she could tell that he was frightened a bit by her surprise hug. He had so quickly pulled her in and accepted her display of emotion that she knew immediately they were made for each other. Not only had he held her like she was a precious jewel, but he had released her slowly and gently, and when their eyes had met, she felt their souls connect.

This is so right, she thought. Then she realized how it would look to her father, should he catch them in this embrace. "We'd better back off before Dad gets here."

"Okay," he managed to choke out. Tim hadn't even thought about that until she brought it up. He had completely lost himself in her but was thankful she had awakened him.

Just as they let go of one another, they noticed Roger's car pulling into the driveway.

"Oh no. Do you think he saw us?" Tim asked.

"I think he did, but don't worry about it. When he hears why, he'll forget about it." She took his hand and led him through the house to where her father would shortly emerge from the garage.

Roger walked in to find an ecstatic Jessica blurting out the great news. She was right; Roger didn't even ask what was going on out there on the porch. All he could do was thank God and start praying. The three of them huddled up on their knees right there in the hall and prayed for God to enter Tim's life. Tim surrendered his life to Christ by accepting his free gift of salvation through the sacrifice of Jesus's life for his sins. He prayed to the Lord to change him and to help him become the man God wanted him to be. They all were in tears as Tim broke down under the liberating feeling of God's forgiveness and love and acceptance. Tim could feel God's grace, and he couldn't stop thanking God for giving him Roger and Jessica to share this moment with.

Though they told Angela about Tim's decision, she did not show the excitement they had all hoped she would. She said all the right things, but they could all tell it wasn't really that big of a deal to her. Tim knew she had no faith in God and that his decision to follow Christ would be of no consequence to her. She loved him dearly, so she would be happy for him. However, she couldn't possibly understand the enormity of his decision to follow Christ. Tim didn't hold it against her, but he didn't accept it either.

Roger, Tim, and Jessica began praying for her together every night before Tim would head home on his bike. They also prayed for her throughout the day ceaselessly. Tim knew that his mother needed the Lord more than anything. He knew it was the only way for her to truly be happy. Roger knew it too.

From the day he accepted Christ until his arrest, Tim never had any regrets. Tim searched God's Word feverously. He and Roger tried to search out every answer they could. They read the Bible together and countless books over the next few years. Christ was what Tim's life was all about for the rest of his life. He would always ask himself if Christ would be happy with whatever it was he was doing. At no time did he ever falter, though he almost did right at the end. He became a model Christian from that point forward, and his bond with Roger was as strong as any two men's bond to one another could ever be. Tim was not without flaw, but he was definitely a new, forgiven believer from the day he accepted Christ forward.

CHAPTER 18

ROGER arrived at Angela's house about ten minutes 'til 7:00 p.m.—ten minutes early, as usual. Angela had told him she was cooking him a special dinner and that she had rented a movie for them to watch. They had been dating for several months, Tim had accepted Christ, and their two families were practically spending all their free time together. Angela was deeply in love with Roger now, but they had still not been together romantically. It was eating her alive.

When Roger had asked if he should bring Jessica along, Angela had told him Tim would not be there, as he was staying over at a friend's house. She went on to say that she was really hoping they could be alone. It sounded innocent enough to Roger, but he had avoided situations like this with her so far, and he was feeling a little uneasy. He could tell she wanted to take their relationship to the next level by the way she had been acting lately, and now she was inviting him over for an evening alone.

Just before he left his place, he had spent some time on his knees, praying that he would have the strength to respect her and to not take advantage of her. He wanted to be with her so badly that he knew he would need God's help if she were to throw herself at him. She was so attractive and had been such a great friend since they had started seeing each other that he wasn't confident he could keep himself from going for it. He had been alone for over two years, as had she.

Roger really loved talking to Angela, and he wanted nothing more than to continue what they had started. He wanted to be with her all of the time, and he was sure he was in love with her. Still, for them to be romantic, she would have to be his wife. That was the only way for him. He just hoped he had the strength to stick with his conviction. He hoped he could explain himself to her in such a way that she would not be offended. He was praying for the right words as much as he was praying for strength. He understood that he was running the risk of hurting her by continually rejecting her advances, but he saw no alternative. If she made it so blatant that he could do nothing but push back, he knew she would be hurt. She was all he could think about anymore, and hurting her was the last thing he wanted to do. He felt joy every time they spoke and wanted nothing more than to get closer to her.

Angela had been planning this evening for weeks. She felt confident that Roger would not be able to resist her if he saw her in sexy lingerie. Chuck never could. She felt like it was time they slept together. She had to please him, as she had no other way to show her affection. For Angela, sex was the only way she knew how to please a man. She had finally noticed Roger checking her out a couple of times, but every time he started to look at her, she noticed him forcing himself to look away. Whenever they spoke, he always kept his eyes off her body. He'd stare right back into her eyes. Every conversation felt special with Roger, though. He always paid attention to what she said. He seemed to care so much about her that she couldn't help but feel like he actually did. She wondered why, as no man had ever liked her for anything other than her looks.

Angela had prepared a grilled shrimp and pasta dish that Tim had told her was the best thing he had ever eaten. Roger had taken her out for seafood several times, so she was betting he'd enjoy her best shrimp dish. When they had gone out to seafood restaurants, he almost always ordered shrimp. The movie she had rented was a real tear jerker that she felt would make him want to comfort her. The trick would be finding a way to reveal her seductive lingerie.

She didn't even let herself think that he might turn her down. He might be a good, honorable man, but he was still a man, she told herself. How could he turn her down? Her body was irresistible. Chuck had told her. If Chuck, who could and did have anyone and everyone he ever wanted, felt that way about her body, how could Roger resist? Angela was a bit of a workout junkie. She did sit-ups, push-ups, and ran every day since she had turned nineteen, and Chuck had made a comment that she was getting soft. She dressed modestly, as she never wanted to attract other men. She never wanted to advertise to strangers; her past had left her petrified of men anyway. That night was different, though. She wanted Roger turned on to the point that he couldn't say no to her. Now that she had noticed him looking at least twice, she felt like it was time to make her move. She needed him.

Roger sat in his car for a few minutes, asking God for the ability to restrain himself as well as the ability to explain himself to Angela, should the situation arise. He felt nervous walking up to the front door, as if this was their first date. Before he could even knock, Angela opened the door and embraced him.

"I'm so happy you're here, honey."

He was too. He felt so right about her, and, feeling her in his arms, he knew he was in for a night of temptation. She was wearing a tight black dress that showed off all her curves. Her makeup was perfect, as was her hair.

Why would she get so done up if she wasn't trying to seduce me? he thought.

He figured she wouldn't put so much time into getting ready to stay at home if she didn't have big plans, and it scared him.

"I'm happy to be with you too, Angela," he said while they were still in their embrace.

All of his senses were being overwhelmed as he fought off the urge to be inappropriate with her. She felt so strong and so soft at the same time. Her smell was something he had already begun to fall in love with, and with her in his arms, he was being overcome by it. He didn't want to let go of her, and he knew that he would not forget her smell ever. The thought crossed his mind that her smell would still be on him when he got home. He loved that thought.

"Come in and sit down. Dinner is ready."

As she loosened her grip, she suddenly felt unworthy. *This guy is too good for me. Maybe I'm pretty enough, but I'm not anything more than that,* she told herself. *What have I ever done to deserve him? He has never treated me like my looks are that important. Why not? If he's not into my outer beauty, maybe he will soon figure out he is wasting his time.*

He answered, "Great," as he entered the house and found a seat at the table.

The dinner was already on the table in covered pots and dishes. As he sat down, he picked up her sudden cooling and wondered if he wasn't giving her the compliments she deserved. Though he was afraid of what he was almost sure she was up to tonight, he decided he'd better not let his concerns keep him from praising how good she looked and how excited he was to be there with her.

"You look amazing tonight, Angela. You are the most attractive woman I know. There is nowhere on the face of this earth I would rather be right now than here with you. There is no one I would rather be with either. Sometimes I wonder how you could be attracted to an average guy like me."

"You must be kidding, Roger. There is nothing average about you. You are the best man I have ever known. I'm the one who is average. I'm average or below average in every way."

She really felt that way and was not looking for him to tell her otherwise. She wouldn't listen to him anyway. Angela knew she had underachieved in her life. She couldn't help but feel like a failure as a mom, as a wife, and in every other way. She knew she was pretty, but comments on her looks were the only positive feedback she had ever gotten. In her eyes, Roger was amazing. He was so able to love, had tremendous conviction, and was the best father she had ever met. All of those things made him incredibly sexy and desirable to her.

"Please don't ever say that you are average, Angela. You are a wonderful person and a great mother."

He got up and hugged her again. To his surprise, she started to cry, not a whimper, but sobbing cries. He felt so good that she trusted him enough to cry like this, as she had been unemotional with him since they had started to date. He just wanted to take care of her. How could he make her feel safe? How could he make her feel worthwhile? He wanted her to understand how special she was, and he knew there was only one way this could happen. She would have to realize that she was God's unique creation and that God loved her unconditionally. If she understood how much God loved her and knew that she was forgiven, she would finally be able to forgive herself. Standing there with her sobbing in his arms was melting his heart. He felt like he was feeling God's love for her. It was overwhelming.

Suddenly, Angela felt embarrassed. "I'm so sorry, Roger. I'm so worthless."

She felt like a failure and couldn't imagine why Roger would want to be around a wreck like her. Until now, though, she had held back her feelings from him. He loved that she was finally beginning to trust him with her most sensitive parts, but it really bothered him to hear her put herself down.

"Don't say that, Angela. You mean the world to both Tim and me. Neither of us could live without you. You are everything to us."

He knew this was true. Tim might have some issues respecting her due to the poor example his father had shown him, but Roger could tell that Tim loved her with everything he had. The part about him not being able to live without her was all he had been thinking about over the last few weeks. Every day he felt even more attracted to her. The physical attraction was there from the beginning, but the more important emotional and relational connection was the predominant attraction. She dominated his every thought, so much so that he was beginning to worry about her not being a Christian, as he could see himself marrying her and taking care of her forever. He just knew she was his destiny. He knew it a couple of dates in but had been fighting it all along.

"You might be nuts for wanting to be with me, Roger. I think I'm falling in love with you." *Oh my. Did I just say that?* She meant it, but she hadn't even considered telling him. *How desperate*, she thought.

"I love you too, Angela." Now he too was crying.

Hearing him say that he loved her in return to her reviling her love for him was exactly what she needed to hear. They re-embraced and held one another for what felt like eternity. In actuality, it was about five or ten minutes. Then they exchanged several small kisses, still no tongue, to Angela's dissatisfaction. Eventually, they sat back down at the table right next to one another and ate what they could of the dinner. Neither of them felt hungry. Throughout the meal, they held hands, exchanged light kisses, and shared their hearts with one another.

Angela was really opening up. She told him things that made him feel like she must be starting to trust him. Between the tender, the embarrassing, and the awful things in her past, it was easy to see why she had held back so much. She shared with him how she was constantly being tormented with feelings of worthlessness—how it was sometimes so crushing that she didn't want to leave her room. She also confessed that he was beginning to change that in her. At times, though, because he was so good to her, she felt even worse about herself, as she felt so unworthy of his love. He had sensed her feelings for some time, but he knew that her telling him was a step toward the healing she so desperately needed. Her honesty was making him feel like a part of her life. It was something he had been praying for, and he was thankful it was finally beginning to happen.

Though Roger felt like they were making tremendous progress, he warned himself that she still had a lot to sort through before she would be comfortable enough with him to tell him everything. He searched himself to see if there was anything he was not telling her. Was there anything he could share with her to make her feel that he too was vulnerable? He knew he was vulnerable to her already but felt as if she would feel that he was not.

Finally, he said that the only thing he could think of that made him really vulnerable. "I meant what I said earlier. I really do love you. It's a love that will only grow, and I want to do whatever it takes to make it stronger. Believe it or not, if you stopped seeing me right now, I would be a huge mess. My work would suffer, and Jessica and Tim would know you had broken my heart."

He hoped she would believe that he really meant what he was saying. It was true. His fear was that she would have trouble believing that he was this into her. She had been lied to for so much of her life. He wondered if she could accept his vulnerability.

This is it. He just gave me the go sign. It's time, she told herself. *I will give him a night he will never forget. I've got to make my exit now.* "I meant what I said too. You are all I think about all of the time."

She was having trouble believing that he would be a mess if she stopped seeing him, but she wasn't going to challenge him or call him a liar.

"I've got to use the ladies' room. I can clean up the table later. Please get comfortable on the couch and we can watch the movie when I come back."

She got up and walked away so quickly that he couldn't get a word in edgewise. She didn't want to mess this up, so she jumped on this opportunity. He had just told her he loved her. People who are in love make love. She wanted him badly, and this was the time.

Roger was glad to hear her reply that she had meant what she had said as well. He loved hearing her say that she loved him. What seemed strange to him was that she had almost run away rather than talk this over. It struck him as odd until he realized what was likely happening.

Oh no, he thought. *What can I do so I don't hurt her feelings?* It even crossed his mind that he should just make love to her. She was amazing, and he had never wanted anything like that. *Where is this coming from?*

He had to stop himself from considering defiling her. As much as he wanted her, he knew it would be better for both of them to do it God's way. If they didn't, they might condemn any chance for a healthy relationship going forward. Sex has a way of changing things. He knew that maintaining the innocence was the only way for this to work.

Should I say something to stop her? he wondered. *No*, he decided. *She might just be using the restroom. I have no right to assume anything. Why am I so high and mighty? I have no proof that she's taking her clothes off or planning anything. It is only my own fear of what she might do. I have to give her the benefit of the doubt.*

Then it occurred to him that perhaps he was letting her get undressed just so he could get a look at her. Man, he wanted to see that body more than anything. He had done his best to keep his mind off her physique until now, but it was driving him mad. He had fought the urge to defile himself while thinking about her. He had even awakened to dreams of them together. He felt as if this too was a test, as if the devil himself was trying to get him to stumble. He felt like it would destroy his witness with Tim, Jessica, and Angela, as well as at church and everywhere else if he were to fail that test. He knew that he had to stand up to this temptation. He began to pray again just as the door opened and Angela walked out in a full-body coat.

She was smiling from ear to ear, but instead of coming into the living room, she walked around the room, shutting off all the lights but the TV and a low light in the corner of the room. Roger couldn't, or wouldn't, speak. He was so excited that he could actually hear his heart beating.

She could tell he knew what was about to happen. He actually looked like he was scared, though.

Finally, he spoke. "Angela, please come here."

He wanted to put his arms around her before she opened her coat. He figured that he could talk her out of it far easier if she didn't show him what he was sure was the best body he had ever seen in real life. He had avoided undressing her in his mind for weeks now, and he knew he would have her naked or seductive image of whatever was under that coat burned in his mind if she dropped her coat. He knew he was at risk of worshiping her body if he ever saw it. It would be burned in his mind. The image he had crafted just from their hugs was so tempting that he could hardly bear it. Seeing her body with his own two eyes would be a big mistake.

She gave him a big smile and dropped the coat. His mouth popped open at the same time. He was stunned. She was wearing a see-through outfit that left nothing to the imagination. One of the first things he noticed was the high heels.

Oh my. That's really sexy, he thought. Everything was perfect. He could see no flaws. *How has she concealed such large breasts?*

He had never noticed that they were that large. Her hips were thin, and everything was so well toned. His eyes quickly examined every inch of her, and he couldn't get himself to look away. Her body had actually exceeded his expectations, but his reaction quickly crushed hers.

He jumped up and covered her up with the coat. He wrapped his arms around her and kept saying, "You are beautiful. You are so beautiful…" He wanted her to know she was gorgeous, but he didn't want to lose control.

She began to cry again. That time it was much worse than before. She was crying out, "What is wrong with me?"

He could feel her body trembling, and his heart was breaking. *Why did I hurt her like this? This is the last thing she needs. Who do I think I am?*

Then it hit him.

This is exactly what she needs.

He had to let her know his love for her was not about her looks. It wasn't about how she could please him with her body. He knew sex had been a big part of what her relationship with Chuck had been based on, but their relationship could not be based on sex. She needed to understand what was going on, though, or she would likely misinterpret his actions. Now was his chance to explain it.

"Angela, part of me loving you is me not taking advantage of you. I can't get over how sexy you are, but that is not why I love you. You have the most amazing body I have ever seen, but I want much more than your body. I want your heart and everything else. I want you to feel loved as my equal. If I sleep with you, all of that is gone. I believe in doing things God's way. His way is for people to get married before they have sex. Sex within marriage is a beautiful thing. That's what I want for you, for us." He hoped what he was saying was making sense to her. He prayed it did.

She was still trembling, but she seemed to be listening so he continued.

"I love you, Angela. I want us to be together. It's just not right for us to do this out of wedlock."

"I want to please you, Roger. I want you to please me. I need you to have sex with me. How can you say that you love me and then refuse to have sex with me?"

"Angela, please believe me when I say that there is nothing I would like to do more than make love to you. You are perfect, and I'm madly in love with you. I think about you all day. I worry about your day, and I pray for you constantly. Tim and I have just begun a very healthy relationship, and I want to be a part of both of your lives. Having sex right now would destroy my witness with Tim. It would also hurt us, as you might feel that is all you are to me. I want you to be my wife when we make love for the first time. Believe me. It will be far better that way." Roger kept praying to God for wisdom with his words while he spoke.

"I need you to want me, Roger. I have nothing else to give you. How can I please you if you won't let me? You won't even look at me. I know you are better than me. Quit trying to prove it. Quit being so perfect, please."

None of it was computing for Angela. She heard what he was saying but could not make herself believe it.

"Are you only with me because you feel sorry for me? I don't need your charity." Right after it left her mouth, she wanted to take it back. She would never have said anything like that to Chuck. Chuck would definitely be mad, and she wouldn't have been surprised if Chuck had slapped her for something like she had just said.

It brought him to his knees. He welled up just as heavily as she was welled up. "No. I love you. Please believe me. I don't want to hurt you, Angela. Yes, I feel bad for you. It's because my heart is yours and it's breaking for you."

He had been somewhat controlled up until she challenged him about his motives for caring about her, but, at this point, he was completely losing it. Her accusation really hit him, as it brought his thoughts to his dead wife and daughter and the accident. He suddenly felt like he was cheating on his wife. He had strong feelings for Angela, and he almost wished he didn't. There was some guilt, but he had pure motives in getting to know Angela. Now she was in his heart. He was addicted to her now. If she only knew the grip she had on him.

She told him to let go of her, and she ran into her room to change. She felt embarrassed and confused.

Roger stood at the door, pleading with her that he loved her and hated offending her in that way. He told her he wanted her to be his future and that he could not have sexual relations before marriage without ruining their future together. She stayed responsive while she changed out of her sexy clothes into a pair of loose sweats and a T-shirt.

After only three or four minutes, she opened the door and they embraced again. Roger kept saying, "I love you, Angela. I love you, Angela."

Angela was telling him that she loved him too, but she felt confused. She felt a heavy damnation that she was not worthy no matter what Roger said. Still, she held on to him and didn't want to ever let go. She felt safe in his arms, but her head was telling her to run. For some reason, though, she believed he was being honest. She just didn't get it.

Why wait until marriage? What difference does that make? she wondered.

They sat on the couch together and talked for about two hours before Roger finally said that he'd better get home to Jessica. He had fully explained his reaction and outlined what he saw for them in the future. She told him she would do whatever it took to be his. Though she never really fully enjoyed sex, she knew it was what men wanted. If Roger was being honest, he wanted to have sex with her, but he felt like it would ruin their chances for a real future. She really wanted to believe that. To Angela, it sounded impossible to be together and marry without ever having sex. She hurt inside for the physical affection she needed from Roger. While they sat together, she could not take her hands off him. More than once, Roger had to push her back. He held her lovingly and even caressed her arms some, but he completely avoided anything that might have led to deeper physical intimacy. It was a night that neither of them would ever forget.

As he left, he told her he would come by in the morning to check on her. He promised to lay awake thinking about her, and he was confident he would do so whether he promised to or not. Angela told him that she might show up and jump him in the middle of the night and then giggled a bit. He loved hearing it but knew that the result would be the same as tonight's had been if she actually came over with that intention. He couldn't believe what a prude he had become. He was sure he was doing the right thing, but it sure wasn't easy.

Right after he left, Angela began drinking the bottle of wine she had bought to share with him that evening. She knew Roger didn't drink alcohol, but she bought the wine anyway, as she thought she might need it. Within an hour, she felt so alone and terrible inside that she felt as if she just couldn't go on. The voices and forces in her head kept telling her she was worthless and that she would only ruin a good man's life. If she stayed with Roger, she would only disappoint him.

Her feelings began to take over and she started swallowing sleeping pills along with the wine. In just a few minutes, she had swallowed the entire bottle of pills.

If this guy loves me, he will check on me, she told herself. *How could he leave like that if he really loves me?*

When her head hit the table on the way to the floor, it made such a loud bang that it woke her up for a few seconds, but she was out again in a flash.

CHAPTER 19

ROGER lay in bed as uncomfortable as he had ever been. Something felt wrong to him. He knew Angela was suffering, and he knew it was his fault. *Had I been too high and mighty? Could I have handled it better somehow?* he wondered. *Maybe I should have stayed and slept on the couch or something? I'm just too afraid of what I might do if she and I are alone in the dark.*

He couldn't get that body out of his mind either. It was burned in his mind—every beautiful inch of it. Just thinking about her aroused him. He didn't even believe that someone as beautiful as Angela wanted to be with him. He had never been the type who could attract a woman like her. Now she wanted him.

"Please, God, help me. Give me strength," he prayed.

Finally, after staring at his ceiling fan for more than an hour, he decided to give her a call to make sure she was okay. Something was telling him that she wasn't. It was such a heavy sinking feeling that he just couldn't ignore it anymore.

The machine picked up, and he urged her to answer. When she wouldn't pick up, he began to panic. *Were my fears correct? Has she done something to herself?*

He jumped in his car and headed her way. About halfway there he told himself that she was fine and he was jumping to conclusions. Why would he think she would do anything to herself over him? He decided it was the best thing that he drove over either way. If she was okay, he could let her know how much he loved her again.

As he drove into the driveway, he noticed the living room light was still on. Angela had purposely done her drinking on the living room couch. She wanted to be where she and Roger had been on the couch. If he loved her, maybe he would show up and save her. If not, maybe the voices were right and he didn't really love her. If that was the case, she was ready to give up. She couldn't bear losing him, and, without him, life was just too hard.

After a couple of knocks, Roger looked through the window and noticed Angela lying on the floor. His heart almost leaped out of his chest when he realized she was laying there in a lump, likely unconscious. He burst through the unlocked door, surprised that it hadn't been locked.

She was completely unresponsive, but she appeared to be breathing and wasn't cold. Her head was bleeding from where it had hit the table. He quickly picked her up and put the empty bottle of pills in his pocket. As he carried her out the front door, he didn't even turn to close it. He knew he needed to get her to the hospital as quickly as possible.

Roger drove as fast as he could and was thankful that the hospital was only a couple of miles away. If he would have passed a policeman, he would have certainly gotten pulled over. When he got to the hospital, he parked in the emergency room roundabout driveway and ran in carrying her lifeless body in his arms.

The next thirty minutes felt like seconds to Roger. Things went so quickly that he never really got his thoughts together. *What if she doesn't make it?*

The hospital wasted no time attending to Angela. They pumped her stomach and told Roger she would be okay, mainly because he had gotten her there so quickly. She was alive but incapable of any sort of conversation.

Roger slept in the waiting room, as they would not allow him to stay in her room. When she awoke, he was back in her room, sitting in the chair next to her bed. She noticed him and smiled as she reached for and took his hand. As she squeezed his hand, he told her he would always be there for her and that he would always love her.

"I know. I believe you." She gave him a smile that he could tell was her finally believing in his love for her.

The hospital told them she would need to be evaluated and that she would need to stay one more night. Roger agreed to take care of Tim for the evening and told her not to worry about anything. It wasn't going to change a thing, though he knew someone would be looking into Tim's home life as a result of this.

Before he left to go find Tim and to talk to Jessica, he kissed her on the forehead and told her that he loved her. He promised to return as quickly as he could. She felt oddly relieved and assured but had to have one question answered.

"Roger, if I gain weight, will you still love me?"

"Of course I would, Angela," he answered without hesitation.

She believed him and inside began to change. Her eyes were finally beginning to open. For the first time, she really began to believe that his attraction to her was not purely physical. The question might have seemed silly to Roger, but it was vital to Angela that he answer it the way that he did, and that he did it with no hesitation.

CHAPTER 20

TIM was angry when he heard the news but didn't act surprised at all. Of course Roger had started out by saying that Angela was okay when he told Tim where his mother was and why. Tim processed the information so quickly and responded so mildly that Roger was impressed. His response was insightful.

"I thought something like this was coming. Mom has been struggling since Dad died. Since you came along, everything has gotten better. Knowing what I know about you and your faith, I figured it would only be a matter of time before her lack of self-worth would collide with the way you were treating her. It was only a matter of time until it pushed her over the edge. I only wish I would have told you about my fears before this happened. I failed you both."

Roger was not sure how to respond, though he did have a question. "How did you know that my faith would cause her to go over the edge?" *This kid is amazing. How can he see so much?*

"My father used to tell her that she had better stay sexy or no one would ever want her. He was constantly telling her that her job was to please him. He picked on her every flaw, knowing that her nature was to try at all costs to make him happy. Now you come along and actually respect her by treating her like she was much more than she believes she is. You treat her like she is something special, and you never put her looks above your respect for her.

"She even started telling me you weren't attracted to her. I told her she was crazy if she thought you weren't. 'How could he not be attracted to you?' I asked her. I told her you wanted to get to know her and didn't think looks were the most important thing about someone. I told her you were a man of faith and that meant you were accountable to God, which meant you had nowhere to hide. I explained that God knows everything and that we are without excuse. Most of this fell on deaf ears, though. I could tell she was beginning to feel unworthy around you. She thinks you are too good for her. She's even told me so. I should have told you. I'm really sorry I didn't."

Roger was impressed. *This kid is only fourteen*, he kept telling himself. When he was that age, he was only worried about himself. This kid was different. Tim was definitely mature beyond his years, and his heart was for God already. Roger was already sure that Tim would do great things for Christ with his life.

"Tell me, Roger, did she throw herself at you before the suicide attempt?"

Tim knew his mother well. He had seen what his father had done to her and knew his mother would express her feelings for Roger with her sexuality. It was part of what made Tim feel like she was who his father had told him she and every other woman really was. Tim had begun to understand how God viewed women as equal coinheritors in his kingdom, and he knew Roger saw his mother that way. To him, his mom had a shot to come out of her wrong thinking about herself only through her relationship with Roger and eventually and ultimately through a relationship with God. He had only kept his mouth shut about his concerns because he felt like Roger was so bright that he would surely understand what was going on inside her. He didn't want to make Roger feel bad about what his mother was going through. Now he knew that had been a mistake.

"Yes, Tim, she did." He felt out of place telling a fourteen-year-old that his mother was trying to seduce him, but he wasn't about to lie to him. "I want to be with your mother more than I've ever wanted anything, but it's wrong to do so outside of marriage. I told her that, and she still tried to end her life. I tried to make her understand that I love her too much to sabotage this relationship and both of our purities for immediate pleasure. Before I left, I thought she and I had an understanding. She agreed that we needed to wait and told me she understood why I had to wait.

At the time, I believed her. I think she believed herself. The wine, along with the condemnation she was feeling, must have gotten to her. I still haven't had a chance to process all of this, but I do know it's something I probably could have prevented if I had been just a little more perceptive. I wish I would have taken the wine away from her. I've seen her drink a few times. It always gets her down. I wish I could get her to stop drinking."

"If I had told you I knew this was coming, this would have never happened. I agree with you about drinking. My dad always got worse the more he drank. My mother knows the dangers, but she seems to crave the escape from sobriety when things get tough."

Tim felt guilty for letting it happen. He was beginning to feel that it was his responsibility to take care of his mother in response to God's commandment to honor your parents. The more Bible study he and Roger did together, the more he felt that his mother was his responsibility. She had no one else now, except for Roger, of course.

Tim struggled to respect his mother due to the years of training he had gotten from his father. He almost never told her what he was doing or where he was going. She never bothered him much with rules and restrictions, so he was pretty much on his own. The more time Tim spent with Roger studying the Bible and learning about the true value of others, as well as the commandment to honor parents, the more he felt responsible for his mother and sorry for not being more respectful.

How did I allow my concerns to become reality? If I had just spoken up, Roger could have had a chance to head this off before it happened. My weakness almost cost my mother her life. It was a valuable lesson, he decided.

"Tim, you did nothing wrong by not telling me. I might have been blinded a bit by the way I feel about her. I honestly felt like she was feeling loved by me. I knew she was getting frustrated because I was running away every time she tried to get intimate. I should have realized that intimacy was her only way to express her love for me. Please don't blame yourself; it was her choice, neither of ours."

He hoped Tim could accept that it wasn't his fault. He really liked how Tim was able to take responsibility for things, though. Tim never seemed to point at others; he always looked at what he was doing first. It may have actually been his biggest flaw, as he always took the blame, believing it was something he had done that had led to the undesirable result. Whenever there was conflict or a reason to blame someone for an undesirable outcome, Tim always took responsibility. Though it was true that changing oneself is usually all that needs to be done to fix a situation, considering yourself to be personally responsible for every undesirable situation is a heavy burden to bear. In most cases, Tim ended up beating himself up over things he actually had very little control over.

Roger went on. "It needs to be her choice to stop drinking. She knows I don't drink, and I have explained to her why I don't. I've told her it's not because I believe God says it's a sin, though I do think it's clear in the Bible that we are not to allow our minds to be altered. My main reason for not drinking is because I do not need it in my life. It does nothing good for me or for anyone I care about. It's one of those completely selfish activities that is only damaging to those around us. No one has experienced more pain from being in love with a heavy drinker than your mother. I'm sure she will start to turn from it if we keep loving and praying for her."

"Okay, Mr. Brooks. I think we might need to team up on her from now on, though. She needs God in her life so badly. How can we make that happen? When I try to talk to her about the things you and I are studying, she glazes over and quickly changes the subject. I think she might actually feel like God couldn't care less about her. She has no idea about his love, and I know she doesn't understand what Jesus did for us. How can we make her see the truth? That's all she really needs."

Roger's admiration for Tim grew every time he spoke. Not only did the kid know what was going on, but he knew exactly how to fix it. Tim was strong—the type of person people would follow. Roger couldn't help but wonder about the great things Tim would achieve in his life.

"You are dead right, Tim. We need to get her surrounded by God's love, and she needs to choose to seek for answers in his Word. It is our responsibility as her loved ones to bring her to the answers. You should have seen her this morning. She seems to have won her first battle. When I was leaving, she really looked happy and kind of relieved."

"I'm with you, Mr. Brooks. What are your plans for tonight? I can stay at my place alone if I need to."

He was hoping to get to see Jessica but didn't want Mr. Brooks worrying about him and his daughter on top everything that was going on with his mother.

"No. You will stay with Jessica and me. We'll go get her after we visit your mom. My mother went over last night to take care of her, so she's in good hands."

Roger knew Jessica was into Tim, and he could definitely tell that Tim was sweet on her. Both times he had seen them hug; he had felt like they both believed that they were destined to be together. He knew he would be powerless when the two of them began to officially date and was thankful for the man he was sure Tim would become. Right now, though, they both seemed so shy about it. Actually, he was happy about that part.

CHAPTER 21

THE visit was short and sweet with Angela. Tim hugged her and told her he loved her while Roger left the room to give them some privacy. Angela cried while she tried to explain herself to Tim. He told her he understood what she was going through but shared with her that it was a fact that her feelings about herself were wrong. He told her he and Roger had just prayed for her to get to know the Lord and that Roger really loved her. He even tried to explain the depth of Roger's love for her—that it was the real thing, like nothing she had ever known. Tim was perceptive, and Angela knew it.

Tim was positive that Roger would not quit his mother. He knew Roger would always be there for her, and he also knew Roger had never been in a relationship with anyone who looked as good as his mother did. He could tell that Roger practically worshiped his mother. On top of all of this, Tim also understood that Roger was helplessly attracted to his mother's personality. Tim knew how bright his mother actually was, though he was positive she didn't. He was certain that Roger loved his mother's wit, her drive to do whatever it took to take care of and provide for her family, her dedication to her job, but more than anything else, her desire to make the one man in her life happy while not caring at all about her own happiness. He was thankful that Roger was such a great guy. A lesser man would only take advantage of his mother's compulsion to make her man happy.

Angela was still feeling a bit cloudy from the emotional roller coaster she was on, but she knew Tim was speaking the truth. He was really laying it on her about how important it was that she begins to start seeking God and quit hiding from him. She began to cry even deeper as she realized how passionate Tim was about her seeking God. She knew inside that she needed something to fill the emptiness in her life.

When Roger returned, Angela was really a mess. She had fallen apart completely and was sobbing uncontrollably at that point. She could no longer hide her internal struggles by acting strong on the outside. Both Tim and Roger knew it. Things were starting to change. From now on she would be much more transparent to them. It was as if a wall was beginning to crumble and she was letting them in. Angela could feel her defenses crumbling, and she was feeling some embarrassment over it. Something kept telling her that they were both too good for her. Although they didn't use judging words or say anything to condemn her in any way, it still felt to her like she was being judged.

From the time Tim was very young, Angela had known he was special. He had always handled things like a much older person. Now that he was learning God's Word, she knew he was becoming much more like Roger than her. She didn't want to get left behind but was unsure if she was capable of becoming the person she knew they wanted her to be.

Her new vulnerability enabled them to push their way into her inner thoughts and feelings. The three of them prayed together, though it was really Roger and Tim praying. Angela felt strangely comforted as they prayed for her. It was like everything was going to be okay. Though the feelings of not being worthy of the prayer and these two great men were still in the background, they were not dominating her thoughts anymore. She saw the love in their eyes, and she began to wonder about this God they both worshiped.

Roger told her on the way out that he planned to take the kids to dinner later and that he'd be back to visit with her by 7:00 p.m. She loved that Roger would be back; it was written all over her face. They were definitely connecting at the next level.

CHAPTER 22

DINNER was great. Tim felt sorry inside for his mother but knew that things were going in the right direction for her. He was changing, and he knew God could do the same for his mother. Although his mother had just attempted to take her own life, Tim was feeling like things were better then than at any point in their lives. They had hope now. None of it was dominating his mind during dinner, though. Jessica was. It was Saturday night, and he was with Jessica. That was what was great about dinner: Jessica.

Jessica clearly felt for what Tim was going through. He could tell by the way she had acted when they came face-to-face that night that she genuinely cared about him and his mom. She had given him a hug and told him she was so sorry for him. One didn't have to be Sherlock Holmes to see how caring she was, and Tim could tell that she was equally concerned for her father. Jessica was sharing a side of their booth with her dad while Tim sat across from them. Tim couldn't help but admire how loving she was toward her father. She kept leaning on him, joked with him, and even rubbed his back for a little while. He wanted his mother to have that kind of relationship in her life, and he knew Roger would give it to her.

From the instant Jessica had touched him with her soft, loving hug, any fear or pain he was feeling had disappeared. She was like medicine to him. He was beginning to think she was his soul mate.

How could anything be wrong with her around? he thought.

The conversation was all over the place but kept returning to the Bible and God. Jessica was a great listener, and she felt like she was learning from both her father and from Tim. She knew he was a believer now, and she couldn't stop herself from thinking about him being her husband someday.

Does he ever think about me that way? she wondered. *Mrs. Jessica Wiseman.* It sounded really good to her.

"So your birthday is next Friday, right, Tim?" Roger knew it was, but he wanted to set the stage to announce his offer for a really nice birthday dinner at the finest steak place in town.

"Yep. I'll be fifteen, just like Jessica." He looked her right in the eyes, and they both smiled so hard that Roger thought they might tear face muscles.

"Well, I was hoping to take the four of us to dinner at Pasqual's to celebrate." He knew Tim had heard of Pasqual's. Everyone had. He was also pretty sure that Tim had never been there.

"Seriously? That would be great!" There was no better gift than that in Tim's eyes. "Do we have to dress up to go there?" Tim knew it was a fancy place, and he was pretty sure he didn't have anything nice enough to wear.

"Not really. You can wear a nice shirt and blue jeans, and so will I." He already had a plan that he wasn't ready to reveal, so he left it at that.

"I will wear that new dress you bought for me," Jessica told Roger.

He hadn't bought her a dress, but she was taking a shot at getting a new dress. Actually, she was only kidding.

"What dress? Is this a setup?" He knew she was only kidding; Jessica was not into material things at all, though she did like to dress up.

While Jessica and Mr. Brooks went back and forth, Tim had some time to think. It amazed him that things seemed to be getting better and better even though his mother had just tried to kill herself.

God is so good, he concluded.

The other thing that crossed his mind was Jessica in a dress. He could hardly wait for that. The steak would be a great birthday present, but Jessica in a dress would be an even better present.

I'd better stop thinking like that, he told himself. His fears over whether he could control himself and treat her like the amazing young woman that she was were always haunting him.

As they piled into the car to head back to the Brooks' house, Tim refused to sit in the front seat as he had done on the way to the restaurant. It was Jessica's place, and he valued her way too much to not insist that she sit next to her father. Jessica tried to resist by saying that he should sit up front since he was so much taller than her, and she argued that he could use the extra leg room, but he refused. She couldn't help but feel good about it. Most jerks she knew wouldn't put her ahead of themselves. She was beginning to notice that with Tim even the little things mattered. He was attentive to others in everything he did. She didn't even know adults who acted that way. Her feelings for him only grew whenever they were together.

When they got to the Brooks' house, Roger told them he needed to get to the hospital to keep his date with Angela. He promised to return when visitors' hours ended and that they would play a game or something when he got back.

"I should be back at about nine fifteen."

When Roger left, they were alone, but neither one of them felt uncomfortable. Jessica trusted Tim completely. She felt comfortable in his presence, and she knew that, inside, she could trust him to respect her. She led Tim up the stairs to the room that would be his for the evening.

"You'll be in here tonight, Tim."

It was a very neutral guest room. If it had one day been her sister's room, he couldn't tell.

"Wow. That's a really nice bed." He couldn't help but run and jump on the queen-sized, sturdily framed bed. Jessica stood at the door and giggled as he jumped around like a little kid. She was amazed at how he never seemed to care what anyone thought about him. She had never seen him try to impress anyone. He seemed so strong and self-assured that he just didn't need anyone else to tell him he was okay. The more time Tim spent with her dad, the easier it was for her to be around him. He was becoming an even better guy, or maybe she was just beginning to get to know him. Either way he was the only guy she ever thought about.

It has to be him, she told herself.

"I'd better leave you alone on your trampoline. I've got a couple of things to do. I'll meet you in the living room in a little bit."

She wanted to go check her makeup and make sure she didn't have food in her teeth or a booger hanging out of her nose. Jessica had no interest in being apart from him but needed to attend to herself. She also knew it was wrong to be alone in a bedroom with him.

"Wait. I want to see your room. Can I get a quick tour?"

He had dreamed of it. He wondered what she had on the walls. In his mind what someone put on their walls told you a lot about where their mind was.

He had no selfish intentions and certainly didn't want her to feel uncomfortable, so he added, "I'll just stand at the door and look around. I don't want you to feel threatened."

"Sure. Come take a look. It's not that impressive. I hope you know that I'm kind of a slob." She was worried that he might see what she had been writing on her notebook, so she ran ahead of him to cover it up.

"It couldn't be any worse than my room," Tim shouted down the hall as he rose to his feet.

That wasn't true, though. Tim was very simple and never left a mess anywhere. With his dad being so hard on his mother over the tiniest little things, he had become very conscious of picking up after himself. He didn't want to see his mother get punished for his laziness, so he was careful not to leave things in a mess anywhere he went.

Tim couldn't wait to see what it was that Jessica thought about. Her room was something he wanted to explore. He wanted to remember everything about it. Just being able to picture where it was she was lying at night was something he would cherish.

As she had just admitted, Jessica had a tendency to be pretty messy. She ran around, picking up clothes, paper, and other junk as he approached the door. She couldn't help but feel a little embarrassed. What would he think of her?

"See. Just a regular old room."

She was standing in the corner in front of a full-length mirror. She and the girl in the mirror both looked amazing to Tim.

Tim looked around and tried to take it all in. He didn't want to be too intrusive or make her feel uncomfortable, but he couldn't help himself from entering.

"I hope you don't mind if I come in to get a better look." He was careful not to get to close to her, as he didn't want her to think he was up to anything. He had no intention of making her feel threatened in any way.

"No. My place is your place." *How stupid was that?* she thought to herself. If he tried something with her, she knew she would have to resist, but she never felt threatened at all.

He was combing the place with his stare and wasn't even looking at her. He seemed to be taking lots of time exploring every detail. It was not at all what he had imagined. Jessica's room was very plain. She didn't have any posters of any kind, only pictures of her mother, sister, and their family together. She didn't even have a white board, chalkboard, or poster board on the wall to write on.

Why did I think that she would?

He was kind of hoping to find something written about him on a wall or somewhere. Any sign that she too was thinking of him would have been nice. Then he noticed the notebook on her desk. It was obviously covered up intentionally as its covering was an upside-down DVD cover. *What had she been writing?* he wondered. He wasn't sure, but it gave him hope. She had run ahead of him to do something, and he assumed covering her notebook was likely that task.

Jessica's bed was plain as well, as was her desk and chair. Both were messy, as the bed was unmade and the desk had ruffled papers and half-empty glasses all over it, as well as that suspiciously covered notebook. Her walls were plain white, and it felt to him that her room was that of a much older woman. The room was quite large and had its own walk-in closet and bathroom.

"This is not what I expected." He hoped that didn't sound bad.

"Why not? What did you expect?" *Oh no. He thinks I'm a boring slob.*

"You are so perfect all the time that I thought everything in your room would be too." What he had just said was exactly what was going through his head; he applied no filter. "I don't mean that I'm disappointed. I had just imagined something perfect."

"I'm not even close to perfect. I've always been a bit of a mess. My father might have it all together, and from what I've seen, so do you, but I don't. I do lots of housework for my dad, but I can't even take care of myself most of the time."

It was so easy to tell Tim the truth about things. It felt as if he would know if she were putting on airs anyway, so why even try? Something told her he wouldn't care that she was a mess. It was the truth about things that Tim was always looking for, and giving him anything else just wouldn't work.

"I stand corrected. It is perfect for you then. You are a rare beauty who deserves to be taken care of." Her room really hadn't let him down at all. It just wasn't the way he had pictured it. He hoped she believed that he wasn't disappointed at all. He hoped the compliments about how perfect she was made her understand what he thought of her.

"Don't be silly, Tim. There is nothing perfect about me, and I can take care of myself." She hoped he meant it, though.

"I disagree. You are perfect. I'll see you in the living room," he said as he left for the stairs.

He wanted to be careful not to make her feel self-conscious about her room or about him telling her she was perfect. As he hit the staircase, he thanked God for her.

She will be my wife, he told himself while he wondered if he was just being a stupid kid. *Can I really trust my instincts about the future? Either way she's all I think about and want.* He wanted to make her proud of him, and he wanted her to be happy all the time.

"I'm right behind you," she screamed down from her room. *He just told me I was perfect*, she repeated over and over again in her head. *I'm not at all, but I'm glad he thinks so.*

The thought of him dating anyone else petrified her. Up until then, fifteen and a half years, she had never felt like that about anyone. *If he's the one, am I meeting him too early in life? Will he want to wait around until I'm an adult? This is crazy*, she told herself. *You are fifteen years old. Stop it.*

After five or ten minutes in front of her mirror, she headed down to be with him. He was watching some sort of sports show, but when she hit the bottom of the stairs, she got his total attention. He immediately muted the volume and tried to hand her the remote.

"I can change the channel or shut this off if you like?"

He didn't really even care about the show. He wasn't much of a TV watcher anyway. The only thing he ever watched was sports. Tim was just happy the waiting was over and that they were together now.

"No. It's fine. We have about two hours until Dad gets home. Maybe you can explain football to me."

She didn't care at all about football, but she did hope to see him play and figured it would be pretty handy to know what was going on out there. She had a pimple on the left side of her chin, so she sat in the big chair on the left side of the couch so he wouldn't have to stare right at it while they spoke.

"No. Let's talk about something else. I'll try to explain football if you really care about knowing how it's played; otherwise, I don't want to waste any time on it. We have two hours to talk, and I want to make the most of it."

He knew she was only trying to be nice by not asking him to change the channel and asking him about football. He suddenly felt kind of silly about how big a deal sports had become in his life.

Is it really that important? he thought. It had become his identity. It was what everyone knew him for. He spent all of his time previous to Jessica and her father, thinking about sports and working to become the best he could be at them.

"I really want to learn something about it so I can come to watch you play. You do have one more game, right?"

She had wanted to go watch him play for a few weeks, but all her friends only went to the JV games, and he was on the freshman team. Even the JV guys talked about him, though. They all said that he was going to be a monster and that no one could stop him. It was almost like he was legend more than an actual person. The way everyone built him up, it was like he was only a myth.

"Okay. I'll give it my best shot. Do you think your dad would come too?"

He was excited to hear her say she wanted to see him play his final game. He knew he would impress her on the field. The physical abilities, intelligence, and the size he had inherited from his father were the only things he was proud of the old man for since he had studied what the Bible had to say. Oddly, though, he was feeling some guilt over wanting to impress her. Drawing attention to himself was something he was learning, through the Bible study, that was not in the character of the type of person God wants us to be.

For the next two hours, the clock seemed to run at hyper speed. He outlined the entire game of football, including all the penalties and strategy. Then they talked about how things made them feel and about what motivated them. The conversation came easily to both of them. As their time together ticked by, both of them grew more infatuated with each other.

Jessica couldn't help but notice Tim's powerful arms and chest. His legs were stretching his jeans to their limit, and she couldn't help but feel physically attracted. Even his hands were bigger and stronger than anyone else she knew. Tim was unusual in so many ways, but his physique was just not natural. She couldn't help but wonder how big he would get.

How could such a powerful guy be so gentle? she wondered.

Tim too was caught in thoughts about Jessica's looks. He forced himself to stare into her eyes, not that it was hard to look at those gorgeous green eyes, but because he wanted to look at her curves so badly and knew he shouldn't. He and Roger had already had a talk about sexual purity. The fact that Tim had lived with a sex addict as a father for so long had been more than enough to make Roger's talk believable. Tim knew well how ugly sex without love could be. He had seen the damage it could do to everyone in its path with his own eyes. He knew it was evil, and he wanted no part of it in his life. From what he had already learned, sex outside of marriage was not God's plan. Looking at Jessica lustfully made him feel like a bad guy. He was glad it did. Jessica deserved the best, and God's way was definitely the best. Still, it was a struggle for him.

Before they realized it, Mr. Brooks was home. He walked in to find them heavily engaged in conversation.

"Hey, guys. Angela is doing well. She even asked me if I could help her get to know God. It was amazing, and we both cried." He was so happy about it that he couldn't help but show his joy all over his face. He had his fears about leaving Tim and Jessica alone, though.

Was it wise to leave the two alone, especially with what I know about Jessica's fondness of Tim? I've got to let her know I trust her and that I know what an unusual young man Tim is, he decided.

"That's great, Dad," Jessica answered.

"It sure is, Mr. Brooks. Thanks for taking care of my mother. Let's get her saved now."

He meant it. He knew Mr. Brooks could bring his mother to the Lord, and he knew Mr. Brooks would never relent. He had seen it in his eyes earlier. Mr. Brooks would marry his mother. To do so, he had to bring her to the Lord.

"Dad, can you and I go watch Tim's last football game Thursday night?" She knew he would go. He had even asked her if she wanted to go to one of them with him, though he had not yet been to one.

"That would be great. I'd love to go see the legend play."

Even Roger had heard all of the hoopla about Tim. People were saying he was the best player they had ever seen. From what Angela had told him, his father had been that kind of player as well.

"By the way, I told your mother about the birthday dinner next weekend. She was excited about all of us going together. She asked if Saturday was okay instead of Friday. Apparently Tim never misses the varsity football team play on Friday nights. Why didn't you say anything, Tim?"

"Priorities, Mr. Brooks. Priorities." He had thought about saying something, but he had decided against it. He could miss a game, especially for that. He'd rather see Jessica and eat steak than watch football. Football had not really been in its proper place, but things were definitely changing now.

They all sat around the kitchen table and played games, talked, and had a great time until almost midnight. Jessica even made cookies. Tim went on and on about how great they were, but he knew they were only cut and bake. He did love them, though.

Tim thought he would have trouble sleeping with the love of his life right down the hall, but he was wrong. Almost as soon as his head hit the pillow, he was out. In the morning he decided that he must have been too comfortable and secure in their house to have trouble sleeping. He felt at home, finally.

The evening was not as easy on Jessica. She was so excited about her connection with Tim that she lay in bed wide awake until her alarm went off and it was time to get ready for church. She kept running the time they had been together through her head. It was all so perfect. Even though Tim was there because of a tragic event, she felt like all of that was behind them. Surely Angela and her dad would eventually get married. Tim might be living with them in the future. It seemed like a dilemma to her.

What if he becomes my brother? What would become of our love then? She wanted him as a boyfriend, not a brother.

Mr. Brooks couldn't fall asleep at first, but once he finally did, he slept like a rock. He had laid out the plan for the kids. They would wake up, go to church, and then go pick up Angela. Then the four of them would have lunch together.

Everything went as planned, and no one would have ever known what had happened Friday night by watching this attractive family dine together. They were all smiles. They joked and laughed together as if nothing had ever happened. Strangely, none of them acted like it didn't happen. They spoke about it as if it were way in the past, as if they had all grown and were totally past it. They all believed it was something that would never happen again, even Angela.

When the game rolled around on Thursday night, Tim was so pumped up that he felt like he might kill someone out there. He prayed to God for control over his passion and for respect for his coaches and teammates. Though he didn't know it, Tim was a much better player than his father had been because his teammates all looked up to him. He was their leader, the defensive captain. Everyone on the team had tremendous respect and admiration for Tim.

Jessica, Roger, and Angela couldn't wait for the game to start. Tim had made a trip over to the fence to wave and say hello to them before the game. None of the other guys did this, but Tim didn't ever care about what anyone thought. He cared about the people in his life more than what someone he didn't even know might think. All he could think was how impressed Jessica would be, but he kept telling himself to not be proud. It was quite a struggle for him. He wanted her to see how he cared for his teammates and that he wasn't all about himself.

From the kickoff, Tim was playing on a higher level than everyone else. Some of the other parents were saying things like, "He really shouldn't be playing with these other freshman," "He's too big and too aggressive," and, "He's going to hurt someone." In the end, Tim made about fifteen tackles. Five of them were sacks of the quarterback. He did actually hurt a couple of people, but he tried to help them both up once he knew they weren't getting up.

What struck most people about him was what his teammates had to say. They all felt like he was there for them. He had helped them all at one point or another, and most of them felt like he could have hurt them at one time or another but he hadn't. Tim never blamed other players or pointed fingers. Whenever Tim noticed someone inferior, he would simply blow by them and make the play. He didn't hurt people just for the sake of it. Everyone appreciated it, even the coaches.

Seeing Tim play always brought back memories of Chuck to Angela, but even she could see the differences between her son and his father. Chuck used to stand by himself and never helped anyone up. Tim was the complete opposite. Everyone flocked to him. He was their protector. Everyone was Tim's friend, while no one ever liked Chuck. They were all afraid of him. Being afraid of Tim was only possible if you didn't know him or you were on the other team. Even then, no one on the other team felt he was a dirty player. Sure, he occasionally hurt someone, but it was only incidental. They could all tell by the way he always helped anyone he had put down. Actually, he helped anyone he saw hurting on either side.

Jessica kept asking her dad what was going on all game long. What she saw Tim doing looked pretty amazing, even to her. It seemed like he was able to do whatever he wanted. When the quarterback got the ball, it seemed like Tim was already back there with him every play. The announcer kept calling his name after every play when he was on the field, and it seemed like everyone was talking about him. When he was off the field, he and one of the coaches seemed to be working as a team to coach the others. The coach always had Tim stand with him as they spoke to the others, and it always looked like the coach was relying on Tim to get his point across.

Jessica even noticed some of the varsity team in the stands watching the game. It looked to her like they were just there to see Tim play. She heard some of what they were saying, and apparently it wasn't just a good game for Tim; it was how he always played. They kept pointing at him and seemed impressed. In the end, she was happy for him that they won.

All through the game, Tim kept looking up into the stands to see if Jessica was watching. Every time he looked, she was either staring at him or talking to her dad. He hoped she saw him helping his teammates. He didn't want to look like a brute to her. He was just really glad she was there. When the game ended, Tim ran over to catch them when they reached the bottom of the stairs.

Roger spoke up first. "You were awesome out there, Tim!" It really was more than he had expected. He felt proud to even know Tim.

"Thanks, sir."

Jessica wanted to let him know that she too was impressed, so she gave it a shot. "I loved it! I am so proud of you." She tried to show him with her voice and her eyes that she was his. Though she didn't fully understand what he was doing on the field, she did understand that he was clearly the best player on the field. Her pride for him made her feel like she might explode. It felt so good to see him so happy.

"Thanks, Jessica. I hope you remembered everything I taught you about football." He was just playing with her, but inside, he was overwhelmed with his feelings for her as well. "Thanks for coming, everyone. I'll see you as soon as I can get out of the shower, Mom."

Angela had seen most of his games. She had been watching him dominate everything he tried all of his life. Even when Chuck was around, she was the only one who went to his games. Whether it was football, basketball, baseball, or track, Angela always tried to be there for him. He knew she was his biggest fan.

"Sure, baby. I'll see you by the locker room."

Tim hated when she called him baby in front of people, but the older he got, the less he seemed to care.

"Thanks, Mom. You're the best."

Angela loved how Tim made her feel, especially since Roger had entered their lives and helped her see that she had value. Tim really seemed to value her more and more as he and Roger continued to study the Bible.

In the locker room after the game, Tim was visited by the varsity team's coach, Coach Briening. "Great game, Tim. I've been watching you for a while now, and I'd like to invite you to dress for the varsity game tomorrow night. I can't promise you any playing time, but I think you will be on the varsity team next year as a sophomore, so I think it would be good experience for you to see how we run things. What do you think?"

"Yes, sir. I would love to do that." He was really excited about it and couldn't wait to tell his mother.

"Great. Be here at five p.m. tomorrow night. We hit the field to stretch at six p.m. Your father played for me when I was a young coach. You play like him, and he was one of the best who ever played here."

"I'll be here, sir. Thanks for this opportunity." He wanted to make sure the coach knew he was a good kid. He wanted him to know he was not at all like his father, on the field or off it.

"I hear you are also a straight-A student. I like that."

Coach Briening had been watching Tim for a few years. He had even gone to watch him play in junior high school. When Chuck passed away, he began to believe that Tim might have a chance to escape his father's legacy. He was really pulling for Tim. Coach Briening knew if Tim could keep it together, he would be a star; it was all up to him.

"I want to make something of myself, sir. God's given me a lot of gifts. I need to make the most of them for myself and for my mother." He spoke proudly about his belief in God and wanted the coach to understand what kind of person he was.

"That is great to hear, son. I'm looking forward to great things from you and for you."

Coach Briening had heard what a great person Tim was from his coaches and from the other players. He had never spoken to him face-to-face before, though. The brief discussion filled him with hope for the team's future.

Tim quickly showered and headed for the door. He couldn't wait to tell his mother about this great opportunity. Just before he opened the door, he noticed two of the starting players picking on one of the team's weaker players. As he always did, he stepped in.

"Come on, guys. What are you trying to prove? Jeff gives it all he can. Get off his back or I'll get on yours."

"Sorry, Tim. We were just having fun with him."

Both of them backed down and apologized quickly, not just because they were afraid of what Tim could do to them, but also because they respected him. Tim almost never needed to actually do anything to get people to do what he wanted. In most cases a few words were all that were needed. Everyone who knew him knew he was good to everyone. If he was on them about something, they knew he meant business and that he was likely on the right side of the issue. He was always fair, and when he was wrong, he was always the first to apologize.

"Well, he's not having fun. Please stop it. I'll see you guys in class tomorrow. Try to enjoy our win and the great season."

The freshman team had only lost one game. Unfortunately, there were no playoffs for them to look forward to. Only the JV and varsity teams could go to the playoffs.

Coach Briening witnessed the whole thing and could not have been more impressed. That was the type of guy to win championships with. He had never seen a better example.

This guy has it all. How could he be Chuck's son? Chuck was pure evil and a total screw-up. He was always fighting authority. He fought everyone and everything. Tim is not at all like Chuck. Thank God, he thought.

Angela was not alone when Tim finally broke from the locker room. Jessica and Roger were standing there with her. Angela opened her arms and reached out to hug Tim. Without hesitation, he embraced her. She couldn't help but think of his father whenever they embraced. Tim was already developing his father's build. He felt like a rock and was already so tall.

When Tim let go of his mother, he kept going down the line. Roger was next. The big hug was actually a little intimidating to Roger. The thought crossed his mind that Tim was already bigger and stronger than he was. If he ever had to try to restrain him, he was pretty sure he couldn't. Thankfully, that didn't seem like a likely scenario, as Tim already treated him like a father.

Jessica was next. She wanted to hug him more than anything, and she was hoping he would give her a squeeze next. Tim felt the same way and was really looking forward to hugging her again. The other hugs had been spontaneous and brief. Tim remembered them well, but the present was always better than the past. The first one had been awkward and somewhat forced, but it had been amazing and would never be forgotten. The second one was nonsexual and spontaneous and occurred as a result of him telling her that he was accepting Christ into his life. The third hug had been when his mother had tried to kill herself, and it too had been brief. They were all monumental to Tim, and he often thought about each one. This one was going to be him hugging her instead of her hugging him. It was going to be the best yet, and he knew it. He wanted her to know through this hug that she was the only girl for him.

With Roger still in his grip, he noticed she was already on her toes, ready for him. As he released her father and started her way, Jessica lunged and leaped for him. He wrapped his powerful arms around her, picked her up, and swung her around in a circle. He knew his mother and Roger were watching, so he kept it as playful as possible and dropped her quickly. They both awkwardly giggled a bit as she stumbled about.

It was only the fourth time he had touched her. Yes, he was definitely counting, as was she. That hug had easily been the best yet. She had literally jumped up into his arms, and she had squeezed herself to him with everything she had. It was officially the best night of his life now. Jessica felt so tiny in his arms, but her affection for him was not small at all. He could feel it in her grip. She wasn't holding on for dear life when he spun her, she had opened her hands to hold his back while completely trusting him not to drop her or hurt her in any way. She had never felt anything like his body. All of the different muscle groups in his back had sprung into action when he picked her up and again when he had spun her around. It was like his muscles had muscles, she thought. It made her feel like he could crush her if he wanted to, but she felt absolutely no fear. Instinctively, she knew he would never hurt her and that he would do anything in his power to protect her.

When Jessica's feet hit the ground, she shyly said, "Thanks for the ride, Tim."

Roger could see her affection for him. Anyone could see her affection for him. Tim sensed Roger's discomfort with the situation, so he began talking about the opportunity he had just been presented with.

Angela missed the first part of what Tim was saying, as she was caught in a flashback to the time Chuck had tossed her over that wall the night they had first met.

Is Tim starting to look at girls as his father did?

She knew how Jessica must have felt, though. It was the way she always tried to remember Chuck. He was so powerful and so into her that she had no power to resist him. For Angela, it was love that first night.

Is Jessica feeling the same way I felt about Chuck for Tim now? she wondered.

After Tim had shared the good news, the three of them congratulated him.

Then Roger added, "Good thing your mother had the forethought to change your birthday dinner to Saturday night."

CHAPTER 23

TIM'S three biggest fans were back for an encore to his big performance the previous night. Though they were told that he would likely not see the field for any real action, all three of them were betting he would. As the team came out of the locker room en route to the field, Tim waved up into the crowd that was much larger for the varsity game than it had been the night before for the freshmen and JV games. Jessica knew he was waving at her, so she waved back. Her dad started to poke at her a bit but knew not to go too far.

It was the varsity team's final game as well. They had a fairly poor season, and regardless of what happened in that final game, they were not making the playoffs. Coach Briening had told Tim that he would likely not play but secretly planned to let him start in the third quarter and let him stay in for at least two series. After that, though, he wanted to let his seniors get the remaining playing time, as it was the final game of their high school careers.

At six foot two and two hundred ten pounds, Tim was not the biggest guy on the field anymore. He hadn't even noticed, though. He told himself that if they called his number, he would not play any differently than he had played the night before.

Too bad I will not likely get the chance, he thought.

As the game began, it quickly became apparent that the two teams were evenly matched. Tim started to feel like his chances of ever getting on the field were becoming even slimmer.

Why would they put in a freshman when they have a chance to win the game? he wondered.

Tim couldn't help but feel like he could get to that quarterback, though. Watching the defensive ends play the run every play while the quarterback made a fake and threw most of the time was really starting to eat at him. He also noticed that the quarterback was standing under the center differently on pass plays than on runs. Tim was a master at reading the quarterback, as well as reading the man he was playing across from and the backfield. He told himself that if he got in there, he would be past that tight end before he could even get his hand off the ground. He was sure he could.

Halftime came quickly, and the team was down 14-7. The opponent had just led a scoring drive that ended with only thirty seconds left on the clock. The team seemed somewhat down on the way into the locker room, so Tim hollered out, "Let's go!" and started a full run into the locker room. He wanted them to be excited to be playing football and knew they weren't.

Where is the emotion? he wondered.

Something just took over inside him, and he began to lead a team that he had never played a down on the field with. Every one of them had seen him play, though. He was like a legend already, and they all admired him. They knew he was different. No one thought of him as a freshman.

The team followed him, practically at full speed, all the way to the locker room. When they got there, Tim started in on them.

"We can beat these guys. You guys are better than them. I've watched you play every week, and I know you are more talented than any of you believe."

They were all engaged; no one in the room was ignoring him. He began to go through the things he saw and turned to Coach Briening to ask if he should shut up now.

"No. Please continue, Tim. I agree with everything you are saying."

Coach Briening stood there in amazement that these juniors and seniors would give the kid their complete attention. He had heard about Tim's leadership abilities and had heard how he was like having a coach on the field, but this was unbelievable.

Tim went on. He pointed out every opportunity he saw and where he thought they could take advantage of what he was seeing. Then he went into detail about all of the great things he was seeing out there, calling out each payer by name for their strengths. To wind it up and get them ready to go, he got very emotional.

"You seniors have the opportunity to play one more half of football before you move into the next stage of your lives. You can either get through it and move on to the next thing like it never really mattered or you can go out there and leave everything that makes you who you are on the field so you can always look back at this game and remember what you were once capable of. I would play on broken legs tonight if it were my final game. Give us all something to remember."

The team exploded with excitement. Some of them were even visibly emotional. The energy level was so high that the players would long talk about the feeling they had that night. They were all completely focused on playing their hearts out.

Coach Briening stood up and announced that Tim would be starting the second half. Everyone was behind the decision and began yelling and clapping for him.

"Let's go get 'em!" Coach Briening hollered as they broke for the field.

Tim felt like a gladiator leading the team back out onto the field.

When Jessica noticed him leading the team out and being surrounded by the team in the center of the field while they were all chanting, she turned to her dad and Angela and said, "They have all been infused with Tim's attitude. I bet you he plays now." She was right.

Tim was so excited to be on the field that he could have run through a brick wall on his first play, and he practically did. Just like he had pictured it, he was across the line of scrimmage and in the backfield before the tight end or tackle could even move. He collided with a stout fullback at full speed. He'd never been hit that hard before, but his momentum and aggression carried him right through to the quarterback, who was attempting to hand the ball off to the tailback. The fullback he had just run into fell hard backward into the quarterback exchange, and the ball popped loose. Though Tim didn't recover the fumble, one of his teammates did. They were now on their opponent's eighteen yard line.

Tim was a bit stunned from the hard hit, but the team was going wild for him, and the excitement kept him from showing any pain. His teammates were jumping around on the sidelines, and the players on the field were all congratulating him and smacking him on the butt.

Jessica was so excited for him that she stood up and screamed for him. Angela and Roger were cheering as well and soon joined Jessica on their feet. The stands were going nuts, but someone near Tim's family hadn't seen what happened.

Answering their inquiry, Jessica yelled, "Tim Wiseman, the freshman, just ran someone over and knocked the ball loose."

Roger began to realize that he was in big trouble. Tim had better be the great guy he thought he was because Jessica was helpless over him. He had no doubt in his mind that Jessica was already Tim's, and he could see that Tim was already Jessica's as well.

Tim was a terror for the rest of the game. When they did manage to block him, someone else was always free to make the play. They assigned two linemen and sometimes sent a back too to keep him out of the backfield. It didn't always work. He still managed to sack the quarterback, make several tackles, and completely throw off the other team's offense. Watching Tim play inspired everyone on the team. He was vocal and always positive. He always seemed to know what was coming next, and he seemed to always be in the right place. Though there was never any anger on his face or in his words, it appeared to everyone in the stands that he was almost out of control with anger. It was just how he played. So inspiring was his play that Coach Briening couldn't bring himself to take him out. From that game forward, Tim never missed a defensive play while playing for Coach Briening. Coach would later say that the first game Tim ever played for him was the first time in thirty years of coaching that he had ever felt as if he was in the presence of greatness, though over the next three years, he must have felt that feeling a lot.

Tim played with a complete disregard for his body. God had given him a sturdy, durable frame, and Tim did everything he could to test it. He slammed himself into double teams and massive fullbacks with a full head of steam. Nothing intimidated him. His body was always beaten and bruised, but he refused to be injured. Even when the injury was bad, Tim never let on. He simply didn't allow it to affect his play. This first varsity game was no different for him. Though he broke a finger and tweaked his back during the game, no one ever knew until after the game.

When the game ended, they had won 17-14. Tim was given the game ball, and everyone was talking about how the freshman won the game singlehandedly. Tim knew differently. He never did anything on his own. He was in constant prayer, and he was the ultimate team player. He fully understood that they won together and lost together. They were a family, and he would treat every one of his teammates as family. He felt the weakest player on the team was a part of them winning, as they had been a part of creating the team that was playing on the field by giving their all at practice every day. He played no favorites, and his closest friends were not at all predictable. He befriended whomever he felt a connection with whether they were popular or not. Tim had friends in almost every clique at school. They were all God's people to him, and he knew God loved them all. So would he.

Still, in the locker room after the game, all Tim could think about was Jessica. Was she proud of him? He wanted her to be impressed, but he also felt self-conscious about it. Was it right for him to want to impress her? He just wanted her to feel for him the way he was feeling for her. Did she? All the signs were there that she did, but he was starting to get antsy about not having talked to her about how he was feeling. He knew it was something he would need to do, and he'd need to do it soon.

While he was still showering and celebrating with all of his new teammates, Coach Briening was outside searching for Tim's mother. He had wanted to talk to her the night before but simply hadn't gotten out in time to see her.

Angela, Roger, and Jessica were practically mobbed after the game. Everyone wanted to congratulate them and tell them how great they thought Tim was. Jessica's friends were sitting with them, and they could all see how proud she was of Tim's performance. Not arrogant pride, just happy-for-him pride. They all knew how she felt about him. No one had to ask. Her closest friends, the ones from her church, were praying for her. They had never seen anyone captivate her like this. What if Tim isn't this great guy she and everyone else thinks he is? What if his status and soon-to-be fame change him? As soon as she had left their Wednesday night meeting two days earlier, her closest friends had prayed together for her. They discussed how helpless she seemed to be over him, and they were all afraid she could get hurt by Tim.

Seeing her now with stars in her eyes over Tim, her closest friend, Michelle, tried to get her alone for a short chat.

"Jessica, you know I love you, right?" Michelle asked.

"Of course I do. You have always been there for me. Why would you say that? Are you about to lecture me?"

"I just want to let you know we are all concerned about how vulnerable you seem to be becoming with your infatuation with Tim. I'm not saying this to hurt you. It's just that none of us have seen you this way. We always thought of you as the one who would be there for us when we got smitten by some guy. I hope he's everything we all think he is. Please don't get crushed. Just be careful." Michelle was shaky delivering the message, but she felt like it was her duty as her best friend.

"Thank you so much for caring this much about me. You're right; I've never felt like this. He probably could hurt me right now by just walking away. I know that, and so does he. He's the smartest and most perceptive guy I've ever known. He's not like

179

anyone else. He's better than everyone else, at everything and in every way. He respects me like my father respects me. I can find no fault with him and only wish I could love the Lord the way he does. Still, we are only fifteen; actually, today is his fifteenth birthday. I'm really scared, but I'm much more excited and happy than I am scared. I know who he is; he's my future. It's easy to be around him, and it feels like this has all been made in heaven. I have no doubts at all about him. He is the one."

She had absolutely no fear sharing her deepest feelings about Tim with Michelle. They had been best friends for years, and it had been Michelle who had been closest with her through her mother's and sister's death. Michelle would always be there for her. She could count on it.

"Wow. It's worse than we thought! I'm so happy for you, Jessica, but I can't help but be scared for you too. I will be here for you either way."

Michelle was blown away. She had always admired Jessica's passion. Over the last year or so, she had watched Jessica change physically into a beautiful young woman. She had not blossomed in the way Jessica had, but Jessica had always told her she was beautiful. Michelle often wondered if Jessica was blinded by her affection for her or if she was just being nice. She had come to the conclusion that it had to be something she believed, as Jessica seemed incapable of anything false.

"I love you, Michelle. I always will. I better catch up with Angela and my dad now. Thanks for being my best friend."

They exchanged a quick hug, and Jessica caught up with Angela and her father before they reached the locker room exit. As the three met near the door to the locker room, Coach Briening caught them.

"Mrs. Wiseman, do you remember me?" He figured she would.

"I sure do, Coach. What do you think of my boy?"

She was so proud of Tim. In the back of her mind, the meeting she had had with Coach Briening where she had begged him to say something nice so Chuck could get a shot at college football and a new life was playing through her head.

"He is like no player we have ever had. He's even better than his dad was. I didn't think I'd ever see a talent like that again. Tim is so much more, though. He's the most mature freshman I have ever seen, and I'm not talking at all about his physique or playing ability. You have a very special person living with you. I just wanted you to know that." He was feeling excited for the program's future and even more excited about closing his career out with a state championship, which he felt Tim could bring them.

"I do. You mentioned his father. I wanted to thank you for what you did to get him into Sam Houston State sixteen years ago. Thanks." She really did appreciate what he had done, though it hadn't worked out for the best as nothing ever seemed to for Chuck.

"Well, Mrs. Wiseman, that is something I wanted to talk to you about. I wanted to let you know that I did meet with Coach Jones, but I didn't tell him what you wanted me to tell him. I told him about the talent and gave him a ton of film, but I couldn't give him my word that Chuck was going to stay out of trouble. I didn't think he would or could. Chuck got in because Coach Jones wanted to win. Since he only lasted three years as their head coach, I guess he made a mistake or two."

"Thanks for telling me. Why bother telling me, though?" She was pretty uncomfortable talking about Chuck in front of Roger and Jessica anyway.

"I'm telling you because I feel like I can finally say something good about a Wiseman. I'll say it to any coach, news channel, or anyone else. I've been coaching all my life. I've been here more than thirty years now. Never have I seen anything like your son. I want you to know how special he really is. What scares me is how good he will be. If he gets as big as his father, he'll be playing on Sunday someday."

He really believed every word he was saying. It felt good to say it, but it felt even better to be at the start of it. The next three years were going to be great. He could hardly wait to get back on the field with Tim on his team. From what he had seen and heard, Tim was the hardest worker in the gym any of the coaches had ever seen. He had even witnessed Tim helping others, inspiring them, and pushing them. Tim would stay around and pick up weights if other lazier or unaware athletes left them out. From what he had seen, Tim was as close to selfless as a high school kid could be.

"Thank you so much for the kind words, Coach. We all feel the same way that you do. I know he's everything his father wasn't." She felt good and bad all at the same time. She began to wonder how all this talk about Chuck was making Roger feel. Though she would not have been attracted to Roger when she first met Chuck, he was definitely the man of her dreams now.

Jessica was proud to hear all of this about Tim. She too wondered how her father was feeling with all of this talk about the man who had hurt the woman he loved so much for so long.

Then Roger spoke. "Thank you so much for sharing this with us, Coach. Tim is everything everyone is saying about him. He's becoming better every day. He's dedicated his life to becoming more like Christ. That's the real reason for the light you see in him. He has a huge heart for God and for other people. We all love him so much."

"Are you his uncle or something?" Coach Briening asked.

"No. I'm the guy Tim does Bible study with and the guy who is in love with his mother." He hoped saying it that way wouldn't make Angela feel uncomfortable.

"That's right, and I love him too," Angela replied.

She was so happy to hear him say it out loud. She had never heard him tell anyone other than her. Tim had told her that Roger told him he loved her all the time, but she had never actually heard Roger say it to him. There was no chance she was losing the guy. He was her rock now.

Roger was suddenly emotional hearing Angela's reply. He even had to excuse himself before Coach Briening left.

When Tim emerged from the locker room, it seemed like the entire freshman football team was there waiting for him. He hugged most of them and declined their offers to go hang out. He had only his new family, but primarily Jessica, on his mind.

Jessica was waiting for him, but she didn't rush him like everyone else did. She just stood there with Angela and her dad. She noticed how all the girls who had been standing around outside of the locker room were trying to get him to look at them. Just the way they were looking at him made her feel kind of angry.

One or two of the girls actually went up to talk with him, but he treated them no differently than he had treated his freshmen football teammates—without the hugs, though. More than one of them tried to touch him, and she saw with her own eyes how he avoided the contact. She knew that at least one of them was a cheerleader, and Tim hadn't even glanced at her inappropriately. Even that made her proud.

Where are his flaws? she wondered.

Tim went directly to her. He had to hug her first. He was too full of joy to pretend she wasn't the priority of his life. It was her with whom he wanted to share his success, and he couldn't pretend otherwise. He needed her, and he could feel she needed him to let her know she was the one for him. When the others were mobbing him, it was only her eyes he felt on him. As everyone turned and watched him go to her, Tim's actions made it clear to all of them that she was who he was with.

As the hug went on, Angela and Roger looked at each other, feeling more than a little concerned about where it was going. In no way was he being inappropriate with her, but he was clearly giving her preference, and it was easy to see his affection for her. As he pulled her tightly to his body, she whispered, "Happy birthday," into his ear. She was right; it was very happy. Upon hearing her birthday wishes, he let her down, and the two of them stared into each other's eyes while they spoke. She was telling him how great it was watching him, and he was asking if they had a good time and if she was learning football since she had been to two games. It was as if they were alone on a desert island for a few minutes. Angela couldn't help but remember how his father used to make her feel that way.

After what seemed like an inordinate amount of time, Tim turned to his mother for a hug and then to Roger. They both congratulated him, and Roger offered to take everyone out for pizza to celebrate.

"As long as it doesn't affect our plans for tomorrow night," Tim answered. He really wanted to see Jessica dressed up even more than he wanted a fancy steak.

"It will have no effect. Also, even though we are celebrating it tomorrow, it's your birthday today, Tim. We have to do something."

Roger took Angela by the hand, and they all headed for the car and a night of pizza and great conversation. Tim's favorite part was sitting in the backseat with Jessica. Sometimes they just looked at each other without talking at all. Neither of them was ever uncomfortable in each other's company after that night. Tim seriously considered taking her hand in the darkness of the backseat but decided against it, as he wanted to talk to her about his feelings before he made any moves that might be misconstrued.

CHAPTER 24

TIM was dressed more than an hour before Roger and Jessica were due to pick him and his mother up for dinner. He was a bit nervous, as he had laid awake most of the previous night dreaming about football and his future with Jessica. The nervousness was coming from what he had decided to say to her. He would have to get her alone to say what he wanted to say.

When Angela finally got out of the shower, he told her he was going to help her prepare for the big night. She quickly picked up that he was dealing with something by the way he was acting.

"What's going on with you, Tim? You seem so nervous." She knew it likely had something to do with the obvious crush he had on Jessica, but she didn't want to assume anything. "I don't need your help getting ready. Thanks for the offer, though."

"Mom, I love Jessica." He wondered how this news would go over.

"I know, Tim. Anyone can see that." She thought it was kind of cute that he thought no one had noticed.

"No, Mom. I really love her. I don't like her or have a crush on her. She is the one for me, and I'm going to ask her to marry me tonight." He wasn't really looking for advice; he had decided to tell her because he wanted her to know. He just wanted to share it with her.

"What? You are just turning fifteen. You have got to be kidding. I just listened to a coach tell me how mature you are, but this is ridiculous." She really was stunned and was trying to laugh it off so he would drop this crazy idea.

"I'm not asking her to marry me tonight, Mom. I'm telling her I'm pledging to keep myself pure for her until we can be married when we are both old enough to marry. I don't want anyone else ever, and I'll die if she ever goes on a date with anyone else. I've been thinking about nothing but her since I first met her. The more time I spend with her, I fall even deeper in love. Every time I'm around her, I feel at peace, and I'm certain God has sent her into our lives to become my wife. I don't want either of us to make any mistakes that could destroy our future together. If she turns me down, I will be a wreck. Please support me on this."

He hoped he didn't still sound like a joke to her. He was dead serious. If he and Jessica were going to be together, it started that night. He was convinced and wanted to make the commitment so he wouldn't be tempted. It would be the covenant he would make with her before God. It was no joke.

"You never cease to impress me, Tim. I guess you have thought it all out. Please realize that not all people are capable of making a commitment like this at fifteen. Do what you feel is right. You know better than I do. You always have. I love you very much, and I know you'll do the honorable thing. She is an amazing girl. I love spending time with her, and I know you are all she thinks about too. What do you think she will say? What about Roger?"

"I think she will be happy that I'm asking. I know she wants this too, Mom. I only wish I could offer her a ring. Roger is a different story. I don't want to disappoint him. I'm hoping he sees my pure intentions. I'm not doing this to get with his daughter; I'm doing it to honor her."

He knew Roger would feel that it was way too soon. How could anyone know someone well enough to marry them in only a couple of months, especially a fifteen-year-old? Roger was the biggest risk; he knew his mother would never try to stop him. Jessica would likely understand that he was protecting them both from this world with the proposal, but Roger almost certainly would have trouble swallowing it.

"You are so good at everything you set your heart on. I bet even Roger will be on board." She wasn't sure, though. It could even set her and Roger's relationship back some, and that scared her a bit.

Tim left the room and continued to rehearse his marriage proposal. Before he knew it, Jessica was at the door and her father was a few steps behind her, trying to catch up to his anxious daughter. Tim opened the door to his beautiful bride-to-be. It was better than he had even imagined it would be. She was in a soft white dress that he knew he would always remember. It showed off more of her figure than her father had wanted, but it was classy, and he just wasn't able to say no in spite of his reservations.

Jessica sprung at him, and when their bodies came in contact, she was surprised, as usual, how solid he was. It was like running into a statue. He was so solid and powerfully built that she practically bounced off him, and she would have had he not wrapped his loving arms around her.

"Happy birthday, Tim," she said softly into his ear as he picked her from the ground like some sort of rag doll.

Having her in his arms, he took the opportunity to breathe in her aroma. She was wearing some sort of perfume, but not too much. He could smell her natural smell too— the smell that would forever make him feel at home.

Sensing the awkwardness of the situation, he regrettably set her down.

"Thanks, Jessica. There is no one I'd rather celebrate it with. You too, Mr. Brooks."

It was true; they really were his two favorite people. He felt underdressed until he realized that Mr. Brooks was wearing blue jeans as well. Mr. Brooks did have on a really nice sport coat, though.

"Tim, I have a gift for you that I'd like to give you before dinner and another from all of us that we'll give you after dinner."

He handed Tim a brand-new sport jacket.

"Here you go, big guy. I bought one I thought was big enough for you. Hopefully you can get a couple of years out of it. The way you are growing, it might not fit next week, though." Roger loved giving gifts to people, especially to people he loved like Tim.

"This is great, sir. I look almost respectable in it."

He loved the way it looked on him. He looked much older in it. Jessica absolutely loved it on him too. She told him how great it looked on him, and he decided that he'd never take it off.

"How is your mother coming?" Roger asked.

Angela never seemed to be ready on time. Roger was a structured type of guy, but thankfully he was even more patient than structured.

"She's almost ready. I just checked on her a few minutes ago. She looks beautiful. I think you'll agree that it was worth the wait once you've seen her."

Tim was proud of how hard his mother worked to stay in such great shape. Being a hard worker himself, he had always admired this characteristic in his mother.

"I bet she does. She always does." Roger too had been looking forward to seeing her in a dress. As usual, he was praying to God for restraint. *Please, God, don't let me violate her with my eyes and my mind*, he prayed.

Just then, Angela made her entrance. She looked amazing even to Tim. She was only about five minutes late—almost a record, Tim pointed out. She had only worn the dress she was wearing one other time. It was too formal for anything in her life, so it just sat in the closet. Angela had owned it for many years but hadn't worn it in at least five years. It made her feel a little uncomfortable, as it kind of accentuated her figure. She felt as if people were looking at her naked. By no means was it inappropriate. "You look fantastic," said Roger.

"I second that," said Tim.

"Yeah, Mrs. Wiseman. You are beautiful," added Jessica.

"Thanks, everyone. Let's get going. We don't want to be late. At least that's what everyone is always telling me." She was trying to be funny to take the attention off her dress. She gave Roger a hug, and the four of them headed to Pasqual's.

Roger and Jessica had been to Pasqual's several times, but they hadn't been there for quite a while. When they got there, the place was full, as usual, and most of the people were pretty dressed up. Jessica and Roger felt comfortable while Angela and Tim were a bit uncomfortable. They had never been to a place like that before, and both of them were afraid of screwing it up for their hosts.

They were seated in a corner booth in the dimly lit restaurant. The booths were like private rooms, which helped put Tim and Angela at ease. Now it was just the four of them; no one else could see them. Tim and Jessica sat together on one side while Angela and Roger sat on the other side.

Tim was impressed with the size and weight of the menus. He was also impressed with the waiter, who appeared to have at least two helpers. The prices, though, were by far the most impressive thing. All the steaks were at least forty dollars, and none of them came with a soup, salad, or any type of side dish.

"Wow. I had no idea this place was going to be so expensive. I'm not sure I deserve anything like this." He was starting to feel uncomfortable and unworthy.

Angela was feeling the same, and she added to what Tim had just said. "Are you sure we should be spending this kind of money on a meal?"

"Please don't look at the prices. We are here to celebrate Tim's birthday, and I don't want anyone worrying about the prices. Let me worry about that. We wouldn't be here if I didn't feel everyone here at this table is worth this type of treat. Tonight will be amazing. You have never had a steak like you will get here. Please enjoy it with Jessica and me." Just the thought of them being distracted made him feel uncomfortable.

"Okay. I'll just think about the meat," said Tim.

"I won't think about the prices either, but I won't forget them either. Thanks for bringing us here," added Angela.

Tim was so preoccupied with what he was planning to say to Jessica later that he was hardly able to pick out a steak. "Can you help me pick the right steak, Mr. Brooks? I think I know the cuts pretty well, but was hoping you could give me some guidance."

He had never had a filet. Although he knew it was the best cut, he didn't know if it would be a good steak for a hungry guy to order. It looked like he could order a big filet that would be almost as many ounces as the rib eye, but he decided to go with whatever Roger recommended.

"Well, for you, I would say size is more important than for the rest of us. Jessica always gets the smallest cut of filet, and I usually get the fourteen-ounce bone-in filet. The bone-in filet is the best steak I've ever eaten. For you, though, I think you should take a shot at the twenty-four-ounce porterhouse. It's got a good-sized filet on one side of the bone and a really good-sized New York strip steak on the other side of the bone. It's huge, and I'm sure it's delicious."

Roger had actually given that some thought. He was pretty sure Tim could do some serious damage to the porterhouse. Tim was a growing boy, or maybe a growing man was a better description.

"Porterhouse it is then. Thanks!" He knew how he liked it cooked, medium rare, so now he was good to go.

Jessica was so happy to be there and to be sitting next to Tim that she could not stop smiling. Every time she made eye contact with him, they both just smiled knowingly at the other. Though she had no clue what Tim was planning, she believed that he was just as much into her as she was into him. His heart was pounding, and his mind was racing. He was completely consumed with his plan. He could hardly wait to get her alone, though he still had not figured out how he was going to get her alone.

The meal was amazing. It was better than advertised. No steak Angela or Tim had ever eaten was like that. Everything was perfect, and Angela hardly even felt unfit to be there. She hoped she was starting to change inside. Maybe Roger could get her over her feelings about herself.

"It's time for us to give you our gift, Tim," Jessica said while she winked at her father.

"You guys bought me a nice jacket and took us to dinner at this unbelievable restaurant. I don't think I can accept anything else." He really felt this way but was curious to see what they had gotten him.

"Don't be silly, Tim. I picked this out just for you. My dad paid for it, but it's really from me." She actually looked a little angry.

Now he really wanted to see what it was. *It's probably more clothes*, he figured.

Roger couldn't help but add, "It's actually from all of us, Tim. Your mother had a part in this too."

"Sorry. I'd be happy to take everything you guys are willing to give me." Tim tried to lighten the mood so they could all enjoy him opening their gift.

Roger reached into his pocket and pulled out an envelope. Tim was pretty surprised to see an envelope. He had no idea what it was, but now he could rule out clothes.

"Tim, Jessica knows what your favorite thing is, so she found you this on eBay." He handed the envelope over, and Tim reluctantly took it.

He opened the envelope to find four tickets to a Monday night football game, Indianapolis at Houston.

"This is great! When is the game?"

He could not be more excited. He couldn't even imagine going to an NFL game.

He was reading the tickets to find the date when Roger answered, "It's this Monday night. We told your mother before we bought them, and she gave us the go-ahead. We'll all drive down together Monday after school. The game starts at seven p.m., but the doors open at five thirty p.m. We'll drive back home after the game since it's less than two hours away. We'll all take Tuesday off to recover. You and Jessica get to miss school."

That was sudden for Tim, but for the rest of them, it was all they had talked about all week. Roger purchased the tickets that Jessica had found on eBay the night before. She had bid on the seats on Wednesday night but hadn't officially won them until they got home from pizza the night before. Had they not won, they planned to pay whatever it took to get seats.

It really was a great night. Tim couldn't imagine things being any better than they were at that moment. His life had been a mess only two years before. Since his father's death, there had been some really dark times for him and his mother. Now they were both happy.

Angela was hoping the gift would change his mind in regard to asking Jessica to marry him, but she knew better. Tim was the most focused person she had ever known. Once he made up his mind, it seldom changed. Actually, he could be downright stubborn at times. Her concern wasn't that Jessica would reject him; anyone could see that she wouldn't. Her biggest worry was that Roger would be set back by it. How would that affect their relationship? She wanted to be his wife. Would it set them back? She feared having to deal with it if it did.

CHAPTER 25

WHEN they got back to the house, Angela asked Roger if he would sit out on the porch with her.

"We can sit on your porch swing and talk. I'll make us a couple of coffees with that fancy machine you have."

Tim felt the weight being lifted off his shoulders when his mother asked Roger to be alone. Now he wouldn't have to come up with a way to get Jessica alone. It had to be that night. He had to talk with Jessica about their future that night. He was incapable of waiting a second longer.

"Sure. That would be nice," Roger responded.

Once she made the suggestion, Roger felt like she had read his mind. He was hoping to get to spend some time one-on-one with her.

In about twenty minutes, Tim and Jessica were alone in the living room. They sat on opposite ends of the couch, but they were locked in conversation and never even pretended to watch the TV that was blaring away right in front of them. Tim reached out and hit the mute button before he started his proposal.

"Jessica, I have something very serious to discuss with you."

She suddenly felt sick. *What is it? Is he going to tell me he likes me, or is he going to tell me that he doesn't think us being together would be a good idea because we will soon be brother and sister?* "What is it, Tim?"

She desperately needed to hear what he wanted to say. He could tell from her demeanor that she was worried, so he decided to jump right in, as he knew she wouldn't feel that way very long once she heard what he had to say.

"You are the only girl for me, Jessica. I happen to believe that you make your own destiny, and I know you are mine. I don't want to scare you with all this, but there is something I feel I need to present to you."

She was jumping for joy inside but honestly had no idea where he was going with this. The worry left her face in an instantly. Now she was relieved and happy, and it showed.

Tim could see she was ecstatic with his statement that she was the only girl for him. He continued.

"I know we have not known each other that long, but as long as I've known you, I have not thought of anything else but you. Not just the way you look, though I love everything about the way you look; I think of you on every level. It's who you are that I'm in love with. Your personality is a perfect fit for mine. Your heart for others amazes me. Your smile is burned into my memory, as is your smell and your laugh. I want you to be mine, and I want to promise to be yours." He paused for a moment when he noticed the tears in her eyes but jumped right back in. "I can describe every wrinkle in your face from memory, and I want to know everything that makes you happy so I can make you smile the rest of your life. When I'm doing well at anything, it's you I want to impress. If you were disappointed in me, I wouldn't be able to do anything until I had fixed whatever it was that was disappointing you. I know you are the one God has picked out for me to be with. I have no questions about that."

He stopped again because she had gotten off the couch and was trying to reach for him. He looked out the window to see if Mr. Brooks was looking and was happy to see that their parents were not even visible from the living room couch.

He stood and embraced her. Things were so perfect that it was almost painful to Tim now.

"I feel the same way, Tim," she managed to weep out. She was shaking in his arms, being overwhelmed with her feelings for him and the thought that he was telling her that he would always be there for her.

"I know you do, Jessica. We were made for each other. My attraction to you from the very beginning was inescapable. That's why I have to make a commitment to you. I want you to be my wife."

194

"Yes, I want that too, Tim." She didn't understand how he could be saying it so soon, and she knew it was just not possible for them to marry anytime soon. Her answer came so quickly because that was all she had thought about for weeks. There was no hesitation because she, like he, knew it was right.

"I'm not suggesting we get married right now, Jessica. What I'm saying is that I would like to commit to you that I will stay pure until we are both ready to marry. I won't date anyone. I won't even talk to other girls if there is any chance it could lead to anything that would destroy our future together. My hope is that you too will commit yourself to me. Can you?" He was pretty sure she would, but he wanted to make it official for both of them.

"Of course I can. I think I was planning to wait for you even before the deal. There is no one else for me either, Tim. There never will be. You are right; you are God's gift to me. It would kill me to see you dating someone else. I want to know you are mine and not have to worry about it."

She was holding his face in her hands now. He was almost a foot taller than she, so he had to look almost straight down at her as they spoke. They were staring deeply into each other's eyes as they spoke.

"I feel exactly the same way. It's a deal then. We are now both banned from any social life that would lead to any sort of distraction to our promise. We will stay pure until our wedding night. You will someday be Mrs. Wiseman." He felt great saying that.

Jessica felt such a relief that she could only nod in response and softly buried her face into his chest. As she began to realize that she might ruin his new coat, she started to pull it off him. When he recoiled a bit, she explained that she was trying to make sure his new coat didn't get ruined.

"Oh, you freaked me out. I thought you hadn't taken the purity part seriously."

They both laughed.

Once his coat was off, she sat him down and leaned into him.

"Can we have one small kiss since we just got engaged?" She really needed a kiss. She had never kissed anyone before.

"I think we can do that, but let's not let it get too sexy."

He was more worried about what he might do than anything else. He feared that he might not be able to control himself if it got heavy. Almost before he finished his sentence, her soft lips were on his. She had crawled up his lap to get her mouth to his. Her lips were so soft and sweet, but he couldn't have been more uncomfortable. He brought her in and kissed her back, but he was careful not to touch her anywhere that could lead to anything more. It was amazing. It was better than anything he had ever experienced, and he felt nothing but concern for her. He was somewhat relieved as he began to feel that he could control himself. He might have gotten a little too comfortable as the little kiss turned into more of a long make-out than a small peck on the lips. Before he knew it, he began to take the kiss to the next level. Thankfully Jessica was not losing control.

He had spent the first twelve years of his life with a father who had taught him that women were for sex first. His dad had pointed out every perversion he could, and no female body had escaped his father's lust. Tim always knew it was wrong and inherently knew that women were of equal value to men. Now, with all of the Bible study and with a positive role model like Roger to learn from, Tim was learning to hate sexual sin. He had discovered that it was true, that we all did have a fallen nature and were all plagued with the burden of sin. In the area of sexual purity, Roger had told him that the best defense was to run from temptation. The more frequently you exposed yourself to sexual temptation, the more likely you were to get snared by it, Roger had told him. Tim was learning the lesson firsthand now.

Jessica was feeling so much love for him that she just wanted to curl up with him and never let go. As their tongues began to caress one another's, she suddenly caught herself and backed off a bit. As she pulled away, Tim caught himself and was stunned that he was that close to doing much more. He was pretty sure she had no idea that he was starting to lose it, but he was wrong. She had sensed it was about to go to the next level when Tim's tongue started licking hers. It was a beautiful moment for them, and they were both relieved they had backed off when they did. For her, that was all she needed, but she could see in his eyes that he was up for another kiss or more.

"I'm sorry I jumped on you like that, Tim."

"I loved it, Jessica. You are everything to me. Until we are married, I don't want to ever do more than that. I'm quite sure I'll need your help, though. I want to respect you, but I'm only human. You are unbelievably sexy to me, so I'll need your help to stay pure. Please keep me in line."

It had scared him a little that he had gone from thinking he was under control to pushing her to do more than they should. Consciously, he didn't want to do anything to damage their purity, but now he was sure that he would fail if he allowed himself to be tempted. Thoughts of her naked body and intercourse had entered his mind, and it made him feel weak and dirty.

"Sorry, Tim. I really needed to kiss you. I'll be the brakes from now on. I want to wait for you more than anything. I have to wait."

She knew she could always stop before things got too far. She had felt the rush to escape before she had withdrawn from him. No doubt, she would need to help him through a long, painful wait. The thought of him forcing her to do more never even entered her mind. It was Tim, and he would never do that. She believed it.

It amazed Tim that his mind was so susceptible to rationalizing away an obvious sin like premarital sex. In the blink of an eye, he had learned that his mind would allow him to ignore his reservations in the favor of immediate gratification even when the results could hurt the person he cared the most about.

In other areas he had never noticed such a weakness in his character. It had been an eye-opening experience, one he prayed he had just learned from. From that moment on, he would not allow himself to get carried away in the moment like he just had. The thought crossed his mind that it would have been impossible to reason with himself had he been drinking.

What a risk people take by drinking alcohol, he decided.

Drinking would never be an issue for him.

Tim had thought through all of the possible implications of his decision to ask her to marry him. Once their amazing kiss was over, he pressed on with the rest of his thoughts.

"I will leave it up to you to decide if we should tell your father about our commitment to each other. My preference is to tell him right away, but I want to let you make that decision. I have already told my mother, but that's a lot easier than telling your dad. I just don't want him to think I'm trying to pull anything with all this. I know how much he loves you, and I suspect he'll think this is a pretty foolish commitment for anyone our age to make. He'd be wrong, though." Tim kind of hoped she would choose to tell her dad. He had such respect for Mr. Brooks that he wanted him to know.

"I want to tell him, but I want to do it alone. Can you let me do that?" She could already tell that Tim would let her do whatever she wanted, not that she would ever take advantage of it, but knowing he would was a huge positive to her.

"Sure, but I think he already knows how we feel about each other. Do you think it's okay to hug and kiss on the cheek when he's around? I think that should be the furthest we let it go, even when we are alone."

He knew he would lose it if they went any further than that. He wanted to do things to her he knew were only appropriate for a married couple, and he knew enough to know that he could not trust himself if they got too physical with one another. He figured Jessica could probably go much further without compromising, but he hoped she would understand that guys and girls were just different with this kind of stuff.

"I completely agree, Tim. We should only hug, hold hands, and kiss on the cheek. Let's not do any of it in front of my dad tonight, though. Is that okay?"

She hoped he would understand that she would be uncomfortable touching him in any way in front of her dad. She was his little girl, and she wanted it to stay that way.

"No problem, future wife." He was having some fun with her now, but he also meant it.

"Okay. Thanks, future husband."

She couldn't even believe it was really happening. *What if he believes in purity now but can't wait as long as it will take? The girls are already all over him.* She decided she had his word and that would have to be enough.

"I will think of you every minute of every day, Jessica. I want to become like your father and, more importantly, more like Christ. Thank you for loving me." He knew it was real. He never had doubts about his feelings. The fears he had once had about becoming like his father had left the day he had accepted Christ. It had been wiped clean. Even his thoughts had been forgiven, though they still occasionally strayed. Tim knew that what had been was now gone and that he was now Christ's. It was his thoughts that occasionally wandered, not his feelings. They never betrayed him.

"Tim, I have never kissed anyone before. I want you to know you were my first and that you will be my last."

She wanted him to understand how pure she actually was. She knew how important it was that he saw her that way so it would be easier for him to honor her purity.

"I know, Jessica. That's why we had to talk as soon as we could. I had to keep it that way even though I knew you would stay pure either way. I really needed this commitment. I've made a couple mistakes already, nothing too serious, though. My dad exposed me to some things that are still stuck in my head. He used to show me naked women and always had *Playboy*s and other dirty magazines he would show me. It really messed with me then, and after he died I really struggled with those images. It wasn't until your father and I started our Bible study and I accepted Christ into my life that I was able to get past that stuff. I used to imagine what it would be like to be with every good-looking girl I saw, and now I simply look away or change the channel. It's something your dad told me to do. He's the best role model I've ever known, and I thank God every day for bringing him into my life, almost as much as I thank God for bringing you into my life."

He always wanted to tell her the truth about everything. He wanted her to know he wasn't perfect. He felt like he was past a lot of stuff that had really affected him, but he was in a good place in his life now. He now knew how he should live.

"I will be here for you, Tim. I'll be here as long as it takes, and you can always know that I'm yours. I'm so sorry for what you have been through, but I know that it's what has made you who you are. You are the most perfect person I have ever met. Good women might be hard to find, but good men are even harder to find. That's all I hear from older women. I can't wait to live my life with you."

Her heart was aching for what Tim had been through. She knew she would never fully understand what he had been through, but she was sure it had been evil in origin. Tim had seen evil and claimed victory over it in the name of Jesus, just as we are all supposed to do. For her it was just another reason to be impressed with her boyfriend.

That's what he is now, she told herself, *my boyfriend.*

They spent the remainder of their time alone, telling one another how perfect the other one was.

Neither of them wanted to be apart for even a minute, but when their parents came in, they said good-bye and Jessica actually gave him a big hug and said, "Happy birthday, Tim," right in front of their parents.

He could feel her heart beating alongside his, and he knew they would be okay. He knew his heart had led him in the right direction, and knowing she was now pledged to him made him feel calm inside.

"Happy birthday, Tim," said Roger. "We'll pick you guys up for church tomorrow morning and then the game Monday. It's almost as if we are a real family now." He wanted them to all be together, but he knew that Tim and Jessica would end up as more than brother and sister.

Tim and Angela talked about Tim's proposal on the way home. Angela was still worried about how Roger might handle it, but she was happy for Tim when she heard how Jessica responded. She really liked Jessica and could see everything her son saw in her. Angela thought that Jessica was the cutest little thing she had ever seen. From the time they had spent together, she knew Jessica was also a great person. She would think Tim was crazy to not be into her.

Things were actually a little tense at the Brooks' house after the Wisemans were gone. Roger knew that something was up, so he kept pushing Jessica for information. She was really worried that he might lose some of his respect for her if he knew she had just agreed to marry Tim. It sounded nuts to her every time she tried to play out the conversation she would have to have with her dad. Finally, she decided to just tell him.

"Dad, I love Tim. He just asked me to marry him, and I said yes." She knew the direct way was the best, but she knew she would quickly need to add more detail.

His face said it all; he was in complete disbelief. "Are you serious?"

"We aren't getting married right now, Dad. I just agreed to save myself for him, and he promised to save himself for me. He told me he wants us to both be committed to purity until our wedding night. He wanted to tell you, but I asked him to let me do it alone. I hope you can understand, Dad."

She knew inside that it was her decision. It was her life. No matter what her dad had to say, she was going to marry Tim. The commitment started then. She just didn't want to disappoint him.

"I think it's great, Jessica. I love Tim too. I just don't know if I believe that two fifteen-year-old kids should be making this type of commitment, though I understand why Tim would. He's told me some pretty bad things about his past, and I know he wants to honor God by remaining pure until he's married. It will be a real struggle for him. Anyone can see how you two feel about each other, and with anyone other than Tim, I would tell you this would be impossible. I just don't want you to get hurt, baby. Tim is like this force of nature or something. He's got more going for him than anyone I've ever known. He's as smart as anyone I've known, he's as talented in almost every way as anyone I've known, and he's already a better man than almost anyone I know. I've been praying for God to bring you someone special who will treat you like the precious person that you are. Tim certainly fits that role, but I was hoping I would be engaged to Angela before you would be engaged to anyone." He was trying to stay positive and support her. He didn't want to destroy the open, trusting relationship that they had either.

"Thank you for not being mad, Dad. You are the best!" She hugged him and ran for the stairs to avoid any further discussion. She couldn't wait to get to her room to start thinking about her future with Tim.

Roger stood in disbelief at what had just happened. When he finally got his wits about him, he called Angela to see what she knew. Knowing Tim's character, he figured he had told his mother what he was planning to do before he had done it.

Did she set me up by asking me to swing with her on the porch? he wondered.

His guess was right. Angela knew everything. She also insisted that Tim would honor his word.

"This kid is like some sort of saint. He always does the right thing. I never have to tell him what to do. He loves Jessica, and he knows what that means. You can count on him not to hurt your daughter, Roger."

She was bracing herself for his reaction. Would this finally set him off? She had never seen him express anger of any sort. She had seen him get depressed and even annoyed, but he had never let it change the way he treated other people. How would he handle this? Now she would finally see how he really was. When the pressure was on, would Mr. Perfect crack?

"I'm betting you are right, Angela. I hear he has a great mother. This kid never ceases to amaze me. I don't think I would ever bet against him." He wanted her to know he wasn't angry, just concerned. He went on. "It just seems so impractical to me. They are so young. I do like the idea of them staying pure for each other until the night of their marriage, though. Like I told Jessica, I always thought I would be engaged to you before she would be engaged to anyone."

He was a bit worried by the tone he heard in Angela's voice. She sounded like she was afraid of him.

"So you're not mad?" She felt relieved. He really was everything she believed him to be. She liked hearing him say the part about them getting engaged. She wanted to wear a ring for the first time in her life.

"I'm not mad at all. I'm dazed and unsure how I feel about this. I love Tim too, but he's just a boy. I suppose I'll learn to live with it. It's nice to know that she will end up with a great guy." His worry over how Angela was feeling was really getting to him. He wanted to be able to reach through the phone line and give her a hug.

"We'd better get to bed, Roger. We'll see you guys in the morning."

The next few days were great. The four of them were really coming together as a strange kind of in-love family. They had the time of their lives at the football game, and the four of them were together almost every night from that point on.

CHAPTER 26

FOR the next few months, things seemed to be progressing nicely. Tim and Roger kept studying the Bible together, and Angela started reading it too. Both Tim and Roger spent time with her talking about it, and she began to wear down. God was definitely working on her. She still struggled with her feelings of inadequacy, but Roger and Tim were always there for her.

Finally, one night, while she was being attacked by feelings of inadequacy, she opened the Bible and read in Romans "If thou shalt confess with thy mouth Jesus as Lord, and shalt believe in thy heart that God raised him from the dead, thou shalt be saved: for with the heart man believeth unto righteousness; and with the mouth confession is made unto salvation" (10:9-10, ASV).

Knowing that she was ready to accept Christ, she jumped in her car and drove to Roger's house. As she pulled into the driveway, she texted him, "I'm in your driveway and need you to help me accept Christ." Though it was 2:00 a.m., she immediately saw his light come on. His silhouette appeared to be getting dressed when the reply came back, "Come in."

By the time she got to the door, he was there. They embraced, and she broke down, telling him about how she had been feeling and that she could actually feel God's love for her.

"I know he's real, Roger, and I want what the rest of you have in your lives."

He was both happy and relieved. She had just chosen heaven over hell. After all she had been through, God had planned to bring her home all along. Something inside him was telling him that everything she had been through had been that way to bring her and Tim into his life. Tim was a born leader who would do huge things for Christ. God had orchestrated their pasts to get the mold he needed for what they would become.

"I know now that I am a sinner. You and Tim have convinced me that I need to be forgiven. I was really struggling tonight, so I started to read the Bible. Then it just hit me that all I need is Jesus."

Her brokenness was easily visible. From the time they had begun dating to who she currently was could not have been a more amazing contrast. She had gone from being completely closed up to wide open to him. It astonished him.

They hit the floor in front of the living room couch together and began to pray. Roger told her he was going to read her a prayer that he had used many times. It was something he had found on the Internet but was no more than one of many prayers that could be used for her to accept Christ. He told her he would read it to her and she should repeat each part after he read it if she wanted to surrender her life to Jesus. She assured him that she did, and he started reading from his notes. Each time Roger paused, she repeated every word.

"Dear God in heaven, I come to you in the name of Jesus. I acknowledge to you that I am a sinner, and I am sorry for my sins and the life that I have lived. I need your forgiveness. I believe that your only begotten Son, Jesus Christ, shed His precious blood on the cross at Calvary and died for my sins, and I am now willing to turn from my sin. You said in Your Holy Word, Romans ten nine, that if we confess the Lord our God and believe in our hearts that God raised Jesus from the dead, we shall be saved. Right now I confess Jesus as the Lord of my soul. With my heart, I believe that God raised Jesus from the dead. This very moment I accept Jesus Christ as my own personal Savior, and according to His Word, right now I am saved. Thank you, Jesus, for your unlimited grace that has saved me from my sins. I thank you, Jesus, that your grace never leads to license, but rather it always leads to repentance. Therefore, Lord Jesus, transform my life so that I may bring glory and honor to you alone and not to myself. Thank you, Jesus, for dying for me and giving me eternal life. Amen.²"

When it was over, she was full of joy and actually felt God's presence. It was like a heavy weight had been lifted from her. "Thank you, Roger. I love you."

Roger was overwhelmed with how good God was. Holding Angela in his arms after what she had just done was one of the greatest feelings he had ever had. It was almost too good. His fears about their future were vanishing, and knowing where she would now spend eternity was the greatest reward he could ever get.

Thank you, God, he kept praying. "I love you too, Angela. I'm so happy you have decided to follow Jesus with your life."

He was just too happy for words. The predominant thought in his mind was that he could now marry her. She would make his life whole, and he would give himself entirely to her happiness. He could hardly wait.

The two lay against the couch and eventually fell asleep in each other's arms. They awoke quite early, and since it was a school and work day, Angela headed for home. They decided not to tell the kids until they were all together later that evening. Things would never be the same.

Tim was thrilled when he heard that his mother had been saved. He even cried. Right in front of Jessica, he cried. Jessica was touched by his vulnerability. She too was moved by Angela becoming a Christian. Now they were all in God's family.

The evenings remained family time with Tim and Roger studying and Angela and Jessica jogging. It was their together time, and Tim and Jessica spent at least an hour together every night before he would ride his bike home. With basketball in full swing and both of them fully committed to getting the best grades possible, they didn't have as much free time as they would have liked. What time they did have, they spent together. Church offered lots of fun things to do for kids in their age group, and they were there for just about all of it. Occasionally Tim would have a game and couldn't go, but whenever possible, he was there. When he had a game, Roger, Angela, and Jessica would all go.

The weekends were spent as a family.

CHAPTER 27

ROGER had been planning that night for quite some time. Actually, he had been planning it from the moment Angela had accepted Christ into her life. He had even bought her the most beautiful ring he could find. Though it wasn't gaudy, it was bigger than it needed to be. He knew that the size or cost didn't really matter, but he wanted her to have something as special as she was. No ring could live up to her in his eyes, but this one was the best he had found. He would love seeing it on her finger and knew that it would be dear to her.

He drove up to the Wisemans' house with Jessica in the passenger seat, though that was as far as she was going. Tim was actually making dinner for Jessica, and they had some plans for a nice evening of their own. Before he could even get the car parked, Jessica was unbuckled and scrambling to get out. The second the gear was in park, she was out of the car and on her way to the front door.

"Come on, Dad!" she hollered back at him.

Tim was watching for them through the window and was out of the house, on his way to greet her, before she reached the front door. As usual, she jumped in his arms, and he held her off the ground for almost a minute. He had started the habit of giving her little love talks during those hugs, and that time was no different. When he finally set her down, he told her she was beautiful, and he asked if he could have a word alone with her dad.

"Sure. But hurry up. I want to see what you have made for us to eat."

"It will only take me a few minutes," he replied as he started to walk toward her father, who was finally out of the car and on his way up the driveway.

"Mr. Brooks, I know what you are planning tonight, and I was hoping to ask for your permission and help with something."

Tim always seemed to know what people were up to, especially the people he was closest to. He paid attention to the little things and was always aware of others' feelings.

"Oh yeah? What am I up to?"

He was betting that Tim knew but still wanted to call him on it. From the first time he had met Tim, he had felt there was something strange about Tim's ability to feel the truth. From what he had seen, Tim was always right about the truth.

"You are going to ask my mom to marry you tonight. I bet you have a ridiculous ring to give her. She'll love it. She has never worn a ring that she didn't buy for herself. Her answer will, of course, be yes. I've been waiting for you to make a move ever since she accepted Christ. I was pretty sure that was all you were waiting for. When I heard you were taking her back to Pasqual's, I knew it was going down tonight. Thankfully for you, I don't think she has a clue. You will rock her world, Mr. Brooks. Please watch her closely after she accepts. I'm pretty sure she'll start feeling unworthy, especially if you bought her a really fancy ring." He knew he was right about every word he had just said.

Mr. Brooks was impressed, as usual. "You got me, Tim. I'm feeling like a little kid tonight. I can't wait to be engaged to her. I want it to be the shortest engagement ever. If she'll marry me next month, that's when we'll do it."

He was so excited that he couldn't help but show Tim all his vulnerability. While he was talking, he could tell that Tim knew exactly how much his mother meant to him.

"Great. I can't wait to move in."

Tim had been thinking about that part for quite some time now. He was tired of them living apart. Living in the same house with Jessica would be a dream come true, though he knew that that would be Mr. Brooks's least favorite part of marrying his mother. Who would want their daughter's boyfriend living in their home?

"I'm just thankful that you two have a pledge of purity. I've got nothing to worry about, right?"

He was pretty sure Tim would honor his pledge but couldn't help but be concerned. After all, his daughter had accepted Tim's proposal.

"Of course not, but you do know you will be my father-in-law someday, right?"

Tim wanted Mr. Brooks to understand how serious he was about committing his life to Jessica. They had spoken about the deal and the importance of purity to their future too many times over the last couple of months since Tim had popped the question to Jessica for him not to have it fresh in his mind.

"I know, Tim. I actually do believe you. What was it you wanted permission for and help with?"

He was nothing like Tim when it came to knowing what others wanted. He tried to be as attentive to others' needs as much as he could, but it was hard work for him. He had an analytical mind, but his creative ability was pretty low. He cared about everyone, but he didn't always see the obvious the way Tim and even Jessica always did.

"I really want to give Jessica a ring. I know she wouldn't care if I made the thing myself, but I would like it to be something kind of nice. I've looked around and found a ring with a three-hundred-and-fifty-dollar price tag that I think she would really like. I can either find a job or do some work for you to pay for it. I won't buy it until I have the money, the way you have shown me the Bible teaches us to handle money. Can you let me do some work for you? If I have to get a real job, I know it will take away from my time with Jessica. You know how busy I am."

Tim knew how Mr. Brooks was going to respond. He was asking for something that would mean the world to his daughter. There was no chance he would say no.

"I can give you three hundred and fifty dollars' worth of work, but you are not going to like it. Maybe you can consider it part of your workout schedule."

Roger had several projects around the house for which he could use a strong back like Tim's to get done. He was really happy to hear the maturity Tim showed by saying he wanted to earn the money for the ring before he bought it. It just reassured him that Tim was the real deal.

"Thank you so much, sir." Tim could hardly wait to start working. "I can start tomorrow morning early if you have something I can start on."

"Sure, but let's make it eight a.m. early, not six a.m. early."

Tim threw his arm around Roger, and they headed in together.

Roger felt like Tim would protect him and Jessica both if they ever needed him to. *It's a really strange feeling to feel like a fifteen-year-old boy could protect you*, he thought. Tim's grip was firm, and Roger could have sworn the kid had grown from the day before. *How big is this guy going to be?* he wondered.

As they walked through the front door, Jessica opened the door to Angela's room and announced her entrance. She was wearing a tight skirt and sweater—a really nice fire-red sweater.

"Sorry I'm not wearing a dress. I only have a couple of them, and I've worn them both for you now, Roger."

Roger's palms suddenly felt clammy. He was just staring at her and couldn't speak. It wasn't that she was any more beautiful than she had been the two times he had seen her in dresses; it was the fact that he knew she was about to be his wife. The reality that she would soon be his wife was crippling him. Since he was unable to speak, he walked right over and hugged her. Jessica and Tim were so happy for their parents that they felt like clapping. Jessica had no idea what was about to happen, but Tim was already a part of it.

Roger finally got his throat cleared and made a snap decision, which was something he rarely did. He pulled out the ring, fell to his knees, and said, "Angela, will you be my wife?"

Well, he kind of said it; it was kind of muffled by his shaking voice. He had meant to do it at the restaurant, but the feelings that were welling up inside him told him that it was time. He wanted the kids to see it as well. What he and Angela had was real love. He wanted them all to know it. It just went against everything that he was to change his plan, but the plan didn't seem to matter to him in that moment. Remembering how he had done it completely out of character was something that Angela would always cherish.

His proposal caught her completely off guard. She fell down on him when her knees gave out. She hadn't completely passed out, but she had lost control for a second. He did his best to catch her, but he couldn't keep her from taking him to the floor. As they rolled over on the floor, the ring went flying across the room.

"Yes, yes, yes..." she cried out, not even paying attention to what had just happened to the beautiful ring. She was holding him now as tightly as she could with no tears; only joy was on her face.

Jessica was almost as surprised as Angela had been. She had no idea that it was coming, but when she saw that ring fly across the room, she sprung into immediate action and nearly caught it. The ring bounced off the TV screen and into a glass of Coke that was sitting on the coffee table. Not knowing what Coke might do to the ring, she grabbed the glass and ran into the bathroom to dump it out and to wash off the ring. As she dried it off, she got a really good look at it. Her dad had done an amazing job picking it out. He could not have found a more perfect ring. She couldn't wait to hand it to Angela.

Angela and Roger were still on the floor when Jessica came back into the room. She took Tim's hand to show him the ring, and with tears in her eyes, she handed it over to Angela.

"I think you are going to want this," she said as she handed it off.

Tim's thoughts went to how it would be when he gave Jessica the ring he was planning to give her. He could hardly wait. His thoughts quickly returned to his mother's wonderful moment and her future with Roger.

Angela had never seen anything so beautiful. The sight of the beautiful ring broke her down. Luckily, she was already on the floor. She laid back and slid it on her finger. It was a bit loose, but Roger assured her they would fit it to her finger if she took it in to the jewelry store.

"It's too big and too beautiful for me," Angela whimpered out.

"It's not even close to big enough or beautiful enough for you, Angela."

He was so excited that she would soon be his wife. He wanted her in their home. He wanted to wake up next to her and, more than anything, make her happy.

Tim was full of joy for his mother. He was happy for Roger too. Everything was going to be okay for his mother now. It was a huge relief for him to have this finally set. He had known for some time where it was all heading, but it felt really good to have it finally set in stone. He, like Roger, hoped for a quick wedding.

Jessica was so proud of her father. He deserved to be happy again. He'd been through so much, but he never used his suffering as an excuse to treat anyone poorly. To see him this in love and so vulnerable melted her heart.

The four of them had just shared an amazing moment. While they enjoyed the significance of what had just happened, Roger's thoughts went back to their dinner reservations and their lateness. He called the restaurant and was able to buy them a half hour.

They all exchanged hugs, and the kids both congratulated their parents. Then Angela and Roger set out for Pasqual's.

They got pretty romantic in the car, and Angela promised him she would be the best wife she could be.

"Can we get married fast?" she asked. "I want to be married to you right now. I want to go home with you right now." She was tired of waiting. They belonged to each other now; it was official.

"I will leave that up to you. I'm in complete agreement, though. I want to take you home and take care of you right now." He was so happy that she didn't want to wait either.

"Roger, we've not discussed it, but I really don't want a wedding. Can we go to Las Vegas tomorrow or next weekend or something and just get it done?"

"Okay. We'll leave for Vegas in the morning. I'll ask Jessica to find us a flight and a hotel. I can get someone to cover my Sunday school class, and we'll be back by Sunday evening. Will that work?" He was again acting differently than he normally would. He was a planner. It all had to be done the right way or he felt uncomfortable. With Angela, he was able to be more spontaneous than he had ever been.

"Yes, that's exactly what I want. I don't want to sleep alone again after tonight. I love you so much." She just wanted it to be done. She wanted him as her husband. She didn't care what her mother or anyone else would think. If her mother wouldn't approve of Roger, no one was good enough.

They were both in agreement, so Roger sent Jessica a text to let her know that they were flying to Vegas to get married the next day. It really surprised Jessica. It wasn't like her dad to do things without a bunch of planning. He rarely made mistakes because he always took his time and prepared for everything. She actually kind of liked it, though. It fit her personality perfectly. Jessica always followed her heart, even if it meant doing something that didn't make sense.

Before they even sat down, Jessica texted him and told him that she and Tim were going to eat and walk to their house to get on the computer to plan the trip. His reply came quickly.

"Great! All four of us will fly. We'll need three rooms."

CHAPTER 28

NO one was notified. No one knew they were even leaving town. They were only a week into the year 2011 when they got on that plane for Vegas to elope. Although they all knew they were doing the right thing, they all felt like they were somehow cheating the system. It felt right, but it also felt like they were getting away with something.

The wedding would be nothing more than an exchange of "I do's." They would get married with the proper vows in front of God, but nothing else mattered. Marriage was between God and the two getting married. They both felt that way. Although they were in a really nice hotel, the wedding was at a little chapel right off of the strip. It was nothing fancy. They had gotten into town at around 3:00 p.m., rented a car, gone directly to city hall to get a wedding license, bought a nice dress for Angela and Jessica and a suit for Tim, and headed right to the chapel. By 7:00 p.m., they were standing face-to-face in front of the pastor, getting married.

It had been short and sweet, but the kiss was long and hard. They had not kissed like that until then, and it felt really good to both of them. Jessica took lots of pictures of everything, and she would later create an album with them. Her dad was no longer all hers, but that was no concern to her. She didn't feel threatened in the least. She could hardly wait to have both Angela and Tim in the same house with her and her father.

Roger gave Jessica and Tim $300 cash and told them to have dinner and see a show or something. They were only given one restriction: no gambling.

"We will see you two in the morning. Get to your rooms by midnight."

Knowing he wouldn't even have to check on them was very settling. Tim and Jessica both always obeyed.

They had three rooms total. All three of them were singles with king beds. One was for the newlyweds, and Tim and Jessica each had their own rooms.

The newlyweds could not keep their hands off one another as soon as they were alone. Angela told him she wanted him in the car, but he managed to convince her to wait until they were alone in their room. When the door to that room they would both never forget opened, the passion exploded. He could not believe how perfect she was physically. Finally touching her was almost too much for him.

Her hard work had chiseled a body that was pretty intimidating to him. It almost felt as if she could overpower him if she wanted to.

For the first time being in a situation that intimate with Roger, Angela had no feelings of inferiority.

Has the Lord completely healed me? she wondered.

Maybe it was just because she could tell he was amazed by her body. He kept telling her how perfect she was. Chuck had never been that complimentary, but Roger couldn't stop. He went on and on about her beauty and how much he loved her. It all felt great to Angela, what he was saying and what they were finally doing together.

They never left the room that night. Dinner was delivered, and Roger went down the hall once for ice, but other than that, the door never opened. They were so into each other that they stayed up until four in the morning. Roger loved Angela so much that he worked tirelessly to make sure she was being pleasured. She had never experienced anything like it. Chuck had always been so rough, and though he was much manlier than Roger, he had never coerced her body into feeling the way Roger was making it feel. Sex had never been for her pleasure with Chuck, while it was all about her pleasure with Roger. She was finally making love, she decided, and it was wonderful. As much as she tried, she could not get enough of Roger. Nor could he get enough of her. Theirs was truly a marriage blessed by God.

The kids had a great evening as well, but without all the love-making. Tim tried to force sex out of his mind, but he knew he would have it with Jessica someday, and he couldn't help but think about it when he looked at her sexy little body. She was so thin with all of the right curves. Jessica had a maturing little body that was starting to approach that of a woman's. For a couple of months, she had been running with his mother, and it was really starting to show.

Thankfully Tim was not about to let those thoughts go unchallenged. He felt conviction to not violate her that way, so he told her he was struggling and asked her to please pray for him. She prayed but didn't tell him that she too was struggling with the same thoughts. They both knew they could go to one of their rooms and have complete privacy.

No one would know, Tim told himself, *and we are already engaged. Who would it hurt?*

It would hurt both of you and your parents, and I would know that you had done it, came the answer in his head.

It's hard being a Christian, he told himself.

After dinner, they went and saw a really great show that cost over $200 for the two of them. Before they knew it, it was 11:30 p.m., so they sat in the hotel lobby, talking for the remaining thirty minutes they had before curfew. Both of them must have said "I love you" twenty times in that thirty minutes. They were really looking forward to the soon-to-come move-in.

"How long will it take you and Angela to move in?" Jessica asked.

"Knowing my mom, we'll be there tomorrow night."

He knew his mother would need to be with Roger all of the time now. He felt like he had picked up that quality from her. He was the type who could fully devote himself to his loved ones.

"I plan to tell people we are boyfriend and girlfriend, not brother and sister." She wasn't trying to be funny but wanted to make sure they had their story straight.

"Of course, you are my live-in girlfriend. Just imagine how cool I will be." Tim was kidding around, but he knew it was also true.

"I don't think you can get any cooler than you already are, future husband."

She liked reminding him that he was hers. Of course, he never needed to be reminded. Neither of them were the jealous type, but they both strived to keep the other at ease by avoiding any potentially uneasy moments with the opposite sex. Neither of them could help but notice the way others looked at them, though. Tim was somewhat of a hero around campus, so girls always wanted to be around him. Jessica was far less popular, but her looks were undeniable. She was rapidly becoming a knock-out, and boys couldn't help but check her out.

As usual, being the responsible type that they both were, they obeyed the instructions they had been given and were in their own rooms by midnight, as promised. Since Tim still didn't have a cell phone, they were unable to text or anything. It truly was lights out. Their night was over.

The four met for a breakfast buffet at 9:00 a.m. There was an easy-to-see difference in the way Angela and Roger were behaving. They held hands and held on to each other the entire time. They even occasionally kissed in public. Jessica had never seen her father display any affection of that sort in public. Angela was really bringing him out of his shell. They seemed to be glowing, and they were practically incapable of having a conversation outside of their love trance. Tim and Jessica teased the lovebirds all morning.

"Why don't you two get a room?" Tim joked.

"We have one, and we'll leave for it if you two don't stop teasing us," answered Angela.

"Our plane leaves at four p.m., so we need to be in the car at about two p.m. My wife and I will meet you guys in the lobby at one thirty p.m. Please check your bags in at the concierge's desk before noon. We need to be out of the rooms by then."

He had plans for him and Angela that didn't include the kids.

"No problem, Dad," answered Jessica. "Can we have some more money, though? Tim and I spent it all last night. We actually only have about ten bucks left." Money didn't seem to go very far in Las Vegas, and Jessica was pretty sure her father would pay them off to be alone with Angela the rest of the morning.

"Here's a hundred dollars. When we get home, all of this money spending has to stop. I've had to dip into our savings to pay for all of these dinners, football tickets, and travel."

He didn't want to sound the way he just had about it, but he really was worried about how much they had been spending. Roger had always been careful with money. He believed in managing every penny, and he was feeling reckless with all the spending they had been doing.

"We'll see you at one thirty for a hundred dollars then." She gave him her cutest smile and grabbed the money out of his hand. "To the machines!" she joked.

"Before we all separate, when can me and my mom expect to move in?" Tim needed to know. It was all that had been on his mind since the vows had been exchanged.

"Your mother and I decided that we'll go from the airport to your place to pick up some clothes for you guys. You're moving in tonight. You and your mother are officially our family now, and you two belong in our home."

He was so proud to have her as his wife. Part of him felt a little strange, as he had had a wife whom he had loved very much and he still felt like he loved Caroline. She was gone now, and Angela was now his partner for the rest of his life. It was sad that Caroline had died before her time, but it had been almost three years since she had passed. He told himself that he had no reason to feel like he was dishonoring her or his love for her by marrying Angela.

"Can I call you Dad now? If not now, I will once Jessica and I get married."

Inside, he was hoping Roger would adopt him so he could have their same name and not feel like an outsider in any way. He knew that wasn't the right thing to do, though. He needed to keep his father's name, and he wanted to do it proud. It would be too weird for him to be adopted and then marry his sister. Even if it was only a name change without an adoption, he decided he wanted Jessica to have his name when they got married.

Roger suddenly felt a knot in his stomach. He was starting to well up. "I would love for you to call me Dad. I'd absolutely love it, Tim."

He was trying to hold back his emotion, but Tim wanting to call him Dad felt great. He knew Tim wanted to call him Dad because he loved and respected him, and that made him feel honored.

"Dad it is then."

Then he looked at his mother to see if she was okay with it. She looked happy that he was accepting Roger that way.

"Can I call you Mom then, Mrs. Wiseman? Oh, I'm sorry, Mrs. Brooks." She felt like an idiot. *How could I screw that up?*

"You can call me anything you want, sweetheart." She was touched by Jessica wanting to call her Mom. She didn't know if Jessica would feel comfortable doing that since her mother had been such a great mom. "I would love to have you call me Mom."

"Okay, Mom. You got it."

She did feel a little uncomfortable saying it, but she liked Angela a lot and knew it would get easier to say with time. Angela had been so accepting of her. She was her running partner, and there was no one better to talk to about how great Tim was. What she loved most about Angela was that she was her dad's happiness. She had not seen him that happy since before her mother had passed. It felt really good to know there would be a woman in the house again too, especially one as good at keeping a house clean as Angela was. Housework had always been a challenge for Jessica. When her mother was still alive, her dad had said that she was the only person in the house who could upset her mother. It had always been about the state of her room or a mess she had left somewhere in the house. Since her mother had passed, she had pushed herself very had to fight her natural tendencies. Her room was the only room she got to live like herself in.

The two couples split, the new husband and wife to their room for one last memory in the room where it all began and then to a nice private lunch. The youngsters headed to the shops at Caesar's Palace and to a nice lunch at the Venetian hotel. They were all back a bit earlier than the set meeting time and had no trouble making their flight.

That night was the first night that Tim and his mom, Mrs. Brooks, slept in their new home. Tim had slept there one other time, but he had been a guest. Now the guest room was his room. They both slept like rocks, and they knew they were finally home. The past was finally behind them, as was their torment. God was so good.

CHAPTER 29

T didn't take much of an effort to move their stuff out of their old house. When Angela called Chuck's Mom, Kathy, to tell her about her marriage and that she and Tim were moving, she was happy to hear the excitement in Kathy's voice. Kathy was in a happy marriage now and had been praying for the same for Angela. She knew firsthand how her son had treated Angela. No one had felt worse about it than she had. She knew he was who he was because of her. Though it would have been difficult for any single woman to raise a son like Chuck on their own, Kathy knew she had failed at giving him her best effort. She had been to selfish and careless in her pursuit of meeting her own needs that she hadn't given Chuck the love and priority he required. As a result, all her son had ever done was hurt people. The only good thing Chuck ever did was have Tim and pick a great woman, Angela, to have him with.

"I am so happy for both of you, Angela. You guys deserve this." Kathy had practically raised Tim. Her biggest regret was that she and John had only visited Tim and Angela twice since Chuck had passed. She wished they were able to be more involved in their lives.

"I wanted to let you know before Tim sent you an e-mail or told you over the phone. I have never been happier, Mom."

Angela had been calling Kathy Mom for most of Tim's life. To her, Kathy was more her mother than her real mother was. Tim was always sending Grandma e-mails, and he religiously called her once a week. He would talk to both Kathy and John and told them everything. They actually already knew that Angela was on the path to marriage, that she had accepted Christ, and that Tim was also engaged. Tim kept nothing from them.

"Tim told us that this was going to happen soon. He also told us you have accepted Christ into your life. John and I cried together when we heard that news." John was a strong Christian, and he had led Kathy to Christ years earlier.

"It's true. I feel so loved right now. Everything is great in my life. I would have never imagined I could ever have all of this." She was starting to cry a bit, so she decided to move into the business part of the call. "We are selling the house. Do you guys want anything out of it before we sell it? It's pretty much all your stuff." That was true, but it had been eight years since Kathy had lived there.

"No, honey. It's your house and your stuff. You have paid all the bills for years now. I hope you can make some money off it."

It felt great to say that. She felt like she owed Angela for what her son had done to her and Tim. It felt like she was giving her sort of a wedding gift.

"Thank you, Mom."

Angela loved Kathy deeply, and she only wished she could have the same type of relationship with her real mother.

Though she didn't want to even talk to her mother, she went to visit her anyway. As she had expected, it went poorly. Her mother put her down and told her she would always be trash and that Tim would always be like his horrible father, Chuck. The visit only lasted a few minutes, and Angela, for the first time, didn't get angry or reduced to tears by what her mother had said. Instead, she felt really sad and disappointed for her mother, who was completely alone in the world.

"I'm sorry you feel that way, Mom. I'll pray for you, and I'll always love you." As she turned to leave, her mother's reply reinforced her disappointment.

"Pray for me. Why would any God listen to your prayers?"

Angela didn't even acknowledge her. She just kept walking right back into her amazing new life.

Though it took almost two months to sell, Angela was able to come out $35,000 ahead on the house. She had never come out ahead in anything in life until Roger, and now her life seemed filled with blessings. Sure, she still struggled with things and occasionally felt down or even a bit depressed, but Roger was always there to cheer her up. God was always listening to her prayers and refining her through small trials that she could definitely handle. Life was really good.

Roger treated her so well that she truly felt like his equal in their marriage. They kept no secrets, and everything was a completely open book between them. Roger gave her complete access to everything in his life, including his finances, which were now their finances. It was even better than she could have imagined.

Roger worshiped Angela, and she quickly began to feel comfortable as his wife. They were all over each other whenever they were alone, and he even began to work out a bit with Tim to try to improve himself for her. There was no part of their marriage that could be improved. It was all perfect.

CHAPTER 30

ROGER had been pushing Angela to quit her job at the supermarket. He told her that she should be doing something she really loved with her time. Once the $35,000 was in their account, he started pushing even harder. She was finally convinced and agreed that she would go to college, as she had always felt like she should have. Her mother had been right about that. She had no idea what she wanted to study or be. All she knew was that she wanted a degree. Any degree would do.

Basketball season had gone quickly for Tim, and he was almost through with track. He loved to run to work out for football, but he only competed in the throws as a member of the track team. Shot put was his favorite, though he was a pretty good discus thrower as well. As a freshman, he was throwing just over fifty feet in the shot put and around a hundred and twenty feet in the discus. He was now six feet three inches tall, and he had gained another five pounds. With Tim at 215 pounds, Coach Briening was happy with his progress. He was watching Tim closely to make sure he was still growing.

Will he be as big and bad as his father? his coach wondered.

Tim had a goal to break all of his father's records. The school records in both the shot put and the discus were his father's. The shot put record was 59 feet 3 inches. The discus record was 170 feet 6 inches. Both were some distance away from what he was throwing. Tim knew he had only two more seasons to get there, as he was planning to graduate early.

Tim and Jessica had been working on their plans for the future almost every night. Though planning wasn't really in Jessica's nature, Tim planned everything. Most of their talks about the future were really about his plans. He was always seeking for her input, though, as they were, as he put it, "Not my plans, but our plans."

He had thought a lot about them getting married. He told Jessica he could not waste any time getting married once he had become an adult and graduated. Jessica completely agreed with that plan. Tim also spent a considerable amount of time planning college for them. He told Jessica he would go to college wherever she wanted to go. Since they were both straight-A students, he figured she would want to go to whichever school offered the program she wanted the most. For him, it didn't matter. There were lots of acceptable schools as far as he was concerned. It did have to be a division one school for football reasons, but beyond that, her being in the school of her choice was the most important thing to him.

Getting married in the same chapel their parents had been married in was another thing they had already agreed on. They wanted to have only their parents and grandparents there, and they wanted it to be their senior trip. The plan was soon conceived that would allow for the quickest marriage possible under the constraints he and Jessica had set. Jessica was a year ahead of Tim in school, so they would have to wait until Tim graduated. Neither of them felt that a year was doable, so Tim decided to graduate at Christmas time the semester after Jessica graduated. That way he could play his senior year of football before he graduated. He felt confident that, through football, his grades, and his high test scores, he would get a scholarship to whatever school Jessica chose.

Jessica never worried about Tim's judgment. She trusted him completely and had never seen him be wrong about anything he was sure about. His instincts were always right, it seemed. If he said he could get a football scholarship to any school she chose, she believed that he could.

Tim even had the forethought to think that he could probably get Jessica into any school she wanted to get into by letting them know he was going wherever she went. He decided that would be wrong and asked her to not let anyone other than their parents know their plans. He didn't want any scandal around his college choice. They agreed to keep their wedding plans a secret from everyone but their parents and grandparents.

Tim hoped to stay close to home when it was time to go off to college, and he was pretty sure Jessica would want the same. His top choices were Texas, Texas A&M, Texas Tech, or Rice. Jessica always wanted to go to Rice but wasn't sure if she could get in or if Tim would want to go there since she knew that his ultimate goal was the NFL. Thankfully they still had lots of time to decide.

Though things could not have been going better for all of them, the world around them was becoming unstable. Since the war on terror had begun back in 2001 after the 9/11 terrorists attacks, the United States had been struggling economically. The costs associated with the war, along with the ever-expanding US government, had been driving the national debt up more quickly than anything the United States had ever seen before. Causes such as the "global warming" movement were costing the United States in ways no one seemed to be able to calculate. Though it was business as usual for most of America, the landscape had been changing for dozens of years. No longer was the United States a major exporter. No more was the United States the leader in education or almost anything else.

Roger followed the news with an eye toward the heavens. He knew the Bible was all true, which meant the end would not be an easy time for anyone. It would be exceptionally difficult for Christ's followers. He discussed it all with Tim, while neither of the girls wanted to hear about the impending doom.

CHAPTER 31

B^Y the end of the track season his freshman year in the year 2011, Tim had finally put in enough time working for Roger to save up the money he needed for Jessica's ring. Roger even went with him to buy it, and the two talked about his plans for giving it to her. They decided that to do it right, he needed to take her somewhere special. It would take another few weeks of work to earn enough for the date. That seemed like nothing to Tim at this point.

Roger was impressed with Tim's focus, work ethic, and ability to honor his word. He was so proud of the kid. More than anything, he loved it when Tim called him Dad. He was beginning to feel like Tim was his own son and couldn't imagine any father loving their son more or being more proud than he was of Tim.

It had been just over five months since Tim's birthday, and now it was Jessica's. On May 12, Jessica would be sixteen. Roger and Tim agreed that her sixteenth birthday would be a perfect time for Tim's engagement ring. Roger took the opportunity to joke around a bit.

"I always knew she was an overachiever, but wearing an engagement ring at sixteen was even better than I could have ever imagined."

"Very funny, Dad," was all Tim could think of in response.

When Angela sold the house, Roger had convinced her to buy a new car with most of the money. He told her she should buy something with cash that she felt comfortable in with the intent of driving it for five years or more. She could put the rest of the money, which turned out to be just over $10,000, into their savings to help pay for her college tuition. They decided to give her old car to Jessica for her sixteenth birthday. It was a nice car, a 2006 Honda Accord that Angela had just finished paying off. Jessica was happy with the car and could hardly wait until she had her license so she could take Tim out on a date without a drop-off and pick-up.

Tim executed his plan so well that he didn't even have to decide where to take Jessica as she came to him with the plan.

"I get my license tomorrow," she told him. "On Friday night, I want to take you to Pasqual's for my birthday dinner. My dad is giving me money for dinner for my birthday. We can go see a movie after if you want." She was only focused on her being able to drive him to dinner and the great meal at their favorite restaurant. She had no clue what he was planning or what he might give her for her birthday. Though she had noticed all of the work Tim had been doing for her father and that her father had been paying him for it, she always assumed he was saving it up for something else. It never crossed her mind that he could be saving it for her gift.

Roger had been concerned that he might reveal that Tim had big plans by offering to buy them dinner at Pasqual's. When Tim had come to him with the plan, he initially doubted that Jessica would buy it without being suspicious.

"She has nothing to be suspicious about, Dad. You always spoil her. She won't have any clue she's being set up," Tim assured him.

Jessica would have no clue that Tim had done work for the money he instructed Roger to give Jessica for her birthday dinner with Tim. Tim was confident that she would never know it. Roger thought she might wonder why he would send them alone to such an expensive restaurant when he and Angela had already given her the car for her birthday.

Tim had simply asked him, "Why would she be suspicious? You have never denied her anything."

Roger had to agree. One thing was for sure: if Jessica were Tim, she would have probably figured out that something was up. Roger was sure of that.

"That sounds great, Jessica. I hate that you are going to be older than me again. You'll be holding that 'respect your elders' thing over me for the next seven months. What time is dinner?"

He had done nothing but dream about giving her that ring since Roger had told him he could work for him to pay for it. He knew how much it would mean to her to have a reminder of their love and future on her finger.

Tim knew that the delivery was important, but he decided not to make a big production of it. He would simply hand her the ring after they were through eating. What he would say would be much more important than how he would present the ring. He had decided he would tell her, "This ring symbolizes our love and commitment to each other. I hope you will honor me by wearing it for the rest of your life." He and Roger had agreed that keeping it simple was the best way to go.

"Dad made us a reservation for seven p.m. I plan to wear that pretty dress Dad got me to go to your birthday dinner. Do you remember it?" She hoped he would remember. She loved the way she looked in it and hoped he did too.

"That really sexy white dress? Oh yeah, I remember that. I think about you in that dress way too much. It will be really nice to see you in it again. It's finally going to happen again. I've been waiting for this. Are you sure this isn't my birthday?"

He wondered how different she would look in it. It had been more than five months, and Jessica had really been filling out. She had gone from tiny with some curves to a full-blown chesty knockout. She was a full-grown woman now, and Tim didn't think she could possibly get any better looking.

How will she look in that dress now that her body has hit full womanhood? he wondered.

"Now I'll be self-conscious all night long, Tim. I hope my dress won't distract you too much. I was hoping to plan our summer over dinner."

She knew Tim wasn't kidding about how he felt about her in that dress. It really flattered her to hear him say that he had been thinking about that. She loved knowing he thought about her.

Tim was starting to feel bad about how he had been thinking of her body. He never wanted her to think that was the foundation of his attraction to her, but was it? He knew the answer was no, but he couldn't stop thinking about her body, and it made him question himself. The thoughts he was having about her forced him to pray for the ability to block her body out of his mind. At that moment, though, it wasn't working.

"I love how you look in that dress, but it's everything else about you that I really love. I thought we were going to that summer camp to be counselors for the summer?"

He was really looking forward to spending a month of his summer as a camp counselor. The rest of the time he needed to try to make some money and spend as much time as possible getting ready for football. Prepping for football season meant lots of running and weight lifting. The down side of camp was that he had never felt particularly comfortable with young kids—kids under the age of twelve. Jessica was great with them, but he was kind of awkward around them. Tim was good with the adults, though—really good. He was just so grown up, and he thought like a much older person.

"Yes, I want to go to the camp. I just thought we could talk about it over dinner. You have never been there, so I wanted to tell you about all of the great things we will get to do together. We'll have a new group of kids in there every week for four weeks, but we get a day alone without any kids in between each group. That's what I wanted to plan with you."

She had been thinking about camp a lot. Just last year, she had been there alone. She remembered lying there at night, wondering if she would ever meet a guy like her dad. She even remembered praying to God to bring her a man like her father. She hadn't expected it this soon, though.

"That sounds like fun. You know how I like to plan. You are wearing my favorite dress, we are going for the best steaks in the world, and we get to spend the night planning. Are you sure it's not my birthday?" He was kidding, but he was also being very honest. *If she only knew about the ring I plan to give her, how different she might feel right now*, he thought. He wondered if she had even thought about what he might give her for her birthday.

"I'm just happy that you will be happy on my birthday, Tim. Remember, I will soon be your elder. Also, I'm driving. You better be nice or you will walk home. I hope you got me something nice."

"Was I supposed to get you something?" he joked. "Good thing we still have some time."

He didn't want to tip his hand. He knew the ring was going to really touch her heart. There was no better gift he could give her. He also knew it wasn't what something was worth that would impress Jessica. She would rather have him make something and put a lot of thought into it than buy her something expensive. He loved that quality about her.

"You'd better be kidding, though just spending time with you is gift enough for me." Though that was probably true, just the thought of him not getting her anything seemed impossible. He loved her too much and was always about her feelings and needs before his own. She felt like he would take a bullet for her.

"My presence is your present. I like that!" *This is going to be perfect. Everything is just right.*

CHAPTER 32

ROGER and Angela sat in the living room, waiting for Jessica with Tim. Everyone was aware of his gift except for Jessica. As expected, Jessica had passed the driving test with flying colors. That night would be her first time to take Tim out alone. While they sat and waited, Roger and Angela kept smiling in his direction.

"You guys are going to blow the surprise," Tim warned them.

"No, we won't. She thinks we are just happy for her to be driving. It's a big deal, Tim," his mother shot back.

"I guess you are right. I can't believe this, but I'm actually nervous about tonight."

As Jessica came down the stairs, all eyes were on her. When her full body came into view, Roger felt like covering her up. Though nothing about how she was dressed was inappropriate, his natural instinct was to protect her from men's wondering eyes. Thankfully he had the ability to restrain himself.

"You look like a full-grown, beautiful woman, baby," he managed to say.

It made her blush, and she felt a little self-conscious about how revealing the dress was. "Is it okay to wear out, Dad? I don't want to leave the house with you feeling uncomfortable." She could tell he was really uncomfortable with how she was dressed. She had been cautious how she dressed her whole life and didn't want to change now.

"I'm sorry, baby. It's just hard for me to see you growing up like this. I can't believe what a beautiful woman you have become." He was blown away at how sexy she was in that dress. He didn't like it at all.

"You really do look great, Jessica," added Angela.

"Thanks, Mom," said Jessica as the two gave each other a loving hug. Roger loved seeing how close Angela and Jessica were becoming. They spent so much time together, and they seemed to be the best of friends already.

Tim was unable to speak for a while. He was astonished the changes her body had been through in five short months. She had been amazing in that dress when she wore it for his birthday, but now she was filling it in a whole new way. Though it held everything in place and nothing was exposed that shouldn't have been, the dress simply didn't hide a thing. She looked like a twenty-five-year-old fitness model in the dress. Tim was almost embarrassed for her. He wondered if she knew what type of attention she would get by wearing the dress out.

"I agree with Dad. I'm a little jealous too. I hope you don't realize you can do better than me." He wanted to keep it light, but inside, it was feeling heavy. He knew he loved her for the right reasons, but seeing her in that dress, all he could think about right then was that ridiculously sexy body. He had never felt so uncomfortable around her, and his instinct was to cover her up, much like her father's first instinct had been.

"You have nothing to be jealous of, Tim. You must be kidding that I can do better than you. No one is better than you at anything. Don't forget that we are engaged and that I will be your wife in less than three years."

She looked over at her dad as she said all of that and noticed he was nodding in agreement. She still couldn't believe that he was on board with their arrangement, their covenant. He did still have Bible studies with Tim, and he had once told her that he had never met a young man who prayed more for other people's needs than Tim did. Her father loved Tim and admired him as much as she did.

"That's right."

He was still trying to act like her being dressed that sexy was no big deal in spite of all of the praise everyone, including him, was giving her. Inside, he was fighting with himself to not stare at her. She was wearing a necklace with a heart with a picture of him in it that she used to have a picture of her dad in. Her dad didn't know the picture had been switched, but Tim did. When he noticed that it was out in plain sight, he felt like getting her out of there before anyone could ask her about the necklace. It would kill him to have Roger see that she had replaced his picture with his picture in that necklace. He even wished he didn't know that Roger's picture had been in there.

"Before we go, I wanted to show Mom my necklace."

He could feel his heart pounding as Jessica leaned into his mother and opened that little heart to show her his picture. That was really bad. He was shocked that she had not thought about how offensive it would be to her father to know he had been replaced in a necklace he had bought for her.

"It's the two men in our lives," his mother said like it was the sweetest thing ever. Tim was relieved that Jessica had only added his picture and not replaced her father's. She had shown him the necklace with her father's picture in it, and when she told him his picture was going in there so she could have him in her heart, he had assumed that her father's picture was coming out. Thank God he was wrong. What a relief.

As they left the house, Jessica told him she wanted to remember that night, and Roger took several pictures of them climbing into the car and driving off. Tim was thankful she was helping capture memories of the night, as he knew it was a night they would both want to always remember.

Dinner was amazing, but Tim felt himself consumed with what was to come. He knew how much joy it would bring her, so he could hardly wait to give it to her. It represented a lot of hard work, but more than that, it represented his love for her. The conversation was great, and they were able to plan out their entire summer. All the planning helped him get through the meal. He liked that.

Since the time they had first opened the door to the restaurant, Tim had felt uncomfortable with the looks Jessica was getting from men. He hated that he was feeling jealous, and it worried him that he felt like knocking someone out. He had seen his father beat on guys for looking at his mother the same way men were looking at Jessica, but he wanted to be different than his father had been. It hurt him to have men looking at his precious Jessica the way he saw them looking at her, and the experience allowed him to understand why his father had beaten those guys for looking at his mother lustfully.

How could they not stare? he decided.

She was a rare beauty, and he bet most people thought she was much older than sixteen. He didn't know any other sixteen-year-olds who looked as sexy and grown up as she did. It bothered him so much that he had to share it with her.

"I'm so sorry, Tim. When I put the dress on, I felt uncomfortable in it. When my dad reacted the way he did, I knew it was wrong. I love how you look at me in it, but from now on, I will never wear it in public again. This is not who I am. I like nice clothes and to dress up, but my body is changing, and I need to be more careful how I dress. I really am sorry. I feel terrible about this. I felt men looking at me when we came in, and I hated it." She hated disappointing him and her dad, but she was thankful that he was being honest with her.

Tim hadn't even told her it was wrong. All he had said was that he felt jealous of all of the attention she got from men in her dress. He told her it made him feel like fighting all of them. She was his, and he would defend her. His face was full of emotion as he explained his feelings to her.

"Don't feel that way, Jessica. You can't help it if you are perfect on both the inside and outside. Please don't feel bad. I hate other men looking at you like you are some sort of sex object. It's also really hard for me to not fantasize about you when I see you in something like this dress. We have a long way to go before we can be together physically, and I don't want to fail you. It's so hard for me not to think of you sexually. I know it's wrong, but my mind wants to think about you that way constantly. Please understand that it's not your fault. It's your body. It would really help if you would make me wonder more about what's under your clothes. You have always done a good job at this, so I'm not even sure why I brought this up tonight. You are just too amazing for me to keep out of my dreams as it is."

She started to cry and told him she would be more careful. When she thought about it, she realized how careful he was to not show off his body. He always wore loose clothing, and he only took his shirt off when he was alone or in a locker room. She had seen him swimming and had felt his hard body against hers many times when they had hugged, but the more she thought about it, she realized he really was saving himself for her. Even when the other track guys took their shirts off at practice to get their bodies tan, he kept his T-shirt on. His body was far better than anyone else's she had ever seen, yet he didn't flaunt it at all. Even at the gym, he never had his arms exposed and seemed to always have on long shorts or sweat pants.

Seeing that he had upset her really made him feel bad. He decided it was time to spring the ring on her, as he knew that it would make up for the stupidity of his jealousy.

"I have something for you, Jessica." He handed her the open box with the ring exposed. "This ring symbolizes our love and commitment to each other. I hope you will honor me by wearing it for the rest of your life."

It was much more difficult to get out than he thought it would be, but he was so happy to have said it just the way he had planned it that he didn't mind the struggle. Except for his tears, which had not been in the plan, everything had come out as planned.

Seeing the ring hit her hard. It was too much for her, and she began to break as she reached out and took the ring right out of the tiny box. She appeared at first as if she was going into some state of shock, but she quickly snapped out of it.

"This is so beautiful. I'll never take it off. It is perfect, and it will make me think of you whenever I look at it."

He had never seen her smile so hard. Her tears were gone, and only pure joy was on her face. She scooted even closer to him in their private booth, and they kissed on the lips deeper than they ever had. He put his arm around her and told her he would always be there for her.

"I want to set a date for our wedding. Can we do that, Jessica?" He wanted to know when the waiting would be over. He needed to know when she would truly be his, both in spirit and in flesh.

"Me too, Tim. I want to look forward to that day. I want to count the days. I want to know there is one day less to wait every day I wake up. I want to book our hotel and flights too." She had already been looking into it.

"I also want to know what your number one college choice is, Jessica. If it's Rice, I want you to know I would love to go there together. I bet I can get married housing through the athletic department." He knew he could if he could just stay healthy and keep working at both football and school.

"Yes, if I can get in, I want to go to Rice. It's always been my dream to go there, but I want you to be able go to Texas if that will help you make it to the NFL. I have to live with you or I'll explode, so I will go wherever you need to go, Tim."

She had always wanted to go to Rice. Ever since she had heard how hard it was to get in, it had been an obsession of hers. She never told Tim it was that big of a deal to her because she wasn't sure she really could get in and was even more worried that Rice was not even on his list. The truth was that it wasn't on his list until he heard how she talked about it. Then it was number one for him. She didn't really need to tell him how she felt about it; he had picked it up and even talked it over with Roger. Roger told him about her fascination with Rice, so he knew she wanted to go. Since he also understood how difficult it was to get in, he wanted to afford her the opportunity to change her mind about it if she didn't get accepted.

They worked it all out before they left for an ice cream and a two-hour talk in a romantic parking spot with a great view of the entire town. Once the wedding date was set, they began to prepare themselves for their lives together. Tim wanted to play in the NFL, but after that he wanted to do something for the Lord. He even considered becoming a pastor. Jessica just wanted to be married to Tim. The college part was important, but being Tim's wife was all that really mattered to her.

CHAPTER 33

THAT summer brought Tim and Jessica so close that they felt like they were becoming one. They prayed together, went to church together, and had life together. Every meal was together, and they never saw a movie without the other. The more time they spent together, the stronger their young love got.

Roger and Angela quickly became one as well. They had an ideal marriage, and they too spent as much time as humanly possible in each other's company.

Tim's sophomore year was a tremendous success. He made all-state in both football and track and almost broke both of his father's throwing records. His body continued to develop, as did his mind. He was over six feet four inches tall by the end of the summer. His transcript had straight A's every semester he had been in high school. Tim's hard work and determination continued while his chances of going to any college he wanted to actually improved. He and Jessica were a year closer to marriage, and he and Roger's relationship was growing stronger every day.

His sophomore year had also been a strong witnessing year for Tim. He had begun to find his passion for helping his friends surrender their lives to Jesus. Although he completely avoided leading the opposite sex to Christ, he was committed to bringing every guy he knew to the Lord. His method was one of strength. Because he was who he was, most guys respected him. Everyone knew that he didn't drink, and no one had anything bad to say about him. That, along with his status as living legend, made it easy for him to influence those who knew him. Tim's ability to see the details and to see things coming before they happened allowed him to reach people when they were ready. All of this, along with the knowledge of God's Word he had obtained through intense Bible study with Roger, made him a powerful witness.

He and Jessica went to camp again the summer after Tim's sophomore year, and, as before, it was amazing. They continued to stay pure for one another and were both sure they would make it. They felt like God was blessing their commitment to doing things his way by making it easier for them to be together without longing for intimacy.

Tim became so successful at bringing in hurting people that they had to begin structuring the Sunday school and Wednesday night services differently at their church. The church as well as decisions for Christ were growing at such an accelerated rate that major changes were needed to keep up with the demand. Tim knew everyone personally and was a wiz at remembering details that allowed him to reach each one of them. Each soul knew he really cared that they come to Christ. The number of people calling on him was growing so rapidly that it was actually starting to become a major drain on him. He was either at school, practice, the weight room, or church. When he was at home, he was either spending time doing homework or studying the Bible with Roger. No matter what, he always gave Jessica a minimum of one hour of his time every day. They also ate every meal they could together.

Tim's junior year of football was nothing short of miraculous. He just simply could not be blocked. He truly had become a man among boys. Every major program in the country was watching him. His play took the team to the state championship game in which they just fell short of the state title. Tim and Coach Briening were both confident they would win it all Tim's senior year. Coach Briening had grown to admire Tim so much that he had even followed his lead and accepted Christ into his life.

When track rolled around his junior year, Tim knew it was his final shot at his father's records, as he was still on track to graduate midway through his senior year. With his conversion to the rotational technique in the shot put, he was able to take state and break both his father's school record and the sixty-foot barrier. He barely got the discus record by a few inches and finished third in the state by throwing his best distance of his high school carrier of 173'9" at the state meet.

Jessica graduated at the top of her class and decided to spend her first semester at home while attending Sam Houston State. Being with Tim was much more important to her than running off to college. She had maintained her 4.0 grade point average all the way through high school and had been awarded a scholarship to Rice. She graduated with the class of 2013 and was actually number two in her class. The scholarship she was awarded would cover about half her costs, leaving about $25,000 per year that her parents would have to bear. The application and interview process had been grueling, but she was happy with the result.

Rice worked with her to postpone her first semester on a family hardship. Her admittance was to the engineering program, as she respected her father so much that she could think of no better thing to be than what he was. Math and science being her strongest subjects made the decision easy. Everything was falling into place.

After another great summer camp and a final summer full of weight training, Tim reported to the first day of practice for his final season of high school football. Coach Briening was shocked when he saw him. Tim had been through his biggest growth spurt yet. Coach could hardly wait for weigh-in and was ecstatic with the results. Tim was now six feet seven inches tall, and he weighed almost 270 pounds. He was an Adonis.

Tim had visited Rice over the summer with the whole family when they had all gone to see where Jessica was going to be attending college. The coach was happy that Tim would even visit. He had no clue that Tim's girlfriend had been accepted or that she was even applying to come to Rice. When Tim told him he had made up his mind and he wanted to come to school there, he was assured that he would have a scholarship and was told that they could not make an official offer until the national signing day or the day after he had graduated high school. It was an easy decision for the Rice coach, as Tim was listed as the number one prospect in the country, and that was when they thought he was six foot five and weighed about 255 pounds. Add his 4.0 grade point average and off-the-chart test scores, as well as his reputation as a leader and a clean kid, and it was almost too good for any coach to land him. The coach understood Tim's situation and told him the married housing wouldn't be an issue. Tim told him that he wanted to play for three years before he would enter his name into the NFL draft. His intention was to graduate before entering the draft. No one doubted that Tim would accomplish everything he planned to accomplish when he planned to accomplish it.

To make things perfectly clear, Tim told Coach Briening about his decision to go to Rice on the first day of practice his senior year. He also asked his coach to please make it public information so he wouldn't have to deal with all of the college recruiters. Coach agreed and called the paper to tell them about Tim's college decision and his decision to retire after the season. Both were front-page news in the local paper the next day.

It all went as planned. Tim dominated all year long, and the team won the state championship. He had started all season at defensive end, and he broke every record his dad had ever set. Actually, he broke just about any defensive record the team recorded. He also played about half the plays on offense. His great hands and speed made him an unstoppable tight end. He set numerous receiving records, including touchdowns in a season for a tight end.

When the season finally ended and his body was still intact, Tim was relieved. His college plans were set, and soon he would marry his soul mate. They had patiently waited for almost three years. Their love had remained pure, and being married to Jessica was all he was focused on. Graduation day for him would not be graduation day for anyone else, but he really couldn't have cared less about graduation. He cared much more about the weekend after graduation.

Tim was number one in his class, but since he was graduating alone, he got no awards for his achievements. What he did earn was a wife, and he could hardly wait to close the deal. Angela and Roger had worked with Jessica to get everything just right for the trip to Las Vegas. Roger's parents were making the trip, as were John and Kathy, Chuck's mom and her husband. The final couple was Caroline's parents, who had grown to love both Angela and Tim. No friends were invited. That had always been the plan. Only Jessica's best friend, Michelle, was invited. She was the one exception, and it had really been Tim who had insisted she come. He wanted Jessica to have Michelle with her, as they had been best friends all their lives.

Sadly, Angela's mother turned down her invitation to the wedding. Actually, they never got a reply at all from her. She never even responded to Tim, her only grandchild.

CHAPTER 34

ANGELA, Jessica, and Michelle went up to Las Vegas the day before Roger and Tim so they could prepare and have some girl time. They had chosen the MGM Grand as the hotel but had decided to get married in the same chapel that their parents had been married in almost three years earlier. Everyone was staying in a block of rooms on the same floor, six rooms total. Tim would share a room with Roger, while Angela, Michelle, and Jessica shared another the night before the wedding. Michelle would get her own room the night following the wedding, while Angela and Roger would have their own room, as would Jessica and Tim. Angela had grown so attached to Roger that the thought of even one night without him was not a happy thought. The other rooms were for the grandparents.

Jessica had found a beautiful white dress three months before the wedding. She was so happy to be able to wear white. Tim had always loved her in white. She had not even worn anything revealing since the night he had given her the ring. Though Tim had seen her in her one-piece swimsuits many times, she had not done anything to tempt him.

Since it had such an impact on Tim the last time she had worn it, Jessica decided to bring the dress she had worn the night Tim had given her the engagement ring. She planned to wear it the night before the wedding, when the whole group would be together for dinner. She wanted to drive Tim crazy and didn't even care if anyone else looked at her. Yes, she had made a deal with Tim not to tempt him by wearing anything that sexy around him, but she didn't care anymore, as their waiting would soon be over. As far as her disgust at the thought of other men looking at her, she decided that anyone who had the guts to stare at her when she was on Tim's arm would have to have a death wish. Tim looked like a freak at that point. It was almost unreal. People stared at him wherever they went. No one ever messed with him, though he was a pussy cat inside.

Tim and Roger were getting in just before dinner. For that reason, Tim wouldn't see Jessica until he arrived at the family dinner. The dress would be a big surprise for him. She knew it would make their final night alone the most difficult night he had ever endured, and she loved the thought of it.

When Angela saw her, she laughed and said, "That's not fair. You are going to kill him in that."

"I hope so. I want him to not sleep tonight. I want him to want me the way I want him. Do you think this will do it?" She knew it would but wanted some reassurance.

"Oh, that will do it. I hope your dad doesn't faint when he sees you in it again, though." She remembered this dress and the long conversation she and Jessica had had about not dressing in a seductive way after that night. Angela, more than anyone, knew not to tempt men by dressing sexy or flaunting your body. She was painfully aware ever since she had been violated by her uncle. Angela had shared those terrible events with Jessica when she urged her to cover up and to never tempt men with her body or with her words or actions. Tonight would have to be an exception, though. Angela was in complete agreement. She hoped her son would learn how important it was for a wife to have her husband desire her. No one knew how important it was more than she did.

"You will keep Dad's eyes off me tonight. You look unbelievable, Mom. We are both dressing more risqué than usual tonight."

Jessica could hardly believe that the waiting was almost over. She would lay with Tim in bed and hold him for the rest of her life. She would smother him with love and give herself to him as much as he could have her. Though they had agreed that they would not start a family until they were out of college, she couldn't help but think about having children with him. She wanted at least three, and she knew he would give them to her if she wanted them. He wanted a family too, but he didn't have a number in mind. Still, part of Jessica was scared. Finally being with Tim was exciting, but it was also causing some fear of failure that she hadn't expected.

"Yeah, I don't dress this way often. When you said we should do our best to look sexy tonight, I went out and bought this dress. I'm glad you think it looks good on me."

Jessica excused herself to go back into the bathroom to put on the lingerie she had bought at Victoria's Secret when she had snuck away with Michelle earlier in the day. She didn't tell Angela what she was doing and just the thought of Angela knowing about it embarrassed her. Buying the lingerie made Jessica so uncomfortable that Michelle had actually gone to the register to pay for it when Jessica had chickened out at the last minute.

The outfit was sexy. It had two pieces. The first part was a tiny top that would leave her chiseled midsection visible while the second piece was the tiniest little thong she had ever seen. Both were bright red. Her plan was to wear it under the white dress she was wearing to dinner so she could tell Tim what was on under the dress. If that didn't drive him mad, she didn't know what would. Her fear was that it might show through the dress.

As soon as she was alone in the bathroom, she quickly slipped off the dress and began to pull the tiny lingerie on. It didn't cover much, and her chest was really stretching out the bra. Though it wasn't comfortable, she was sure it would blow Tim's mind. While she stood there admiring her figure, she heard Michelle knock on the door. It startled her, and she was suddenly aware of her almost nakedness. She grabbed her dress and climbed into it. Thankfully nothing was visible through it. It felt strangely like she was naked under it. Thinking about Tim looking at her in the dress tonight and in the lingerie tomorrow made her more than a little nervous.

"Michelle's here, Jessica. Are you almost ready to go?" asked Angela.

"I sure am," she answered as she opened the bathroom door.

"You look amazing, Jessica. I'm so jealous of your life." Michelle was more envious than jealous, but neither was a stronger emotion than her joy for Jessica. She thought the world of Jessica and was so happy for her that she had been losing sleep over it. Michelle was also a huge fan of Tim. Though she had initially been suspicious of Tim, as he seemed too good to be true, Michelle came around as time went by and she got to know him better. He was like a dream to all of the girls. To her, though, he was assured happiness to her best friend.

"Thank you, Michelle. I'm so glad you are here for this."

It was relieving to have Michelle around. Other than Tim, no one knew her better.

As they headed out the door, Michelle whispered in her ear, "Are you wearing it?"

Jessica gave her a smile, nodded her head, and put her finger over her mouth in the shush gesture. Michelle gave her a high-five, but Angela hadn't seen a thing.

Angela, Michelle, and Jessica got to the restaurant first. The two Brooks girls were dressed to kill and Michelle felt seriously out of her league. When the grandparents started to show up, the compliments were many.

"Boy don't you two look appetizing," said Kathy.

She knew what they were up to. Not long ago, attracting men had been her specialty.

Jessica suddenly felt embarrassed, and it showed on her face.

"I'm so sorry, honey. I meant it in a good way. You two will have your men's attention all night. It's a good thing. Don't feel bad, honey." Kathy felt really bad now.

"I've never done this before, and I'm really nervous. I hope I do everything right. What if I disappoint him?"

She was suddenly feeling aware of her inexperience, and her face began to show signs of a breakdown coming. She and Tim had done lots of hugging and holding, but they stayed away from any petting or heavy kissing. Truth be known, if they stayed that way, it wouldn't matter to Jessica that much, though she knew they both needed more.

Sensing Jessica's lack of confidence, Kathy followed up with, "Believe me, honey. From what I can see, there is nothing you could do to disappoint him. Just relax and enjoy yourself. He loves you no matter what you do." Kathy gave her a big smile and a hug and sat down right across from her.

Everyone was seated, and they had all been served a nonalcoholic beverage when Tim and Roger walked in. Jessica spotted Tim from across the room and leaped to her feet to wave to him. When he saw her, he immediately noticed she was in the dress from his dreams. It had long been his fantasy.

Jessica ran across the restaurant, oblivious to anyone's stare, to jump into his open arms, and as usual, he caught her and lifted her into the air. Neither of them cared who noticed or who was looking when they were together. Tim was sure it had to be annoying for the people around them, but he was also sure no one ever doubted their love for one another. Swinging in those powerful arms was the safest place Jessica knew.

When he pulled her tight to tell her how much he loved her, she told him she had some sexy lingerie for him she was going to wear under the wedding dress. Then she added, "I'm wearing them tonight too, and it's almost like I'm naked under this dress. I look amazing in them."

"Great. Now I can't let you down or both of our families will see how badly I want you." He wished he was kidding.

"Don't put me down then." She loved the reaction she had gotten but felt terrible for him for the uncomfortable situation she had put him in.

"I'll let you down in the hall."

He announced to the family while he was still holding her in the air that they would be right back, and he carried her into the private hall.

"This is so perfect, but I want it to be over. I want us to already be married. It's absolute torture." He was hoping for some relief, but setting her down and looking her in the eyes only made it worse.

"I can't wait either. I will be your wife by this time tomorrow. I am going to be so rough with you."

He looked so cute and so desperate to her. This hulking man was like a little kid in her hands. She was loved every minute of it.

"This isn't working, baby. You are only making me more excited. Your face is too perfect, and I can't believe you are wearing the dress from my dreams. You have to stop talking about your undergarments and how naked you feel under that dress. I thought we had a deal."

"All deals are off now, honey. We start the new deal tomorrow, and I expect lots of attention from you. My body has been working so hard to earn your approval and you are going to give it to me, aren't you?" She could tell that he was about to lose it.

"Are you kidding me? Please go back to the table. I've got to go into the bathroom to cool off for a bit. Yes, though, I will give your body all kinds of approval. It's all I've been thinking of for more than three years now. I just hope I don't hurt you."

Had he gone too far? He didn't want to scare her. He would never hurt her. If she had pain, he wouldn't do it. He'd stop right away at any sign of pain. *Maybe I shouldn't have said that thing about hurting her*, he wondered.

"Do you think it might hurt me?" She had been thinking about that. He was the biggest, strongest person she knew. If he wanted to, she was pretty sure he could squash her like a bug.

Seeing the concern on her face was almost too much for him. "Of course not, baby. I plan to be gentle. I will never hurt you. I will only hurt those who try to hurt you. I plan to be careful with you. Remember, I have no clue what we are getting into either. I'm scared too, baby."

The lust suddenly stopped, and he was fully able to return to the table with her.

"This conversation has cured my condition, so we can go to the table together now. I love you so much it literally hurts. We'll figure out the sex part together. That's why we waited."

He could see her trying to be strong and sexy, but in what felt like a heartbeat, her demeanor had changed from vixen to a scared little girl. He could feel her fears, and he knew she was afraid of disappointing him.

"You will never disappoint me," he added. "All I can think about is not failing you. Soon we will be a married couple and nothing will ever separate us."

Jessica smiled and pulled him down for a kiss, and they joined hands and walked back into the room where everyone else was waiting for them. Roger had already finished greeting everyone and was seated and clinging to his soul mate, as usual. Angela got up to hug her son. She was so proud. After the hug, Tim went around the table saying hello and thanking everyone for being there.

The meal was great, but Tim could hardly eat. Jessica knew why, and she loved the way he was looking at her. They had previously decided to part after dinner. The plan was to stay parted until it was time to get in the limo to go to town hall to get a marriage license on their way to the chapel, where the rest of the group would be waiting. Tim started to feel like the split after the meal would be a mistake. He didn't want to leave her and not see her again until they met at the limo anymore.

"Jessica, do you still think it's a good idea for us to go our separate ways after dinner? Don't you want to be with me tonight?" He didn't want to let her out of his sight ever again, especially not in that dress.

"It's your plan, Tim. I plan to get this dress off as soon as you leave. I've only worn it for you. We girls have plans."

She wanted to stick with the plan because she knew where she had him. Tim was perfect in every way in her eyes. Even the stuff she did well, he did better. As attractive as she had become, she knew he was more attractive. She loved feeling like he needed her that badly, and she didn't want his passion for her to decrease at all before they were finally alone as a married couple the next night.

"You are the wife of my dreams. You're the only woman I will ever lie with, and you're the only woman who will ever have my eye. I want to honor you with everything I do, but right now, I just want to take that dress off you. I don't want you to take it off; I want to take it off you."

He had whispered it to her so no one else could hear. He knew he was losing control, and he knew that them getting away from each other until it was time for the vows to be exchanged was the smart thing to do. It certainly wasn't the easiest thing to do, though.

They had been leaning into one another, whispering back and forth for most of the meal. Everyone could see what they were up to. They all thought it was great and enjoyed being in the same room with such powerful, pure young love.

Tim left feeling that everything in his world would be right after the wedding. Until then, he was uneasy and was feeling lots of anxiety. It was December 2013, but it would be 2014 in ten days. Twenty fourteen would be the best year of his life, he decided.

The guys went to a comedy show after dinner while the ladies saw one of the big magic shows. Both Jessica and Tim were distracted with thoughts about the other all night.

Neither of them slept much. In the morning, the guys and girls went their separate ways. Tim and Jessica were both anxious, and they both wanted nothing more than to see the other. More than anything, they both just wanted to be married; the waiting had no value and felt like some sort of punishment.

Jessica could hardly pay attention to what the ladies were saying. Lunch had no taste to her, and she barely ate. *Why am I feeling so antsy?* she wondered. She just wanted to be married to Tim; she wasn't really looking forward to the ceremony at all. The result of the ceremony was all she wanted.

Tim was completely out of it. Jessica was distracted, but Tim was almost a zombie that morning. He was so far out of touch that he forgot to zip up his pants, and though he put gel in his hair, he never combed it.

"What's up with the new hairstyle, Tim?" asked Roger

"Oh, man. Does anyone have a comb?" He wasn't even a little embarrassed.

"You might want to zip it up while you are at it, Tim. I think you should just run up to the room for a minute to get yourself right."

Roger was happy for Tim, but he began to think about how young he was and wondered if he really was ready for marriage. People often forgot how old Tim actually was. He was so physically imposing that it was easy to think of him as a much older man. It's not just that he was six feet seven inches tall; he was also very manly looking. If he didn't shave for even a day, he'd have the start of a beard.

If anyone that young is ready for marriage, it's Tim, Roger decided.

Tim was ready for their 2:00 p.m. meeting at the limo an hour early. He was wearing a specially made suit Roger had bought him as a graduation gift. Tim couldn't buy anything off the rack at a regular store. The suit was tailored, but it wasn't a big name brand. On him, though, anything that fit looked amazing.

Rather than wait around in the room, he headed down to the lobby and paced back and forth, waiting for his bride. The family was scheduled to meet them at the chapel at 4:00 p.m. for the wedding. Tim wondered how long they would have to wait for everyone at the chapel or if it would take the full two hours they had allotted to pick up the marriage license and get to the chapel. If things went quickly, he hoped they could move the schedule up so they wouldn't have to wait until 4:00 p.m. to be married.

Jessica made sure she was in the room two hours early to get ready. She had already showered and gotten her hair done. As she climbed into the lingerie, she felt self-conscious. The women in the Victoria's Secret flyer that she found in the bottom of the bag the lingerie had come in looked so confident and seductive. She didn't know if she could pull that off.

As soon as she pulled the dress over the expensive undies, she began to feel more comfortable. Just like the night before, though, she still felt naked under her dress.

Once the dress covered the undergarments, she opened the door and allowed Angela and Michelle to help her the rest of the way.

"How are you feeling, honey?" asked Angela.

"I just want to be married. I wish I could skip all of this stuff and just be alone with Tim for the rest of my life. I'm also feeling some concern that I might let Tim down tonight."

She was starting to show some fear on her face. Angela couldn't have missed it.

"The wedding will be over before you know it. You two are going to be perfect together, and you're right, it will be forever. Tim will not be disappointed with you. He has nothing to compare you to. That's part of the beauty of what you two have done by waiting for each other."

Jessica's expression changed into a happy, confident one. Angela pointing out the fact that Tim had nothing to compare her to had given her the confidence she needed. She now realized that she didn't have to look like the Victoria's Secret models. He would not be comparing her to them or anyone else. He never looked at women and always changed channels when something sexy came on TV. She really had no competition. Though Tim had told her that he had nothing to compare her to the night before, she somehow had forgotten until Angela pointed it out to her.

When Angela and Michelle were done with her, she was done up perfectly. When everyone agreed that she was completely ready, Angela and Michelle escorted her down to the lobby to meet Tim. They hit the lobby at five minutes 'til 2:00 p.m. Jessica refused to be late for anything. Not that she was good with time, but she had been living with an engineer and with Tim. Neither of these guys allowed themselves to ever be late for anything.

Tim saw them coming from the elevator bank. The dress made her look so classy that he suddenly realized how distinguished a look Jessica actually had. She was a classic beauty, and seeing her done up that way made him feel proud. He waved to them from across the lobby and began to wonder if Jessica would still do her standard run and leap into his arms or if the wedding dress would hold her back.

To his absolute joy, the dress didn't hold her back. She came barreling toward him like she always did. Her eagerness to be in his arms had always made him feel great. That time was no different, though it was, and he could definitely feel the difference.

"It's finally happening, Tim," she said into his ear while suspended at least a foot off the ground in his powerful grip.

All he could manage to get out was, "I love you."

He was beginning to go to pieces. Seeing her dressed for the wedding and holding her in his arms was making him feel faint. She noticed it in his voice and started to fall apart herself when she realized how wonderful it was that he loved her that much. He set her down and held her face in his hands. She was touched by the tears in his eyes.

"I will always remember you like this."

His voice was cracking, and he looked like he could be knocked over with a feather. Angela was moved by seeing them like this. She couldn't wait to tell Roger all about it.

The limo driver was waiting outside. When the two climbed into the backseat, they embraced again.

Getting the license was painless, and they were at the wedding chapel almost an hour early. Thankfully everyone else was there by about a quarter after 3:00 p.m. Tim asked if there were any open slots before 4:00 p.m. because their entire party was there and they couldn't wait to be married. The answer came back that they could go right then if they were ready, so they jumped on it.

Before they knew what was going on, the two of them were standing at the front of the chapel with the pastor, reading the vows. Tim was standing there in awe that it was finally happening. His legs were beginning to feel weak, and he was beginning to feel flushed. The seriousness of the moment was overwhelming him. All of his senses seemed to be numbing. Meanwhile, Jessica was standing across from him, feeling nothing but joy.

When the pastor got to the part when he asked Tim to say "I do," Tim dropped like a rock. He had passed out but came to as he was hitting the floor. As he got his wits about him, he quickly yelled out, "I do!" while he picked himself up off the floor with Roger and Jessica both trying to help him. Tim fainting like a little girl would be retold for the rest of his life. Once everyone knew he was okay, they all laughed a bit and the ceremony continued. It had been really strange to see such a big, strong guy drop like he had.

The pastor paused for a bit until everyone was composed. Then he continued with the part that both Tim and Jessica were waiting for. When he told them that they were man and wife and that he may kiss his bride, Tim went down again. That time Jessica grabbed on for the ride and went down with him. He was stunned at what was happening to him but simply had no control. As soon as she saw that his eyes were open, she put her mouth on his, and they began to kiss the kiss they had both been dreaming about for years. He immediately came to life to kiss her back, and the family began to cheer. Even the pastor joined in.

"I've done a lot of weddings, but I've never seen two people more in love than this," he told the family.

The two lay on the floor, hugging and kissing, for quite a while before Tim picked her up like she was a feather and walked right out of the chapel. "We love you all, and we'll see you for breakfast tomorrow at ten a.m. as planned."

Tim was on a mission. He was suddenly feeling super strength, and he felt as if he could walk right through the wall with her in his arms if he needed to. Nothing could have stopped him.

Jessica could feel his power when he had suddenly sprung from the floor with her in his arms. She wasn't even sure how he had been able to raise from the floor with her in his arms the way he had. He just stood up without using his hands at all. She could feel his tensed muscles right through his suit, yet she knew his tenderness. He was perfect as a person, but the outside was pretty amazing too. He was now her husband. She could hardly believe it.

Tim gently set Jessica into the limo and climbed in behind her. The driver was instructed to take them back to the hotel, and he was quickly forgotten. The drive turned out to be one long make-out session for the newlyweds.

After they tipped the driver, they ran through the hotel lobby and desperately waited for an elevator. Both were thankful that they got an elevator to themselves. As soon as the door closed, they started back at it. With the sound of the ding, the doors opened and Tim swept her off her feet and started to run down the hall to their room with her in his arms. Jessica had the key tucked away in a hidden pocket of her dress. It was out and ready to go before they even got to the door.

They opened the door to find a fancy red comforter on the bed and lots of soft, fluffy pillows along with an envelope that said "Mr. & Mrs. Wiseman."

"What in the world?" Jessica said as she reached for the envelope.

Tim was holding her from behind now. His arms were wrapped around her tiny midsection, and his lips were all over her neck. He loosened his grip just enough to allow her to reach the envelope but not enough for her to break free.

"I bet the bed was Mom's idea, and the envelope is probably from Dad," Jessica said as she turned and gave herself again to his passion. She tossed the envelope away and told him to take her now.

Tim didn't waste any time. He had her dress unzipped and was attempting to pull it off all in one motion. She helped him out by pulling it down to the floor and stepping out of it. Seeing her in her sexy lingerie with her finely chiseled body bursting out in all of the right places was too much for him. He couldn't just take her like an animal; he loved her too much for that. Instead, he sat down on the bed, reached out for her, and gently pulled her chest into his face. He laid his head on her chest and told her this was the best day of his life and it was already better than he could have ever expected it to be.

"How come I'm almost naked and you're sitting here in a suit? I didn't know you would turn out to be such a selfish lover."

He hadn't even thought about getting undressed. All he could think about was seeing her body. "I'm sorry, baby. Do you want to help me get undressed?" He needed the help; he had already passed out twice that day.

"Yes. I want you in your underwear right now."

Suddenly, he was feeling a little awkward. "Should I turn the lights off first?"

There she was, standing there with really nothing on, and he was acting afraid to take his clothes off. She thought it was funny but didn't want him to be uncomfortable.

"If you want to, but not all of them, I want to see you too."

He got up and turned off all of the lights except for the bathroom light. It cast a dim light throughout the room. Jessica still had her heels on, so she sat down to take them off. When he saw her on the bed, he walked right up to her and started to undress.

"Do you want to help me, wife?"

She reached up and unbuttoned his suit. In a matter of seconds, he was down to his underwear.

Jessica was impressed and could see that he was excited. The thought of what they were about to do was pretty scary for both of them. While she stared at his body from her seated position on the bed, she began to reach inside his underwear. With that, things escalated quickly and the two were all over each other. Though they were clumsy, they figured things out.

They lost track of time, and it was midnight before they realized they hadn't eaten. Neither of them cared. Everything in life was good for them. They were so deeply in love that they couldn't stop touching each other. Each touch would lead to another special moment. Each one was better than the last. Tim had always wanted to shower with her, so they did. Knowing they were husband and wife made it all so surreal that they kept telling each other they couldn't believe they were finally totally together.

Jessica offered to message Tim's back and shoulders, which only led to more intimacy. It really bothered her how beaten and bruised his body was. Going all the way through the state championship had required the team to play games almost all the way through Christmas. He told her that his body always looked that way during football season. Then he tried to convince her that it looked worse than it actually was, but she didn't believe him through all of his winces.

"Hey, what about that envelope?" Jessica asked.

"Oh yeah. I forgot," Tim replied.

The envelope was stuffed with cash, a gift certificate for one of the hotel's fancy steak places, and tickets to three shows. The note read "We are so proud of you two. You are the best two kids parents could ever hope to have. We know you two will have a marriage as strong as ours, and we want you to know we will always love you both, no matter what. Please use this stuff over the next three days, as we have extended your stay for three more nights. We will see you at breakfast. 10:00 a.m. Don't forget." It was signed "Mom and Dad."

They were excited about the idea of spending three more nights and days together before they would have to jump back into life. They never really liked the idea of flying home the day after the wedding but didn't want to ask their parents to cover the additional expenses they would have if they were to extend their stay.

"This is great, Tim. Three more nights! I hope you can keep up with me."

He was wondering the same.

They made love again and fell asleep around 3:00 a.m. When the alarm went off at 9:00 a.m., they took a look at one another and went at it again, though she wouldn't kiss him.

"Not with this breath," she told him.

They showered and rushed to get ready for breakfast. Everyone would be waiting for them, and they didn't want to be late.

Breakfast with the family was great. Angela and Roger were almost as frisky with each other as Jessica and Tim were that morning. Tim thought to himself that God really knows what he's doing with this whole "one man for one woman" thing.

How could anyone need more than one woman? he wondered.

Jessica was everything to him, and he couldn't imagine ever wanting anyone else. It made him angry to even imagine her with anyone else.

After the meal, the grandparents, Michelle, and their parents all headed for the airport, and the couple was left in the city of sin all alone. For the rest of their stay, they never left their room except for meals and shows. It was the best three days of their lives, and they both knew it was something they would always fondly remember.

CHAPTER 35

RICE was the next chapter of their lives. The two planned to share a car and were all set up to live in married housing through the athletic department. Tim chose engineering as a major so he and Jessica could study together. They decided to wait until they were done with college to start a family. They even agreed that the minute they signed a contract for Tim to play in the NFL, they would start officially trying to have a child.

Their love was so strong that they didn't want to be apart if they didn't absolutely have to be apart. They tried to take all of their classes together, but because Jessica was a semester ahead, it wasn't possible. Tim was the big man on campus, and it didn't take long for people to begin to ask who he was. He worked out with the football team daily and was getting stronger at an alarming rate. He felt like it had to do with how his body had really been maturing over the last half year or so. Every part of his body was getting thicker, and his chest was exploding with hair.

It was in the weight room that Tim began to gain his fellow players' admiration. By summertime, Tim was easily the strongest player on the team. He could hardly wait for practices to start. He and Jessica had spent the first semester submersed in their studies, so they agreed to spend most of the summer back home with their parents. It was an exciting time for them, and they really enjoyed being home.

Angela had completed a four-year degree in business at Sam Houston State University that semester, so they all went to her graduation ceremony. Tim was so proud of his mother. He could hardly even remember the woman she had once been. It was sad in so many ways. Her home environment during her formative years had led to her susceptibility to his father. She had almost no self-esteem when Roger had met her, and she had felt that her only strength was her looks. Now she was this amazing godly woman in a perfect marriage with a perfect husband. Tim thanked God for bringing her out of the ditches and into his kingdom. It seemed almost implausible that she had once tried to end her own life.

Roger was so proud of Angela's graduation that he bought her a beautiful diamond necklace. She told him he shouldn't have, but it went right on. She had no trouble believing he was proud of her, as God had completely set her free.

In the outside world, things were continuing to deteriorate. In spite of the extermination of Osama Bin Laden, the architect and leader of the 9/11 terrorist attacks back in 2001, the terrorist activity in the Middle East had only gotten worst. Now, some three years after his death, it was clear that taking him out hadn't solved anything. The hostility toward Israel was reaching new heights, and the US was starting to turn their attention away from the attackers. With growing world opinion going against the support of Israel, the United States was now only giving lip service as support for Israel.

The US national debt continued to climb exponentially year on year. The only answer the government had was to continually increase taxes. People and companies were now getting taxed in so many ways and from so many directions that many began to feel punished for any sort of success they were having. The companies that had not already left the United States were all seriously considering it. The trend in the United States was quickly moving toward socialism as the government continued to take on more and more of the economy.

CHAPTER 36

WHEN they returned to campus, fully recharged from a summer at home, Tim and Jessica began to search for a church to get involved in. They had already attended several churches during their first semester, but none of them had felt like home. All throughout high school, Tim had been known as "the Wiseman preacher." He had been a leader in the Sunday school department, and he always took it upon himself to share Christ with everyone he could. Being who he was made it easy for him. People responded to his big body, talent, personality, and his big heart.

Tim did his best to make everyone around him better. He was fiercely competitive, but mainly with himself. He never came down on anyone but himself, though he was a vocal leader. When Tim saw someone struggling, he felt for them and always tried to do what he could to help. His kindness had stretched across the entire high school student body. While in high school, he had gone out of his way to know every player on the JV and freshman teams. He always congratulated them for things he saw them do on the football field, in the weight room, or in life. Tim was a big believer in encouraging others, and it had become a part of his character. He had been such a positive example that people often told him they loved him. He loved everyone because he understood that God loves everyone. He did his best to obey God's laws because he knew that's what God wants as a response to his love for us.

Tim's love for Jessica had been an example to the entire student body as well. Not only did the two stay pure until they were married, but they told everyone what they were doing. Early on, no one knew about their engagement. However, when Tim gave Jessica the engagement ring, they decided to make it public knowledge before people started asking about it. Jessica had been popular in high school, but Tim was like a rock star; everyone knew who he was. The example they set was so inspirational to everyone that knew them that they were able to start a group of young people committed to sexual purity until marriage. The group grew daily. The school saw improvements in every measurable statistic over Tim's time there, including decreases in drug use, drinking, pregnancies, and violence. The school's graduation rate actually improved as well.

Now at Rice, the two were hoping to have a similar impact. Rice had an undergraduate program of around 3,500 students when Tim and Jessica first started attending. Only the strongest students were admitted, and obtaining a degree would almost guarantee prime employment. What they had underestimated was the effect that so many years of wrong thinking had had on the otherwise-intelligent young students. It was sad to Tim that so many were so closed-minded. It was ironic to him that so many would claim to be open-minded when, in fact, they were actually quite the opposite.

There were some believers on campus, but the closer Tim got to knowing them, the more he realized that most of them had compromised God's Word with fallen man's views and man's limited understanding. Since Tim knew in his heart that some of these people would earnestly be seeking for the truth, he decided he would love on everyone and speak the truth of God's Word into whoever's life he could.

For the next three seasons, Tim did things on the football field no one had ever done for Rice. He led the nation in sacks over his college carrier and had even been dominant against the big schools like Texas and Texas A&M. In his final season, he led the team, on and off the field, to the Conference USA Championship.

Tim also broke a school record in the shot put when he threw 61'3". The record he broke had been in place since 1973. He won the conference both years he competed.

Tim's outstanding college career had him on the top of every NFL team's draft board, and he was a shoe-in to be selected first overall by the Houston Texans in the 2017 NFL draft. At six foot seven and three hundred and five pounds, Tim ran a sub 4.6 second forty, had a vertical leap of 35 inches, and put up 225 pounds thirty-eight times in the bench press at the NFL combine. Along with him about to graduate with an engineering degree from one of the most prestigious universities in the country, he was the ringer of the century.

As expected, the Texans called his name first. Tim had told the team that he wanted to stay at home in Texas and play for them during his time visiting the team. He had actually agreed to a contract with the team before the draft, so it was no big surprise to him when they called his name.

Tim, with Jessica's blessing, quickly signed the five-year, multimillion dollar contract. While the ink was still drying, they started trying to get pregnant, as previously planned. Their first purchase was a nice home in The Woodlands, Texas, which they were able to pay cash for due to a signing bonus that was also part of the contract. Out of gratitude, they paid off their parents' mortgage as well.

They committed to living like they were making far less money, tithed 10 percent to their church, and gave away another 20 percent to whatever Jessica and Tim decided was God's work. It was Jessica's gift to give to others. She loved finding good causes for their giving. The government got its 50 percent of everything as well.

CHAPTER 37

THE week before Tim's first regular season professional football game, Jessica broke the good news to him that she was pregnant. The two could not have been happier. The due date was May 2, 2018, and as far as they were concerned, it wasn't soon enough. Tim was so excited that they were having a baby that he loaded Jessica into the car and they hit the road to go tell their parents. Practice had just ended, and he had until the following morning to be back on the field. Since they only lived an hour or so from their parents, they arrived just in time for dinner.

As they walked up the driveway, Angela spotted them and came running out. "Is everything okay?" It wasn't like Tim to just show up unannounced like that.

"We have big news, Mom," said Jessica. "Is Dad here too?"

"He's upstairs, changing into his lay-around-the-house clothes. Can you tell me the news, or do we need Dad here first?"

"We definitely need Dad for this. I'll go get him." Jessica took off for the stairs.

Roger was startled when Jessica came bounding into his room. "Is that you, Jessica?"

"Yep. Tim and I are here with some great news." She knew that their first guess would be that she was pregnant.

"You're pregnant, aren't you?" He knew it from her excitement.

"Yes, Dad, I'm pregnant." She was in tears of joy. "I haven't told Mom yet. I was only coming up to get you down there so we could tell you guys together."

They embraced and enjoyed each other for a moment.

"Where are you guys?" hollered Angela. "I need to hear the good news!"

They broke up their hug and quickly started down the stairs. When they hit the final step, Angela and Tim were standing there, arm in arm.

"Did you tell him, Jessica?" asked Tim.

"Did you tell her?"

She could see it in Angela's face.

"Yes, but only because I knew you couldn't keep this from Dad until you got down here."

All four of them huddled and hugged it out.

Finally, Tim said, "Can I buy everyone dinner at Pasqual's?" After all that time, it was still his favorite place. There were just too many great memories there.

"You sure can, Dad," Angela responded.

Just hearing his mother call him Dad got to him a bit. *How great is this?* he thought. "Let's go."

They were all so excited during dinner that they almost forgot about Tim's first NFL game coming up the following Sunday. When a young fan came up to get an autograph, the conversation changed to football. Jessica told everyone how nervous she was for him. She was so scared he would get seriously hurt that she was scared to even go to the game. Tim told her he would be just fine. He'd been working hard, and he felt confident he could play at this level.

Tim had gotten tickets for Jessica, Angela, Roger, and all four of the grandparents who had come to their wedding. Only Chuck's mother and her husband, John, had to travel for the game. Everyone planned to stay both Saturday and Sunday night at Tim and Jessica's place. They had three guest rooms, though one would soon be the baby's room.

At the end of the evening, as the group was getting ready to leave Pasqual's, an attractive Indian woman approached their table. She looked only at Tim.

"Are you Chuck Wiseman's son?"

"He was my biological father, and I got my last name from him, but the man sitting next to me is my real father. Why do you ask?" He hadn't been asked about his father in years.

"My name is Brandi. I have seen you around before, and I've been following the news about you. When I first saw you, I thought you were your father. He actually put me in the hospital once when I was in college. I think it was before you were born. I didn't know him well, but knowing him at all was too well. Getting close to that guy was a dangerous mistake. He almost destroyed my closest friend's life and almost killed her boyfriend, the guy who later became her husband. If this is your mother, I apologize for bringing all this up, but I had to talk to you about this. I couldn't relax and enjoy my meal without telling you how great I think it is that you have become the man you are now. Making it to the NFL, graduating from Rice, openly sharing your belief in Jesus—you are truly an inspiration. You overcame some serious evil to become the strong Christian that I read and hear that you are. I wish your father could see you now. You might have been the only one who could have helped him."

Tim didn't know what to say, so he said the first thing he could think of. "Thank you for the compliments. I've become who I am because God is good and because of the people right here at this table. I'm so sorry for the things my father did to you and your friend. He loved me and my mom, but he tried to do things alone and never looked to the Lord." Tim was painfully aware that his mother was uncomfortable talking about Chuck. She looked like she was about to cry, so he took her hand to comfort her.

Brandi saw Angela's face and immediately regretted her decision to come to their table. "I'm really sorry I brought all this up. Please forgive me," she said as she started to turn to go.

"Don't feel bad, Brandi. We all know he was a bad guy. You have done nothing wrong. Keep your head up and enjoy your meal tonight. We are here to celebrate my wife's pregnancy. Our lives are all overflowing with good things. The past is behind us. We can only control what we do going forward. I was given a second father, and he is the best one I have ever known. Chuck gave me an amazing mind and body, but Roger has given me the truth and love. No one is more blessed than me and my mom. I have the most attractive, intelligent wife any man could ever dream of, and my mother has the best man I have ever known as her husband. Have a great evening and thanks again for your compliments."

Brandi was blown away by how caring Tim was. He had noticed his mother's discomfort and had comforted her. He had also noticed her discomfort after she had made a fool of herself by bringing up the ugly past and comforted her with kind words. Then he went on to compliment his beautiful wife and gave the highest praise to his stepfather. He took care of her and his whole table of loved ones. She was now even a bigger fan of Tim and would tell everyone she knew what type of guy he was.

"Thank you for letting me off the hook. Have a great evening."

Tim had that type of impact on almost everyone he met.

Roger was touched to hear Tim say such kind words about him, but his concern for his wife was his primary concern. "Are you okay, honey?"

"I'm fine, sweetheart. I don't know why that bothered me so much. It just hurt to remember how things were before you, Roger. I forget how perfect my life has been since you came into it. You are a great man, Roger." She was holding his hand.

Roger couldn't wait to get her home, away from the cruel world.

Jessica was still feeling anger that Brandi would say such things to Tim and his mother. The way Tim had handled the situation reassured her that he was the most perfect person she had ever known. She sometimes wondered how he could be so calm all the time and yet such an out-of-control menace on the football field.

"I'm so sorry, Mom. I hated that for you." Tim hated seeing his mother put off like she obviously was.

"It's really okay, sweetie. I'm fine now."

She really was fine. It just affected her for a moment, and she was back now. Angela's faith had grown exponentially over the last couple of years. People who knew her years before Roger had come into her life were amazed at how different she had become. If she had been that person when she first met Chuck, they would have never gotten together. She would have never had Tim or met Roger, so she had come to terms with the fact that it took everything to happen the way that it had for God to get her full attention so he could transform her life.

CHAPTER 38

FIVE years after Tim entered the NFL, things became difficult for the country he loved. The United States had been going through serious changes due to massive national debt. Attempts to provide health care for every citizen, along with a runaway illegal immigrant problem, proved to be the backbreakers to the US economy. Tax rates had been raised on the so-called rich, year after year forcing small business owners to cut jobs, and even fail in the worst cases. The government's attempts to create jobs were miserable failures. By 2022, the US government was not able to pay employees and the Social Security system was completely bankrupt.

That year, 2022, China began selling its US debt and the United States began to spiral out of control. The dollar's value dropped overnight, and the world switched to the OWC, One World Currency. OW, the union that had grown from the European Union, simply called One World, brought the United States into their new cashless society. US dollars were converted into OWCs, and no hard currency was issued.

The stated goal of One World was to bring peace to the world by becoming one people. Tolerance for others beliefs and life choices was a major value for the union. The other driving forces were economic, as the entire world seemed to be going bankrupt. The only growing economies were China, India, and several other smaller nations in Asia. The United States had no other option but to join the One World union. Canada, Mexico, and all of South America had already joined.

To the average American, the switch from the dollar to the OWC was painless and even relieving. For more than ten years, they had watched their country fall apart. Most Americans lost their retirements during that period. They also witnessed their home and possessions values disappearing. Personal bankruptcy rates and foreclosures seemed to set new records every other month. The older generations were losing all of their benefits, including Social Security, Medicare, and Medicaid. Many retirees were forced to move in with their families. As a result, suicide rates were at an all-time high, as were every sort of crime rate. It seemed that only a few wealthy people were still living the American Dream, but they were mostly unsure if they could stay on top.

When companies started to fail, the government had stepped in with more and more assistance. Spending more and more of the taxpayers' money seemed to be their only solution. The fact that it wasn't working didn't stop them.

Though no one would call it what it was, a huge percentage of the American workforce was now working for the government posing as various companies. When the government was no longer able to pay its employees, the collapse was officially on. As the United States began to sink, they were forced to give up on their independence.

As a new member of the OW union, the US constitution was no longer the ultimate authority. International law, controlled by the OW, now trumped the US court system. With the collapse of the government, the entire US court system was only a shell of what it had once been. No longer were judges elected at the state level; they were appointed by the US branch of the OW.

Through all of the world turmoil, professional sports continued to draw huge followings. They were the only thing that the average person had to look forward to. In 2020, the major US sports leagues, including the NFL, NBA, MLB, MLH, and MLS, actually became government entities. Owners were forced to sell, and no foreign ownership was allowed. All existing contracts were guaranteed to be paid out, but new contracts were far less lucrative. The contracts that were being paid were taxed at such a high rate that the players were only keeping about 25 percent of what they were being paid. The years of athletes becoming multimillionaires were over. Tim had cashed in just in time.

The Wisemans had been wise with their resources. Tim's five-year, multimillion dollar contract had allowed them to pay cash for their home in The Woodlands, Texas, and they carried no other debts. They invested wisely, including several million dollars in gold.

Regarding the direction of the United States, Tim couldn't help but relate to something Roger had shared with him early on in their studies. It was something that Paul Harvey had written called "If I Were the Devil."

"IF I WERE THE DEVIL" BY PAUL HARVEY:

I would gain control of the most powerful nation in the world; I would delude their minds into thinking that they had come from man's effort, instead of God's blessings; I would promote an attitude of loving things and using people, instead of the other way around; I would dupe entire states into relying on gambling for their state revenue; I would convince people that character is not an issue when it comes to leadership; I would make it legal to take the life of unborn babies; I would make it socially acceptable to take one's own life, and invent machines to make it convenient; I would cheapen human life as much as possible so that life of animals are valued more than human beings; I would take God out of the schools, where even the mention of His name was grounds for a lawsuit; I would come up with drugs that sedate the mind and target the young, and I would get sports heroes to advertise them; I would get control of the media, so that every night I could pollute the minds of every family member for my agenda; I would attack the family, the backbone of any nation. I would make divorce acceptable and easy, even fashionable. If the family crumbles, so does the nation; I would compel people to express their most depraved fantasies on canvas and movies screens, and I would call it art; I would convince the world that people are born homosexuals, and that their lifestyles should be accepted and marveled; I would convince the people that right and wrong are determined by a few who call themselves authorities and refer to their agendas as politically correct; I would persuade people that the church is irrelevant and out of date, the Bible is for the naive: I would dull the minds of Christians, and make them believe that prayer is not important, and that faithfulness and obedience are optional; *I guess I would leave things pretty much the way they are!*"

At no time in US history had this been truer than it was now; Tim was sure of it.

CHAPTER 39

TIM played ten productive years in the NFL before his arrest. He went to the Pro Bowl eight times and set an NFL record for sacks in a season. His carrier numbers were clearly hall of fame numbers. The arrest ended his career while he was still a productive player who was feared by every other team in the league.

At the time of his arrest, he and Jessica had two children. They named their son Roger after Dad, and the girl they named Caroline after Jessica's mother.

Tim was being interviewed after the Pro Bowl at the end of his tenth season when he was arrested on camera. The whole thing had been a set up by the powers behind the One World union. When he was asked if he still believed that Jesus was the only way to heaven and eternal life, he simply answered, "Yes, I believe what God tells us in the Bible in John 14:6: 'I am the way, the truth, and the life: no man cometh unto the Father, but by me.'"

The international police were on the field ready to take him into custody. Tim had seen them and knew what was about to happen. For years he had been dealing with persecution for his beliefs that the Bible was word-for-word literal truth. When he saw the police on the field, he quickly prayed to God for the strength to stay a strong witness through everything that was sure to come.

Tim had refused to recognize the Acts of Hate laws since they had begun to be passed one by one more than four years prior. The laws were put into place to keep those who took the Bible literally from calling others sinners, even though they also believed themselves to also be sinners. The belief of the One World union was that religion that told people what was right and wrong needed to be eliminated. They pointed to events all through world history as evidence that these differences in beliefs were the cause of almost all of the wars through the ages. The consensus behind the union's thinking was that religion needed to be controlled and reworked to bring peace to the world.

The United States had turned its back on Israel, yet Israel continued to defeat all attackers regardless of how superior the enemy force had been. Though it seemed clear to Christians and Jews alike, somehow most of the world denied that their deliverance had been supernatural each time it successfully defended itself against overwhelming odds. No objective person denied it, though. When the United States had not supported them in their defense, most Christians understood the repercussions of their actions. God's Word was clear that he would bless those who bless Israel and curse those who curse her. In Genesis, God, referring to his people Israel, said, "And I will bless them that bless thee, and curse him that curseth thee: and in thee shall all families of the earth be blessed" (Genesis 12:3, KJV). The blessing that came out of the Jewish nation is Jesus Christ.

Since most of the world had bought into the lie that the Bible had been proven to be full of error, anyone who took a literal view of Scripture was ridiculed. It became difficult for a Bible-believing Christian to work at a university or even to get hired by a church, as most churches had been polluted by humanistic reasoning.

The attack on the Bible began against all speech considered to be hate speech. The assertion that homosexuality was a sin was only the first of many such hate speech examples. Shortly, preachers were forbidden to preach all of God's Word. It seemed like almost weekly, a new passage was deemed to be hate speech. People were rewarded for reporting violations of these laws. Many, hoping to catch a preacher in violation, visited churches for that purpose alone. Though some actually became Christians and were saved, many were successful in their quest.

Sharing one's faith became a risky proposition. If one worked for the government in any capacity, they would almost certainly lose their job for the offense. The effects of all of the arrests of pastors lead to the return of the church to small home groups in hiding.

Tim was constantly being warned about his public faith proclamations. Since he had become a well-known figure as a superstar athlete, he was considered a dangerous threat. Though there were many others who claimed to be Christians, they had quickly agreed to keep their faith to themselves when the league and authorities warned them. Tim would not. His fame and popularity made him an effective witness, and he never missed an opportunity to witness to someone about Jesus. Any time Tim was given a microphone, he spoke about his Lord and Savior, Jesus.

Though initially none of these so-called "hate crimes" carried the death penalty, things were quickly moving in that direction. When the law passed that said it was illegal to claim that any one path was the only way to God, Christians were no longer able to legally share their faith. Anyone who publicly proclaimed that Jesus was the only way to heaven was to be arrested. Tim was the first to be arrested under this law.

To be released, all that had to be done was a denial of God's Word. There would be no trial, as there was no possibility that someone was not guilty, as all they would have to do to be released was to deny that Jesus was the only way to heaven. Though only a few years before Tim's public arrest, Christians in the United States felt that this could never happen to them. It was now a reality. The United States no longer existed in its prior form. Most believers thought they would never face anything like that prior to the coming of the antichrist. "Wasn't the forcing of people to accept someone other than Christ as God supposed to happen during the Great Tribulation under the reign of the antichrist?" was a common question in the mind of the believers. Most believers also believed they would be long gone before that type of persecution even began.

Tim was fairly certain that one day he would likely be arrested for his beliefs, and now it was happening. He had been chosen as an example so that Christians would know that it would no longer be tolerated to push right and wrong on people. Though the penalty for violating this law had not yet been defined, the rumor that it would carry a death penalty was being spread by the One World union itself.

The OW was claiming huge successes toward world peace due to their enforcement of their laws against religion all over Europe. In their eyes, it needed to be forced in all of their member regions, including the United States.

Though Islam was still a major issue, most of the fighting due to Islam was confined to the Middle East due to the strength of the OW union forces. The followers of Islam also hated Israel and Christians. The biggest issue for the OW was Christianity. Almost all of the opposition to the OW, especially toward what they believed would bring world peace, came from Christians.

CHAPTER 40

TIM had only been in jail a few days when the news came that the penalty would, in fact, be execution if he would not deny his faith. He was told that all he would have to do is admit that Jesus was not the "only" way to heaven. He would have to make his denial live on TV to be released.

Tim calmly declined the offer to make a retraction of his belief in Jesus. It really wasn't even difficult for him. There was no chance he would ever deny Jesus. The verse that kept going through his head was, "If we suffer, we shall also reign with [him]: if we deny [him], he also will deny us" (2 Timothy 2:12, KJV).

Immediately after his official rejection to deny God's Word and be set free to go home to his family, he was sent to a maximum-security prison. As hard as the OW had tried to stop Tim's witness, he quickly touched everyone he came into contact with inside of prison. From guards to inmates, he was bringing people to Christ every day. They flocked to him, so he had to be put alone and completely secluded from everyone else.

The news about the death sentence hit the family, their friends, their church, Christians around the world, and many sports fans very hard. The outcry was overwhelming but only played into the hands of One World union. That was exactly what they were going for by arresting a famous person. There was no one better than someone everyone knew to make an example out of.

The worst part about his sentence was that it would be carried out in only two months' time. There was no chance he wasn't guilty, and the OW wanted it to happen quickly so the world would know how serious they were. The OW firmly believed that Tim's public execution would have the desired effect of stopping believers from spreading their poison.

Jessica was proud of Tim for standing strong, but she couldn't bear the thought of him being executed or even not coming home.

How would she live without him? He was everything to her and the kids. Every part of her just wanted her wonderful husband at home with her and their family. That was where he belonged. He was a great man. How twisted were things that preaching God's Word was now a crime that carried the death penalty?

Jessica's faith in a loving God was being tested continually since the arrest. *Why can't he just say that Jesus isn't the only way to heaven and come home?* she thought. She knew the answer, but it was impossible to accept or live with. The pressure was so extreme that Angela and Roger had to move in with her to help with the kids.

Angela and Roger were proud too but couldn't believe it was happening. It was like being in hell to them, and it tested their faith as it was testing Jessica's.

The kids were young, but they both understood what was happening. Tim was such a great father to them that they were almost zombies without him around. Every night Tim had read the Bible and stories to them. Now Grandpa was filling in. Though they loved him very much, it just wasn't the same. The kids were really hurting. There was lots of crying.

The family felt that the world must be ending. How could they lose Tim? He was Superman. No one stood stronger, and no one was a better father, husband, or son. The pain they were all feeling was crippling. They just couldn't understand it. How could God allow this? Roger told the family that was all about the enemy. He explained that things had to go that way near the end and that they needed to trust God. Though they all believed him, it didn't make it any easier for any of them to bear.

The family had not been allowed to see Tim since he had been arrested. Things were different since the OW had taken over. Most rights that Americans had always taken for granted were no longer rights. Thankfully, when it was only one month away from his execution, they allowed the family to come visit him.

They were put through roughly an hour worth of screening and security checks before they were led into a waiting room. A military officer with an OW uniform finally came out to meet them after what felt like another hour. They weren't exactly sure how long it had been, as their watches and phones had been taken away when they were going through the security process.

"You will go in this order: first the wife and the kids for ten minutes, and then the parents will get ten minutes. Then the wife will get another ten minutes alone." The officer seemed business-like and showed absolutely no emotion. Though he didn't say it, he clearly didn't invite any questions. "Let's go, wife and children," he said as he turned and started to walk down a long hallway.

Jessica took little Roger and Caroline by the hand and started to follow their escort. Roger was almost nine years old while Caroline was only seven. They were both mature kids for their ages due to the time and amount of material their father and Jessica had shared with them. Jessica was home schooling them both. Public schools had pretty much fallen apart. When the government fell, schools stopped paying their teachers. The OW quickly stepped in began pushing their curriculum while only rehiring teachers who passed their profile testing. Home school was soon to be illegal, as the OW firmly believed that all children need to get a "nonbiased" look at the "truth" as they saw it.

As Jessica and the kids caught up to the man in the OW uniform, they were just reaching the end of the hall. When they got there, they turned right into another shorter hall. There was only one door at the end of the hall. In front of the door was an armed guard. The man had no expression on his face and never made eye contact with any of them. As they approached, he stepped aside as their escort reached for the door. They heard a buzzing sound just before he touched the knob. The noise apparently came from some sort of electromechanical locking device that was being charged to allow the door to be opened. The door opened with almost no effort.

Tim was standing in the middle of the room with a big smile on his face. He was so happy to see them that the circumstances weren't even affecting him. As he dropped down on his knee so the kids could run into his arms, he said, "Get over here!" They both sprinted into his arms, and he pulled them in tightly. Jessica joined them as he reached out to pull her into the group hug. He also gave her a kiss on the lips, and the kids didn't even care. Normally they would show their displeasure with an "ew" or some other sign of disgust.

"You guys have ten minutes," the OW escort said as he closed the door on them.

Tim was wearing standard prison clothing. The pants were a bit too short, but they had found a shirt that fit him. He had grown a poorly manicured beard and it kind of creeped them out a bit, but none of them said a thing about it.

Tim seemed so happy that it felt a little odd to Jessica and the kids. Sensing it, he decided that he'd better explain himself.

"I am so happy to see you guys. I've missed you so much that it's felt like torture to me. You three are the most important people in the world to me. That's why I'm so happy. Roger, I hope you are taking care of Mommy. You are the man of the house while I'm not there."

They all looked so scared for him. He wanted them to know that he wasn't scared at all and that he loved them very much.

"Grandma and Grandpa are living with us, Dad. It's been really sad." Little Roger's face was full of pain. Tim had always been amazed at how mature Roger had always been. His mother always told him that Roger was exactly like him when he was little.

"Don't be sad, guys. I'm doing what God wants me to do. He's been giving me peace that I just can't explain. I think God is going to do something really big with all of this. I love you guys and hate being away from you. Being without my family is the only thing making this hard. I need you all to be strong. You guys need to all be there for each other. I think about you guys all the time, and I need to know that you are all at home, loving one another. I pray for all of you every day." He was calm, and it helped them all feel like everything was okay.

Tim brought up the visitation schedule, and Jessica confirmed that they had been told the same. The four of them huddled up and loved on each other. Since Tim knew Jessica could come back in at the end, he spoke to the children primarily. Caroline really seemed to open up while Roger just held on to his father's arm quietly. Sensing his sadness, Tim pulled him in tightly.

"Roger, these other prisoners are getting pretty tired of me talking about how great my little boy is."

Roger's big smile quickly appeared. Jessica loved to see little Roger's dimples, and they were in full bloom now. Tim saw Jessica's smile, and his love for her welled up inside him to the point that he almost lost it. Thankfully he was able to control himself and remain strong for the children. He was being honest, though; God had given him an amazing peace. Other than the pain of not being with his family, he was doing pretty well for a guy who was soon to be executed.

In what only felt like a few minutes, the door opened and the OW officer was telling them that their time was up. Tim, knowing that that might be the last time he would ever see the kids, got back on his knees so he could tell them how much he loved them. He did his best to maintain eye contact without showing any negative or sad emotions. "I love you two. You guys and your mom are the three most important people in the world to me. I think about you guys all of the time. Don't feel bad for me. God is in control, and I trust him."

They all told him how much they loved him, and Jessica told him she would be right back as they were leaving.

Tim's visit with his parents, Roger and Angela, was much more emotional that Tim had expected. Roger seemed to be strong and appeared to have accepted that what was happening was part of God's plan. Angela was not at all capable of holding her pain for her son in. She gave him a really long hug and cried uncontrollably. Tim stayed strong and told them he actually was doing just fine and that he was sure that what was going on would bring glory to God. He told them all about the mysterious peace he was feeling and urged them to keep praying for him. He asked them to pray, not for his release but for God's will to be done and for understanding and peace of mind. He told them that he had been praying for them and thanked them for taking care of his precious family.

Roger told him how tough things had been on the kids but that his real concern was for Jessica. He said that he had never seen her hurting like she was now. Not even when her mother had died was she even close to as depressed as she was now.

"What will happen to her if this happens?" he asked.

"I don't know, Dad. I can't even bear the thought of not being there for her. I don't know what I can do about it, but I do know that God is in this. He will make everything work out for the best in the end. I have to trust in him, Dad, because I can't do anything about it on my own. I have always been so in control. Now I have no control and I have to completely trust the Lord."

That was the only answer he could give, and he knew that Roger knew it before he even opened his mouth. Still, Tim had his doubts. He was worried that he couldn't go through with it and ceaselessly prayed for strength.

"We are so proud of you, honey," Angela managed to get out through her tears. She had been so proud of him his whole life, and now he was choosing to do the right thing, even though it was the most difficult thing he could ever do. She knew how much he loved his family.

How much must he love the Lord? she wondered.

"I agree with your mother, Tim. You are an inspiration for all of us. We love you." Roger was forcing out a smile, and Tim could see the admiration for what he was doing in his eyes. After a short pause he continued. "This will backfire on them and bring glory to God."

"Thanks for standing with me. I am who I am because of you two. Thanks for loving me the way you always have."

It felt like a really strange good-bye to him. It was wrong for a child to have to say good-bye to his parents like that.

Is this really going to happen? he wondered.

They did some more hugging before the OW officer broke them up and escorted his parents away. Tim could hardly wait for Jessica to return alone. He wanted to hold her for ten minutes. He hoped he could help her understand that she would be okay.

As soon as the door opened the third time, Jessica came running for her usual jumping-hug greeting. He grabbed her up into his arms, and they both started crying.

"I thought of wearing that old white dress you have always liked so much, but I just couldn't do it."

"You don't need a dress to look unbelievable, baby. You are always perfect no matter what you are wearing."

"Tim, I don't know if I can do this. I don't want to go on without you. I can't. It hurts too badly. The kids need you too. Why do you have to be so perfect?"

He could tell how honest she was being. She really didn't know if she could handle it.

"God is in this, Jessica. I know it will work out for us. Even if they execute me, I know it will be the right thing. You have to trust God and be strong for the kids. They need you now more than ever. You can do this, baby. I know you can."

"Let's not think about it, Tim. Just hold me and tell me how much you love me."

She knew their time was limited and wanted to savor every second of it. As soon as she stopped talking, she put her mouth on his and they kissed and talked for the rest of their time.

When the door opened, Jessica went to pieces.

"I can't leave," she cried.

"Jessica, you have to go. You'll be right here with me every second, though. Don't worry about me. I'm in God's hands. I'll pray for you and the kids every day."

It was a horrible feeling seeing her like that. To him it felt like the worst possible torture he could endure. He hated not being able to make everything better for her.

"I love you so much, Tim. You have been an angel in my life since I first met you. I am so proud of everything you do. Did I tell you they promised that I will get at least one more visit?"

Jessica had been told that she would get at least one more chance to bring the kids in to see him before his scheduled execution.

"Yes, they told me. I'll be dreaming about it. I love you, baby."

As he finished his sentence, the OW officer approached to take Jessica by force if necessary. It crossed Tim's mind that he could completely annihilate the guy with one punch, but he knew it would only hurt his witness and that it was completely against all that he was as a person.

"This way, ma'am," the officer commanded.

As she left, he felt his heart sinking. *Do I really have the strength for this?* Tim asked himself.

Jessica could hardly walk away. Her legs felt shaky as she walked backward, trying to maintain eye contact as long as possible. He was forcing a smile, and she was trying to return it when the door shut and he was gone.

Then she hollered, "Please shave the beard, Tim!"

He heard it and yelled back, "I'll shave it, baby."

He never heard a sound in reply.

CHAPTER 41

ABOUT two weeks before his scheduled execution, Tim got a letter from a man claiming to be his grandfather. Since his mail was limited to family only, everything else was denied. This man was claiming to be his grandfather, so the letter found its way to him. The note had little detail but provided a phone number, should he want to speak with him before the execution. Tim was not sure if the prison would allow the visit, as they had only allowed him to see his family once so far, but he pushed hard for it, as he wanted to understand what it was that had made his father into what he was.

To his amazement, the visit was approved. They were set to meet one week before the execution. Tim was assured this visit would not effect on the final visit with his family.

As Tim waited in the private meeting room with an armed guard, the man claiming to be his grandfather came through the door. Tim immediately noticed that the man had him and his father's face.

There is no way this guy is faking it, he thought.

The man looked to be pretty old. Tim guessed that he was in his late seventies or early eighties. He was a large man, but at that stage in his life, it was difficult to tell if he had been a powerfully built man as Tim and Chuck were.

"Hello, Tim," the old man said calmly. "Thank you for giving an old man a chance to apologize."

Tim was not sure where it was going, but it seemed odd to him.

Why is this guy showing up to apologize?

Tim was impressed by the old man's ability to speak and connect with him so easily. He decided not to jump on the apology. Instead, he would let the man say what he had come to say.

"Your father was a great embarrassment for a man like me, Tim. I was the pastor at the church your grandmother used to come to when she needed someone to listen to her and pray with her. She had been sexually abused as a child and was caught in a pattern of seeking acceptance from men through sexual relationships. She was very young and very attractive. I looked forward to her visits and foolishly began to meet with her alone.

"On one of her visits, we made love. I was a married man and a man of God." He was becoming a bit choked up but continued. "She became very special to me, and our affair was very passionate. We met two or three times a week and had sex in my office at the church or at her place. I was beginning to fall in love with her and planned to leave my wife and the church to be with her when I discovered that she still had several other partners." He paused again.

Tim could tell that it was painful for the old man.

"When she came to me to tell me she was pregnant, I told her that we had to stop. I told her I never loved her and that she needed to leave me alone or I would deny everything."

He broke down at that point. Obviously he had loved her.

"It's okay, Mr. Hatch. That was all a long time ago." Tim was trying to help him out by taking the pressure off.

"Tim, it was not okay at all. To get away, I moved my family to another church in another city. My wife just died last year, never knowing that I had an affair or that Kathy was ever a part of my life. My effectiveness as a pastor was severely affected. My conscious forced me to step down and enter the business world. My wife and kids never knew my real reasons. I've had to live with this most of my life, and I will never forgive myself for what I did to my family, your grandmother, and your father. I'm just so thankful for the way you turned out. It's because of you that I have rededicated my life to Christ. That's why I had to come see you, Tim. You are a great example of what we should all strive to be. What you are doing by allowing them to execute you is huge for the faith, and I admire you very much. Thank you."

The man's emotions had gone from tremendous pain and anguish to sheer joy in only a few seconds. Tim couldn't help but feel encouraged.

"Thank you for telling me all of this. I'm thankful that you are back with the Lord. I forgive you, and I know God does as well. My grandma is a Christian now, and she's in a loving relationship with a great man. God used your life to work in all of ours. I'm happy to have you as a grandfather. Thank you for coming and sharing with me, Grandpa." Tim was hoping to hug him but was pulled back by the chains holding him to his chair.

Having met his grandfather, Tim began to think again about how important it was that people do sex God's way. The purity that he and Jessica had achieved allowed them to have such a beautiful love and a perfect marriage. God really knows what's best for us.

CHAPTER 42

FOR the rest of the week of his execution, Tim was pushed to publically renounce his belief. The OW felt like they couldn't lose either way. If he renounced his belief that Jesus was the only way to heaven, they won. If he held to his beliefs and refused to renounce the Lord, as they believed he would, the televised execution would be a big win.

Two days before the execution, Tim was told they had decided to only allow his wife to visit; no other family would be allowed. Though he was disappointed to not get to see the kids again, he felt that it might be the right thing for them. He knew how disappointing it would be for them, but he felt it might also be easier for them. Seeing him two days before the execution would be even more difficult than their last visit. The good news was that he would get thirty minutes alone with Jessica. He just wanted to hold her and tell her again how much he loved her.

Jessica hadn't been sleeping much since the arrest. She would lie in bed, praying to God to bring her husband home. Though she wanted God's will to be done, she was praying that his will was to bring Tim home. Why wasn't she feeling any peace through this? Tim had told her that he was at peace and that he knew that it was God's plan. Why didn't she feel the same?

Do I not have enough faith? she wondered.

Although the kids were disappointed that they weren't going to get to see their father, Jessica was relieved. Just thinking of them having to deal with what was about to happen to their father was too much already.

On the day of the visit, Tim was so excited to see Jessica that he requested a shave so he could look his best for her. After they cleaned him up, he was taken to a room with no chairs and all white walls. He sat on the floor after standing around for what felt like an hour. The waiting wasn't nearly over, as it was only

289

2:00 p.m. and Jessica wasn't scheduled in until 4:00 p.m. Of course, no one told Tim that.

Tim, being the thinker that he was, alone in that plain white waiting room, went back and forth feeling strong about his decision to stand strong for the Lord followed by fears of failing. He wanted to be home with his family so badly that he actually contemplated denying the Lord. If he did, he would be home with his loved ones in only hours, but his witness and his very salvation would be gone. The thought would only last a few minutes as the calm the Lord was giving him would always return and his conviction to never deny Jesus at any cost would take back over. Waiting in this room to see the love of his life was much more difficult than being alone in his cell.

When he finally heard noise at the door, he leaped to his feet so he would be ready for his usual Jessica greeting. He needed to hold her, he needed to smell her hair, and he needed to look into those eyes. He had been starting at her picture as much as he could ever since he was put into his cell just under two months before. He loved everything about her, and being away from her and the kids had been the worst agony he could have ever imagined.

Before the door was all the way open, she slithered through and came running across the room and jumped into his arms. She was wearing the white dress; he couldn't believe it—the white dress. Although neither of them heard it, the guard told them, "You two have thirty minutes," before he shut the door.

Jessica was happy to see that he had shaven. In Jessica's eyes, he was so naturally good looking that the beard really only served to hide his pretty face. Now it didn't matter what he looked like. He was everything to her, and for the next thirty minutes, he was all hers. She had promised herself that she would focus on their time together and not on the horrible stuff.

Tim was shocked to see her in that dress. It was the way he always pictured her, and she always looked better in it in real life than in any picture. He was just so thankful to have her there.

Seeing her so happy to see him made him believe that she had chosen to focus on their time together rather than be preoccupied with what was almost certain to happen to him in a couple of days. He had hoped she would be able to enjoy their time together.

"I want you right now, Tim."

She was sure he would want her too but was betting that he wouldn't think she would be willing. She had even considered that there might be a camera in the room but had decided that it didn't matter.

She was right; he was shocked that she would be willing. He had been in the room for quite some time and knew he was being watched.

"I want you too, baby, but we are being watched. If you don't care, neither do I."

She didn't answer. Without missing a beat, it was on. They enjoyed each other and laid together in a hump, hugging and kissing. They had both decided to focus on the other and to be in the moment, so they didn't even talk about what was about to happen.

After what felt like only five minutes, the door opened and they were told, "You have one minute."

They told each other how much they loved the other, and Tim told her that he knew God was going to do something amazing with all of it. No matter what happened, he urged her to believe that it was God's will and that it was all for his purpose. Tim was no longer waffling back and forth knowing that Jessica needed to see him strong in his belief for what he was about to do. For the first time, Jessica felt a calm come over her. The fear left her, and she too believed that everything would somehow work out.

They kissed until the OW officer came in and took Jessica away.

"Tell the kids and our parents how much I love them."

It felt like he was saying good-bye, but it no longer felt like it to her. She felt lucky to be his and oddly confident that nothing bad was going to happen to him. She knew it was coming from God, and she hoped Tim could see it on her face.

Tim noticed her sudden strength, and it immediately relieved him. God was definitely comforting her. He was thankful, as her and the families' pain was killing him. He finally felt like everything was in God's hands. It was a peaceful feeling. As she left, he couldn't help but feel blessed to have been married to her. Every moment he had spent with her over the years had been perfect. He had no regrets and was thankful he had done things God's way since the very beginning. God had truly blessed every step of their lives. They both had hardship in their lives, but God always made things better in the end. Somehow Tim was sure he would with their current situation too.

CHAPTER 43

THE day of execution finally arrived. Waiting to be put to death should have been far more difficult than it had been. For some reason he had been sleeping well and had no reservations. He kept hoping that God would miraculously save him, but he was prepared to die proudly for Christ if that was God's will. His thoughts were mainly for his family, though his last visit from Jessica had really helped him feel that God was comforting them and that everything would be okay.

After his last meal, he was brought out by two armed guards as if he was a dangerous criminal. For the meal he had requested a bone-in filet from his favorite Houston-area restaurant, Taste of Texas. As usual, it was amazing. He had no regrets about the meal choice, though he couldn't help but think that it would have been much better at the restaurant with his family. With a full stomach, he was led to the room where his life was scheduled to end.

The method of execution would be lethal injection, though the One World union had pushed for the return of crucifixion as a demonstration of the foolishness of Christianity. Almost no one was being put to death for any crime at that point. The death penalty was thought to be cruel and unusual. Only crimes against the OW, such as Tim's, held a death sentence.

A young, charismatic man, Sargon Adasi, was such a gifted speaker and leader that he was winning the hearts and minds of the other leaders within the OW. Sargon was the force behind the OW leaders that had suggested and was pushing to make an example out of Tim. He was also the source behind crucifixion as the method of execution. No one had ever heard such a convincing speaker, and his charisma was already being talked about all over the world. It seemed as though anyone who had heard him speak became a disciple. His ability to seamlessly speak fluently in almost any language he chose to speak in had amazed leaders from all over the world. Sargon never spoke from a teleprompter and never worked from notes, nor did he use a speech writer. He was truly gifted. Though no one saw it coming, he would soon become a leader like the world had never seen. Though he came from the former United States, there were claims that he was something more than human, something superhuman.

Tim was not given a chance to speak. The only thing they would allow him to do was deny Christ, which he had no intentions of doing. That was it; Tim would die for Christ. He had accepted it and was feeling a settling calm. People were watching live on television, and the commentators were amazed at the joy they were seeing on his face. Tim was being overwhelmed by feelings of joy. He was feeling the presence of God, and it was bringing him relief and joy. It was easy to look happy in the presence of the Lord.

Jessica was in tears until she saw his smiling face. She knew immediately that Tim was not alone. She knew their gracious God was there for him, and it made her feel almost at ease all of a sudden. She too began to feel the presence of God, and actually began to smile as well. It was amazing.

Jessica turned to her left to see why Angela had stopped crying and noticed right away that God was with her too. She sat between her father and Angela. They were all holding hands and praying when Tim had been brought out. Now they were all feeling a strange and wonderful calm. Everything would be okay. They all knew it.

As they strapped Tim into the table he would be executed on, he was looking directly into the camera and saying that Jesus was Lord. He began quoting scripture, so the cameras were instructed to pan out so no one would be able to read his lips.

Moments before the chemicals were to be mixed and pumped into his body, the order was given. That was when it happened. He simply disappeared. He was gone. Only his clothes were left. The guards were caught completely by surprise. They began searching the room but saw nothing.

In the viewing room, more than half of the people had disappeared, just as Tim had. Jessica, Roger, and Angela too were gone. In fact, millions of people all over the earth had disappeared in the twinkling of an eye.

ENDNOTES

1   John 14:6 (KJV)

2   http://www.salvationprayer.info/prayer.html

3   *King James Version*